Two for Joy

About the author

Helen Chandler was born and brought up in Liverpool, and read English at Oxford University before joining the NHS and working as a general manager in various healthcare organisations.

She gave up (paid) work when she had a baby, and wrote her first novel, *Two for Joy*, in any spare minutes she could get when her daughter was either asleep (rare) or could be palmed off onto one of her grandparents for a little while.

Other than reading, Helen's main passions are food – reading about it, shopping for it, cooking it, eating it and sometimes just thinking about it – and London.

She lives in East London with her husband and daughter.

You can visit Helen's website at www.helenchandler. co.uk to find out more and read her blog, or follow her on Twitter twitter.com/HelenLChandler.

HELEN CHANDLER

Two for Joy

HODDER

First published in Great Britain in 2013 by Hodder & Stoughton
An Hachette UK company

First published in paperback in 2013

1

A CIP catalogue record for this title is available from the British Library

Paperback ISBN 978 1 444 76929 6
Ebook ISBN 978 1 444 77578 5

Typeset by Hewer Text UK Ltd, Edinburgh
Printed and bound by CPI Group (UK) Ltd, Croydon, CR0 4YY

Hodder & Stoughton policy is to use papers that are natural, renewable
and recyclable products and made from wood grown in sustainable
forests. The logging and manufacturing processes are expected to
conform to the environmental regulations of the country of origin.

Hodder & Stoughton Ltd
338 Euston Road
London NW1 3BH

www.hodder.co.uk

To my mum and dad, the best parents ever,
thank you for everything.

I

As Julia raised her eyes to Toby's face she realised that he had been waiting for her response, probably for some minutes. The noise of the busy restaurant seemed to have receded, it was just the two of them, and she had to think of something to say. Her hand groped instinctively for the trusty goldfish bowl of Pinot Grigio on the table in front of her and she took a restorative gulp before attempting anything as complicated as the formulation of a sentence.

'Wow, Tobes, that's . . . that's amazing. Wow. It's . . . erm . . . incredible.'

Even to her own ears her voice sounded forced and unnatural.

'Incredibly good, or incredibly bad?' Toby raised his eyebrows quizzically and she could sense that he was a little hurt by her lack of enthusiasm.

She rallied, and willed herself to control the myriad complex emotions which were whirling around her head and concentrate on being a good friend to Toby. But what did 'good friend' mean in this context? Did it mean offering unconditional support? Was she being a good friend if she encouraged him in this insane plan to marry a woman he barely knew and had nothing in common with? Or would a truly good friend try and talk him out of it, point out that marriages were likely enough to fail without the odds being stacked against them to the extent they would be here?

Maybe she could compromise. 'Well, incredibly good, of course. It's amazing that you feel so strongly for Ruby, that you're so happy together.' She paused, and frowned. 'The only thing is, I suppose, that you haven't been together that long. Wouldn't it be better to at least live together for a while first before getting engaged? It's such a big step.'

Toby gave Julia a funny little half-smile. 'That's why I love you, Julia. Your romantic impulsiveness. Listen, it *is* a big step, I am aware of that, but that's not automatically a bad thing, you know. Ruby is so beautiful, so exciting, she makes me feel so alive. I don't want to risk losing that now I've found it – now I've discovered the person I can be when I'm with her. Asking her to move in with me would feel routine and functional. Actually proposing won't leave her in any doubt about what I feel.'

Julia sighed. Surely by this time she was old enough to know that compromise rarely worked. She hadn't, in any way, achieved her objective of making Toby think twice about his rash decision. All she had succeeded in doing was to ensure that she herself appeared in the worst possible light as an unromantic killjoy. 'Well, proposing to her should certainly give her an indication of how you feel.'

Oh God. That sounded sarcastic and bitter as well. 'Sorry, Toby. I don't want to spoil things for you. I just want you to be happy, and it's a bit of a shock, that's all. I had no idea things were so serious between you and Ruby.'

Toby's face lit up as he began to eulogise. 'Honestly, Ju, I've never felt like this before. She's literally all I can think about. She's so beautiful, so passionate. I can't concentrate when I'm not with her because I'm thinking about the next time I'll see her, and I can't concentrate when I *am* with her because I'm just mesmerised looking at her. Do you understand what I mean? All I want to do is look at her.'

Julia couldn't decide whether her feelings of slight nausea were caused by downing half a bottle of wine in five minutes flat, or by Toby's saccharine sincerity. She did understand, though. She herself had experienced very similar feelings in the past. The trouble was, she had been thirteen years old, and the object of her affections was the student teacher assigned to her French class. And while she would happily have proposed to him, always supposing she had been able to muster something more eloquent than a nervous giggle in his presence, with the benefit of seventeen years' hindsight she couldn't help but feel that the relationship might not have lasted. Luckily a spark of feminine intuition surfaced, somewhat later than it might have done, but nonetheless in time to prevent her sharing the comparison with Toby.

She looked at him affectionately. He had changed remarkably little in the time she had known him, and as he sat now, elbows on the table, leaning forward, eyes alight with eagerness, he could still have been the passionate student activist she had first seen holding forth in the college bar, twelve years previously. 'Come on then, Romeo. Let's order some fizz to celebrate. And don't worry, I understand it's top secret until you actually ask her on Friday. My lips are sealed.'

The rest of the evening passed with their normal mix of banter, teasing, chatting and joking, and if Julia felt the need of a little more alcoholic lubrication than might otherwise have been the case, well, at least The Proposal wasn't referred to again.

It was only when they said goodbye in the tube station at Oxford Circus that things felt any different. They stood together for a moment in the crowded-even-on-a-Sunday-evening ticket hall, and Julia was suddenly aware of how tall he was. At five foot eight herself, Julia liked tall men and the way they always made her feel so deliciously feminine and protected, but she had never really considered Toby in that category and he had certainly never had that effect on her. She knew he was well over six foot, of course, and she was in flat ballet pumps that night, which emphasised the difference, but suddenly there seemed to be something else as well. Some awareness of him as a man, of her as a woman. Some slight frisson when he bent to kiss her cheek and his stubble grazed her slightly.

'Well, bye then,' she said awkwardly as they stepped away from each other. 'Maybe see you next weekend, to celebrate?'

Toby appeared faintly embarrassed, but pleased. 'Yeah, that'd be great. I'll talk to Ruby, see what her plans are, and give you a call.'

There was another moment of slightly strained silence and then he was off, loping towards the escalators without a backward glance.

Julia stood for a minute, fancying she could still feel the pressure of his hands on her upper arms. She gave herself a mental shake. Bit of a coincidence that the first time she found herself going all Mills and Boon about Toby's height and the set of his shoulders was the evening he told her he was proposing to someone else. Talk about the unobtainable being more attractive . . .

Back in her own little house later that night, Julia threw herself luxuriantly full length onto her purple needlecord sofa and began drinking the pint glass of water which would hopefully stave off hangover hell in the morning, wincing at the thought of the budget meeting starting less than nine hours later. She knew, though, that there was no point going to bed just yet. Her mind was still buzzing from the champagne and from Toby's news.

Now she was alone in her sanctuary and didn't have to pretend anything for Toby's sake, she tried to analyse honestly how she felt. Not good, she decided. She curled up and cradled a patchwork cushion on her lap. Why was this so hard?

Was it turning thirty that had made the difference? Julia didn't think she was an inherently selfish person. She had willingly, even enthusiastically, submitted to having her hair contorted into unnatural curls and squeezing her curves into unflattering pastel satin at both her younger brother's and best friend's weddings, and was just delighted that people she loved were so happy.

She had been equally enthusiastic a year or two later to return to the scene of the fashion crime, this time hoping that a hasty lunchtime purchase of the best Debenhams had to offer in the way of linen jackets and big hats would say 'responsible, caring yet independent-minded godmother and aunt' rather than 'desperate broody singleton'. She wasn't at all sure that she had succeeded in the latter; there had been, at least to her paranoid gaze, far too many sympathetic glances, although it was only her teenage cousin who had actually voiced what she suspected the rest of the family were thinking: 'Doesn't it make you feel weird, Ju, that your little brother's married with a baby and you haven't even got a boyfriend at the moment?'

Julia was determined not to fulfil the Bridget Jones stereotype (although if it could involve Colin Firth and Hugh Grant fighting over her in a fountain she would be prepared to reconsider), but she was uncomfortably aware that circumstances, not to mention her own unspoken but compelling longing for a baby, were conspiring against her.

Newspapers and magazines were constantly full of articles about the growing number of single households, of women reaching the peak of their careers and then turning forty and producing strings of beautiful babies, and rationally Julia knew that the world had moved on from the days when you married the boy next door aged twenty, popped out a baby every two years until you had your perfect little family, and then got your hair cut and permed, bought a mid-calf-length floral skirt from Marks and Spencer and settled back to wait for grandchildren.

It was just that no one appeared to have shared the news of this demographic shift with her closest and oldest friend Rose – married at twenty-seven, mother to the divine Sebastian at twenty-eight, and be-Bodened stay-at-home mum in her comfortable four-bedroom detached house in an affluent Berkshire commuter village. Or with her younger brother Harry – married at twenty-two to his childhood sweetheart Angela (Julia strongly suspected that Angela's adherence to a branch of Christianity which forcefully advocated no sex before marriage had more than a little to do with that) and now father to adorable Sarah and Ruth.

Or with her mother and father. Eddie and Pat Upton had been happily married and contentedly installed in their suburban Manchester three-bedroom semi for thirty-two years. They were at a loss to understand why their only daughter had moved to London, paid six times the national average wage for a Victorian terrace that only the very kind-hearted (or the polar opposite, an estate agent) could describe as two-bedroomed, and didn't even have a boyfriend.

None of that had really bothered her before, though, and she had been quite content with her little house, her demanding but satisfying job and her role as group mother to a wide circle of friends.

Was Toby just the final straw? He was the last of her closest friends to meet his other half. He was also an ex-boyfriend, if you counted a few half-hearted snogs and gropes at the university bops which sometimes seemed another lifetime ago. Maybe it was that despite making different decisions from her parents, she came from a warm, close, loving family and had enjoyed an idyllic childhood; watching her brother recreate that with his girls sometimes made her feel that she had somehow managed to miss the boat, and Toby's forthcoming engagement just underlined the point further.

One thing which really did bother her was how little she had seen of Toby during the last few months since he had been dating Ruby. Perhaps a key reason why she had never particularly minded being single was that the traditional 'couple times' – Sunday nights, holidays, work Christmas parties – had never held any terrors for her because there had always been Toby, and she had more fun with him than she had ever had with any of the blokes she had been in so-called relationships with. Presumably Ruby wouldn't be too keen, though, on her husband spending his weekends and holidays with another woman, which meant that singledom was going to mean something very different in future.

And then there was Ruby herself. There were no two ways about it: Julia just didn't *like* Ruby, and at the thought of Ruby as Toby's wife this dislike seemed to swell to the point where Julia thought she might burst with angry outrage. Ruby seemed to be Julia's complete opposite – dark where Julia was fair, size 8 to Julia's size 14, petite where Julia was tall. Julia was a hospital manager, Deputy Director of Operations at St Benedict's NHS Trust, one of London's most prestigious teaching hospitals, a relatively well-paid job high on responsibility but low on glamour. Ruby was a ballet dancer, currently performing in what she described as a 'retro yet avant-garde interpretation of *Swan Lake*', working for almost nothing but funding her stylish existence through a generous allowance from her parents. Julia's parents worked in middle-management roles in local government; Ruby's father was a baronet and had the country estate to go with it. The only thing the two women had in common was Toby, and that didn't provide them with much in the way of conversation at dinner parties. At first Julia had been paranoid about referring too much to her and Toby's shared past, and she was scrupulous in avoiding the 'do you remember' anecdotes that she worried could lead to Ruby feeling insecure or excluded. She quickly realised, however, that there was no need to worry at all. Ruby was supremely self-confident. Self-absorbed, even, thought Julia bitchily, and it was only too clear that it had never entered Ruby's head to consider Julia as either threat or competition.

Rose, in a fit of G&T-induced honesty, had once said that Julia was jealous of Ruby; jealous that she was the only one of Toby's girlfriends who had ever seriously threatened her position as number one woman in Toby's life. She had also said that Julia was in danger of being a dog in the manger – not wanting Toby for herself, but not wanting anyone else to have him either. Julia's response back then had been dismissive. 'I've got no reason to be jealous. Just because Toby happens to be shagging some nubile bimbo, it doesn't change our friendship. After all, he's not about to marry the woman.'

Now, facing the prospect of an engagement she had not even allowed herself to consider as a possibility, and filled with something which did feel horribly like jealousy, Julia considered whether there was any truth in what Rose had said. She supposed, uncomfortably, that she *had* always considered Toby to be hers, and had always felt that given any encouragement he would be more than happy to make the transition from best friend to boyfriend. They had made the obligatory agreement at university – 'if we're not married by the time we're thirty-five, we'll marry each other' – and while Julia had never really considered that there was any spark of sexual attraction between them, on her part at least she loved him very much as a friend, and her thirty-fifth birthday no longer felt the impossibly distant event it had at nineteen. Maybe she *had* felt subconsciously that Toby was her back-up option.

Julia cringed at her own arrogance. Why had she imagined that Toby – tall, dark, handsome, successful – was going to be left on the shelf, willing to be her reserve choice should Mr Darcy/Rochester/de Winter not make an appearance in time? After all, no one ever bemoaned the plight of single thirty-something men – if men were single in their thirties, she thought cynically, it was only because they were trying to decide which twenty-something babe to shag next.

Maybe this was just the wake-up call she needed. Looking round her kitchen as she went to get yet another glass of water before heading off to bed, Julia concluded that with her well-stocked spice cupboard, her full range of Nigella cookbooks and her small but perfectly formed herb garden, she was living the Smug Married life, but had somehow neglected to provide herself with that ultimate Smug Married accessory: a husband. She needed to stop spending all her free time having cosy dinners with either Toby or her coupled-up friends, and start getting out and meeting people. As of tomorrow, Things Must Change.

2

Toby regarded himself in the full-length mirror inside his wardrobe door. He had persuaded Julia to go shopping with him a couple of months ago to buy the sharply tailored Armani suit the assistant described as 'cobalt blue', and she had said he was 'gorgeous – almost sexy' in it, which was about as complimentary as she ever got, so that was okay. His shirt was new, white and freshly ironed, and he was practically sitting on his hands to avoid putting on a tie. Suit and no tie was as close to smart-casual as he ever got; Saunders SpencerYork, the management consultancy he had joined as a graduate trainee nearly ten years ago, didn't exactly encourage informality.

He was aware, though, that Ruby's sartorial standards were somewhat different, and although approximately eighty per cent of her salary – not to mention the generous allowance from her parents – went on clothes, he wasn't sure that Armani was a label she would ever consider wearing. Her designers of choice were Chloé or Marc Jacobs, although she was equally likely to put together a stunning outfit after rummaging through the stalls at Portobello Market or braving Topshop on a Saturday afternoon. The contrast between the creative chaos of her world and the relentless drive of his own working life was one of the things he loved about their relationship.

Toby had never intended to be a thirty-year-old management consultant. He had been brought up in Hampstead by bohemian baby boomer parents who had met at art school, swung in the sixties, found and lost themselves several times over in India during the early seventies, and by the late seventies had opened a surprisingly successful art gallery, bought the spacious and stylish flat over the gallery in 1980, and then had him. They claimed to have got married at some point in the proceedings, but had always been a little bit vague on the details.

Now, although they were wealthy by most people's standards, their cash went mainly on travel to increasingly exotic and far-flung places, books and art, and neither of them had a materialistic bone in their bodies. Toby didn't consider himself to be particularly materialistic either – certainly by the standards of some of his colleagues he definitely wasn't – but although his parents adored him, he had always played Saffy to their Patsy and Edwina, and he knew that they were puzzled by a son who worked eighty-hour weeks as standard, travelled the globe but often only saw the conference centre and his hotel room, and thought that never having taken an illegal substance was a good thing.

When Toby joined SSY at twenty-one his intention, like so many bright young left-leaning things, was to work for them for five years, tops, take advantage of the generous salary and telephone-number bonuses and then retire to do what he really wanted with his life. At twenty-one he had no idea what that was, but had confidently expected that it would all fall into place.

Two things then happened. The first was that Toby loved, and excelled at, his job. He had always felt that he moved at a different pace from his friends; his mind seemed to spin, he was full of restless energy, he even talked more quickly than most people. In a top-level management consultancy he finally felt that the world was moving at his speed, and he thrived in the fast-paced, competitive environment.

The second was that at twenty-eight Toby had succumbed to the inevitable for a child of the eighties and had been overcome by an irresistible urge to 'get his feet on the ladder', buying a three-bedroom house in Wanstead, north-east London. Wanstead seemed to him to have all the advantages of more popular West London at a fraction of the cost. It was affluent, comfortable, slightly conservative, but filled with City types like himself who were drawn by the thirty-minute commute down the Central Line, the Victorian and Georgian housing stock, the good schools, the pretty village green and quaint high street where organic butchers fought for space with organic delis, high-end beauty salons and designer clothes shops. It was also a ten-minute drive from considerably less affluent though arguably even prettier Walthamstow Village, where Julia had bought her pocket-sized house. Even with a particularly generous year's bonus covering the deposit, the mortgage still took a considerable slice of his salary, and he knew that very few other jobs would enable him to afford it. Toby currently lacked the wife and 2.4 children which were the usual accompaniments to this lifestyle, but he knew that those were what he wanted one day and it seemed to him to make sense to put down roots now rather than going for a flash bachelor pad in Canary Wharf.

Satisfied that he looked as good as possible, Toby glanced at his watch: 6.15 p.m. Far too early to leave for an 8 p.m. meet-up in town. Toby was suddenly aware that he hardly ever saw his house in the daytime. This evening he had taken the unprecedented step of sneaking out of the office at 5 p.m., wanting to have time to return home to shower and change before his big date. Normally he left work at any time between 8 p.m. and midnight; if it was an earlier finish he would meet friends for dinner and drinks in town.

At the weekend he tended to gravitate towards Julia's house, even though it was approximately a quarter of the size of his, and looking around now he could see why. Julia had bought her little terrace a few years before him, and she had worked very hard on it. The walls were lined with her extensive collection of books, and her cheerfully mismatched furniture was a characterful blend of renovated hand-me-downs, junk-shop finds and Ikea. In summer the French doors were opened onto her tiny patio garden and the scent of lavender and rosemary wafted in. As Julia was a skilled and enthusiastic cook, there was always a well-stocked fridge, delicious cooking smells and, more often than not, a homemade cake around somewhere.

In stark contrast, his house remained much as it had when the decorator he had hired on moving in had left. It had the almost compulsory stripped wood floors, plain white walls with a few black-and-white prints on them, and the kitchen, although stocked with top-of-the-range Smeg fridge and Poggenpohl units, was rarely used for much more than pouring a bowl of cereal or heating up an M&S ready meal. Toby was not a cook, and since meeting Ruby had spent even less time at home. She was utterly disbelieving that any form of civilised life could exist outside Zone One, let alone in Zone Four, and the majority of the nights they spent together were in her studio flat in Islington.

As he helped himself to a beer, hoping to kill time and his nerves before leaving, Toby's heart leapt with excitement. This was yet another thing to look forward to in marrying Ruby – his house would be brought to life, filled with family, friends, hopefully one day children. In his mind's eye he saw long balmy summer afternoons with a barbecue, weekend guests enjoying Eggs Benedict and the Sunday broadsheets, convivial yet stimulating dinner parties. In this vision the inconvenient truths that neither he nor Ruby could cook, and that Ruby in fact barely ate, could be safely ignored.

About an hour later, Toby came out of the tube at St Paul's and glanced up, enchanted as always by the view of the spectacular cathedral. He was planning to walk the short distance across Millennium Bridge and down the river to the Oxo Tower Brasserie where he was meeting Ruby, the best table in the house booked and hopefully the Moët discreetly on ice, ready to be brought out at the appropriate moment. He had chosen the Oxo Tower because as well as its wonderfully romantic views over the river, it was there they had gone for their first proper date, almost four months before.

Although a Londoner born and bred, Toby had none of the cynical indifference to his city which his contemporaries seemed to affect. He loved the very bones of it, the bricks it was built on, and whenever he was anxious or needed to think something through, a walk through London was his go-to solution. Patting for the hundredth time at least his inside pocket which contained the beribboned, distinctively aquamarine Tiffany's box, he set off, contemplating the events which had led him to this point.

Like most educated, successful men in their twenties, Toby had always given more thought to propositioning women than to proposing to them. However, if he had ever speculated on it, his mind's eye had always automatically placed Julia as the proposee. He supposed that on one level he had always been half in love with her. Not in a way that the Victorian novelists Julia loved so much would have recognised, a way which left him pining, disconsolate and celibate, but in a way which half-unconsciously used her as the benchmark by which he judged other girlfriends – and found them wanting. In a way which meant he never really thought any of her boyfriends were good enough for her. In a way which secretly acknowledged that in a purely platonic friendship you shouldn't spend quite so much time appreciating the aesthetics of said friend's truly fantastic tits.

Julia had made it quite clear, though, at university and beyond, that she didn't see him 'that way' at all. At the Christmas ball at the end of their first term as undergraduates together he had finally plucked up enough drunken courage to kiss her, and she had kissed him back at first, before breaking away laughing and saying that they shouldn't do anything to spoil their friendship. He had felt rejected, and had covered that by over-vociferous agreement, and this had set the pattern for their student days. After graduation the drunken kisses had ceased but the close friendship had remained, and Toby had always vaguely hoped that it would become something more. Until he met Ruby.

Ruby was the sexiest, most beautiful woman he had ever laid eyes on. Just seeing her, fully dressed, across a crowded bar was enough to give him a massive hard-on. She had thick, shiny dark hair which swooshed round her shoulders, deliciously full lips always coated in red lipstick, and firm, high, round breasts. Every glance, gesture, word seemed to suggest sex, and when he was actually in bed with her, her supple, agile dancer's body could do things he had never even dreamt of. She was exciting, passionate and unpredictable – in bed and out of it.

Moreover, dating a beautiful ballerina, mixing with her arty friends, making the romantically extravagant gesture of getting engaged after only four months together, made him feel in some obscure way that he was living up to his parents' expectations. They had never put any pressure on him to do anything. In a way that was the problem. Both of them had been born into solidly middle-class families – teachers, accountants, solicitors – and they had fought fierce family disapproval in order to go to art school rather than university, to live together without being married, to travel further than an annual summer trip to Devon or Norfolk. When he was born he knew that his parents had promised themselves that he would never be constrained by the shackles of conventional society in the way that they had been. They would, he knew, have given him their full and enthusiastic support if he had dropped out of school to become a sculptor, or joined a kibbutz, or announced his homosexuality. The trouble was that he was a straight, white, middle-class male without a creative bone in his body. He had a degree in History and Economics from Oxford, worked as a management consultant, had chosen to live in an affluent suburb, and he had always had a vague and uncomfortable sense that his parents rather mourned the fact that he had never in his life done anything that the average middle-class, middle-income couple could possibly object to, and was therefore denying them the chance to show how wonderfully open-minded they could be. Introducing a slightly spoilt, wilful, extravagant, passionate, beautiful, creative but generally impecunious ballet dancer as their future daughter-in-law would give them the perfect opportunity *not* to disapprove.

Julia was feeling furious with herself. Despite her best efforts, contemplation of Toby's forthcoming engagement had occupied most of her waking thoughts that week. She had been irritable and distracted at work and had refused any invitations out so that she could enjoy solitary evenings consuming heroic quantities of hummus, baked potatoes and Ben & Jerry's ice cream while watching her *Friends* box set and avoiding calls from her mother and her best friend. She had told Rose about Toby's plans – Rose had only met Ruby once, and they hardly moved in the same social circles so it didn't

seem to matter – and Rose had seemed distinctly unconvinced by Julia's breezy 'isn't it exciting news' stance,
which she had been practising very hard. To be fair, Julia
wasn't entirely convinced by it herself, but she felt that
Rose could have given her the benefit of the doubt.

Instead Rose had pretty much repeated a toned-down
version of her 'dog in the manger' comments, and had
been far from her usual sympathetic self. Maybe she was
trying to make amends when she phoned back the following evening, and again the one after that, but Julia didn't
feel up to finding out, so she hadn't answered. She had
also been avoiding her mum. Pat had always thought the
sun shone out of Toby's backside and she had never made
any secret of her hope that he and Julia would end up
together. Time enough to break the bad news to her and
cope with the lamentation and recrimination, thinly
disguised as consolation, which would result.

Now it was Friday night, and while her Armani-clad
friend was plying his beautiful fiancée with the finest
champagne, Julia was slumped on the sofa in eight-year-
old Primark pyjamas with a large glass of Tesco's half-
price deal of the week. She was furious. With Toby, with
Ruby, but primarily with herself. She had no idea why
she was letting this upset her so badly, but she couldn't
deny that it was. She gave herself a mental shake. This
had to stop. In an hour or two's time, Toby and Ruby
would be phoning her with the happy news, and when
they asked what she was up to there was no way the
answer was going to be 'sitting alone drinking alcohol
units at levels not approved of by the Chief Medical
Officer'. A few of her friends from work were going out

tonight and she had been asked along but had automatically refused, despite her resolution on Sunday night to get out more. She glanced at her watch. Half seven. They wouldn't really have got started yet. Fired by a sudden energy, she got to her feet and ran upstairs.

Cream lace push-up bra, which made her average 36Cs into something a lot more voluptuous, matching knickers (well, you never know), soft mushroom-coloured chiffon blouse tucked into denim pencil skirt. Wide belt, which she sincerely hoped emphasised her waist while drawing attention away from her tummy. High heels. The look she was going for was sexy but sophisticated, and after applying a little more than her usual amount of make-up and pulling her shoulder-length hair up into a high ponytail, she was inclined to think that she might have succeeded. Julia smiled at her reflection. She felt slightly better already.

3

Ruby wasn't late. Not by her standards anyway. She didn't even think it counted for the first half an hour. Normally Toby was just as bad, held up by mysterious consultancy crises, but tonight she noticed, as she arrived at the Oxo Tower only twenty minutes after their agreed meet-up time, that she had three missed calls from him. That wasn't good. She frowned. If Toby was going to start getting all obsessive, that was going to make life very difficult indeed.

Toby glanced up for what seemed like the thousandth time, and this time was rewarded by a sight which was turning other male heads besides his own. Ruby's original fifties outfit in bright scarlet, complete with white net petticoat and vertiginous heels, was enough on its own to make her stand out, but combined with her slender, graceful figure, her blow-job lips and her L'Oréal ad hair, she was irresistible.

Not even remotely unaware of the effect she was having, Ruby strolled across to the table by the window, gazed out appreciatively at the cityscape below her, and leant over to kiss Toby softly on the lips. He breathed in her musky perfume, felt her hair trailing across his face and tightened his hold on her waist possessively. This was it. He hadn't been going to do things so suddenly, but the twenty-minute wait, the two glasses of wine he had drunk while he was waiting and the sheer overwhelming desirability of her got the better of him. He pushed her gently away from him and sank down on one knee in the classic style. It felt like a cliché to him, but Julia had assured him that clichés generally became that way for a reason. He took both of Ruby's hands in one of his, and with the other one felt in his pocket for the ring.

Ruby realised she was holding her breath. No. Surely not. He absolutely couldn't be about to propose. Her mind searched feverishly for plausible reasons why her boyfriend might be crawling round on the restaurant floor. Dropped something? Drunk? Then, oh God, a Tiffany's box. He was doing it. Nervous tension got the better of her and she began to giggle.

Toby raised his eyes to her beautiful face and saw that she was laughing. He wasn't quite sure that was the response he had been hoping for, but heaven knows he probably looked like a dick right now. Anyway, there wasn't any going back. He slid the ring onto her finger. 'Ruby, you know how much I love you, how happy you make me. Will you marry me?'

Ruby moved away slightly, no longer laughing. 'Sit back down, Toby.'

She moved round the table and took her seat.

Toby sat down feeling a little confused. This was definitely not the response he had been hoping for, expecting even. Out of the corner of his eye he could see the waiter, apparently equally confused, hovering with the bottle of champagne. He waved him away and took another gulp of his wine. 'Well, come on, Ruby, say something.'

Ruby gazed back at him, not quite able to believe she was in this situation. She was twenty-four years old. She was right at the beginning of her career. They had only been going out for a few months! In what parallel universe was Toby living that he thought she might conceivably want to *marry* him? The difference in their expectations left her speechless, but she felt the horrific urge to giggle again. She leant over and took hold of Toby's hand. 'Darling Toby, it's so incredibly sweet of you to want to propose. I'm really flattered. But it's come completely out of the blue for me.'

'That's okay, I understand, I shouldn't have rushed you. You'll need time to think about it.'

'No, sweetheart, you don't understand. I don't need time to think about it. I don't want to get married. Maybe not ever, but definitely not now, to you. I love being with you, but I never thought things were that serious between us. I just want to have fun at the moment, and focus on my career. I literally found out today that there's an opportunity for me to work in Germany for a few months, which I'd love, and I want the freedom to be able to do things like that. I'm not ready, I'm too young, I just don't *want* to be tied down at the moment.'

Toby's life at London's top grammar school, Oxford's top college and the cream of the milk-round employers hadn't given him many opportunities to understand how it felt to be punched, but the way he was feeling now took him back to a cold, wet playing field fifteen years earlier, and a heavy leather football hurtling straight towards his stomach. 'You don't love me.' He almost whispered the words.

She squeezed his hand tighter. 'Oh darling, I do love you, of course I do, I'm just not even remotely ready for that kind of commitment. Maybe it's because I'm younger than you, I don't know. I'm so sorry though.'

Toby took on the demeanour of a kicked puppy. 'But if you love me ... surely that's what it's all about, isn't it? That's what everyone's searching for – meeting The One, being together for ever. That's what I want for us, Ruby.'

Ruby could feel herself beginning to panic. She didn't want to hurt Toby, of course she didn't, but it was starting to feel as though a silken net were being drawn slowly but irrevocably around her, and in her desperation to free herself her voice was sharper than she intended. 'No! Toby, no. No. This isn't what I want. I didn't mean to lead you on, but I never thought this was serious between us. I never meant it to be.'

The sharpness in her tone awoke a frisson of anger in him. 'Not serious? You didn't think it was serious? But Ruby, you've just said that you love me. And that's not the first time, you're always saying it. If being in love with someone doesn't make a relationship serious in your book, then do you think you could explain what the hell does?'

She shrugged gracefully. 'Come on, Toby, it's just something you say. I do love you, but I never expected this. You must have told girls you loved them without thinking that next thing you'd be walking down the aisle!'

He shook his head vehemently. 'No, I've never said "I love you" and not meant it. In fact, I've only ever said it to one other girl.' He briefly let his mind drift back to that warm summer evening in Oxford half a lifetime ago, but then figured that there was nothing in that memory to salve his current feelings and returned swiftly to the present. Deliberately fanning his spark of anger to crowd out the feelings of humiliation and anguish, he glared at Ruby and raised his voice. 'It's just crap, Ruby. At least have the decency to treat me with a little honesty. If you love someone, then you don't care about how old you are, or your freedom, you just want to be with them. It's not like I'm going to stop your precious fucking dancing and turn you into a housewife. It's just bollocks. You don't love me, simple as that.'

'Hang on a minute, Toby, that's not fair. I had no idea you were thinking about marriage, I never intended to lead you on. But if you want honesty, then okay, no, I don't love you enough to marry you, and yes, my "precious fucking dancing" is more important to me.'

Toby scraped his chair back noisily and got to his feet. 'Fine. Well, we both know where we stand then, don't we? I'm going now, and I expect that one day I'll look back and see this as a lucky escape.'

She glared back at him, cheeks flushed, more beautiful than ever. 'Yes, go. And a quick piece of advice, Toby: next time you think about proposing to someone, you might consider their feelings as well as what *you* want. You decided you had to have the house and the wife and the babies, and expected it all to fall into your lap, but I've got news for you. I'm my own person, and I'm going to stay that way.' She pulled off the princess cut ring and flung it at him.

He shoved it in his pocket and dropped some notes down on the table. 'You really are staggeringly immature, aren't you? Too damn right you're too young to get married. You can't even begin to grasp the emotional complexity of making a lifelong commitment to another human being.' He was almost shouting now, and aware with one part of his mind that he was giving the other customers an experience to rival *EastEnders*, but he was past caring. His only conscious thought was to get out of the restaurant and away from Ruby.

Five minutes later he was walking west along the river, thankful for the cool breeze on his flushed face. He felt as if he was in a film – the rejected hero – and he should be walking into a seedy bar and ordering three double whiskies, or possibly throwing himself into the river. His skin was crawling with humiliation. To have made such an open declaration and been so completely rejected was intolerable. She had actually *laughed* at the idea of marrying him. He shuddered.

As he crossed Waterloo Bridge, the Friday night crowds beginning their weekend all around him made him feel vulnerable, as though an accidental touch would bruise him, and he just wanted to find somewhere he could curl up in the foetal position and hide, literally and metaphorically. He felt so ashamed, so stupid. So angry – with Ruby, but also with himself. He just wanted to go home. With this thought in mind, he reached the Embankment and hailed a taxi. 'Grosvenor Road, Wanstead, please. Just off the High Street.'

He sat back and looked out of the window as the lights sped past. For once he could get no consolation out of his city. Normally one of the things he loved was the feeling of hugeness, eight million people each with their own lives, most of them never knowing or speaking to each other but as a collection of disparate, diverse, eclectic individuals somehow coming together to form the homogenous whole that was London. Now that just made him feel insignificant and small. And suddenly the thought of his too large, too empty house didn't seem so appealing after all. Should he go to his parents? No, they were in Morocco. Then a sudden realisation struck him and he exhaled slowly. When he had felt his overwhelming urge to go home it wasn't, he now realised, his own home he was picturing. He had been thinking about Julia's cosy little house. He wanted his best friend.

'Excuse me, mate, change of plan – can we make it Walthamstow instead, please? Eden Road.'

4

Julia was drumming her fingers impatiently on the kitchen table, wondering exactly what you had to do to get a minicab round here, when she heard the car pull up outside. Assuming that it was the taxi she had ordered finally arriving, she grabbed her bag and opened the front door. Then she stopped dead in her tracks. Toby was walking down her path, which was unexpected enough, but also he seemed entirely different from the Toby she had said goodbye to the previous Sunday – the Toby, in fact, whom she had known for twelve years. What was it? He looked older, harder, slightly dishevelled. Actually, she acknowledged to herself, he looked pretty bloody sexy. One of the obstacles to Julia fancying Toby had always been his sheer overwhelming niceness. Although he was undoubtedly tall and dark, he had never smouldered in the way that a girl raised on a literary diet of Gothic heroes felt a man should smoulder. He had never presented any sort of challenge to her. However, there was certainly a significant amount of smouldering going on right now.

'Toby, what on earth are you doing here? I thought tonight was the big night? You're meant to be on the South Bank with Ruby!'

'Past tense. *Was* the big night. Can I come in?'

There was no smile of greeting. In fact he appeared positively morose. His mouth was set in a hard line, his eyes seemed darker and he exuded tension. Hmm. Definitely sexy.

Toby paused for a second as he took in the fact that Julia was definitely not dressed for a quiet night in. 'Oh shit, are you going out? I never thought of that.'

'Thanks, Toby, nice to know your opinion of me is such that you imagine I spend my Friday nights sitting at home, on the vague off-chance that my friends decide to take a break from proposing to their girlfriends and pay me a surprise visit.'

'Come on, Julia, please. I really can't cope with the wisecracks right now. Are you going out, or can I come in?'

Julia felt shamefaced. It didn't exactly take Oprah levels of emotional intelligence to work out that something had gone very badly wrong for Toby this evening, but, hyper-aware of her own equivocal feelings during the past week, she had allowed herself to fall back on her usual self-defence of sarcastic self-deprecation, and in doing so was in danger of letting Toby down. 'Sorry, Tobes, you're right, that wasn't fair. Of course you can come in. I was only meant to be meeting a couple of the girls from work for a drink. I can easily cancel them.'

'Would you mind? Sorry, I wouldn't normally ask you to drop everything for me, but I really need a sympathetic pair of ears. Possibly a sympathetic pair of arms as well.'

Julia blushed, and was unsure why she was blushing, or why her hands had started shaking slightly. 'Well, sympathetic ears and arms are my speciality, so you've come to the right girl. Come in, and just give me a minute to cancel my taxi and text Jo to let her know I can't make it.'

That done, Julia turned to look at Toby, who was still standing awkwardly in the corner of the room. 'Hey, why the formality? Normally by this time you'd have helped yourself to a drink and found a light-hearted documentary on the prevalence of STDs in the Soviet Gulags which you'd be trying to persuade me would enhance our evening and my education!'

She was aiming for light but not flippant, desperately trying to put Toby at his ease a little and somehow recover the usually relaxed register of their banter. A standing source of good-natured teasing between them was that Julia's taste in television tended towards what she grandly described as 'culturally accessible', whereas Toby liked hard-hitting documentaries or the kind of film which never made it to the local Odeon. This attempt at normality seemed to work, to an extent at least. Toby sat down on the sofa, throwing off his jacket. She poured them both a glass of wine and curled up in the armchair opposite him.

'Do you want to talk about it?'

'I don't know. It's pretty fucking obvious, isn't it? One minute I tell you that I'm going to propose to my girlfriend, who I'm madly in love with, the next minute I'm round your house in need of a shoulder to cry on. You're an intelligent girl, Julia, put two and two together.'

'Okay, well clearly you haven't just got engaged. And from your tone I'm guessing that it isn't because you decided not to propose after all. So I suppose Ruby must have told you she wasn't ready to get married?'

'Well done. That's exactly what happened. Or to put it less tactfully, she turned me down. She doesn't want to get married, maybe ever, definitely not to me.'

Julia couldn't stand the hurt in his voice. She felt protective, in the way she remembered from when her little brother was bullied at school, but this was complicated by the fact that somehow Toby's change of mood had led to her being aware of his physical presence as never before. His shoulders, hunched in misery, seemed broader. She looked at his hands, twisting round and round the stem of his wineglass, and suddenly could only think about what they might feel like against her skin. She blushed again and tried to concentrate on how she could make Toby feel better. 'She's mad, Toby. Look at you: you're gorgeous, funny, clever, successful, really lovely . . .' She paused. 'Sexy.'

He laughed bitterly. 'Really? So if I'm that sexy, Julia, how come you didn't want me when we were students? Or ever since, for that matter? How come my girlfriend doesn't want to marry me? I just feel so humiliated. I can't believe I misread things so badly. I can't bear to think of her laughing at me. And everything I've been thinking about – what kind of wedding we'd have, whether we'd want children straight away or wait for a while, how much fun it would be living with someone properly, having someone there every morning . . . it's all just gone.'

He buried his head in his hands and, unable to bear it any longer, Julia went over to him, knelt on the floor by his feet and put her arms round him. Stroking his back soothingly and repetitively should have desexualised her mood, turning him into a platonic object of pity, but it didn't seem to be having that effect at all. Instead her nerve endings tingled and she surreptitiously leant in closer, enjoying his smell, his warmth.

'Tobes, can I ask you something, and you be honest with me?'

'Go ahead – this seems to be the evening for overly honest answers.'

'Do you think that deep, deep down you're really in love with Ruby, and you really want to marry *her*?' She paused. Toby hadn't said anything, but he hadn't moved away from her, or sworn, or hit her, all of which seemed perfectly plausible reactions, so she felt encouraged to continue. 'It's just that what you've said about feeling humiliated and losing your dreams about the wedding and living with someone and all the rest of it, that's all fair enough, and I can totally understand why you'd be upset, but you haven't actually mentioned Ruby personally. It makes me wonder whether you've reached a stage in your life when you feel that marriage is the right thing to do, and Ruby just happened to be in the right place – or wrong place, I guess – when the music stopped.' She paused again, and glanced up at him. His eyes were opening wide in what seemed like startled recognition.

'I don't know,' he said slowly. There was a pause while he turned the idea over in his mind. 'I think you're right to some extent. I have got to a point where I want to be married; I want to have a deeper level of commitment than a toothbrush and some clean underwear in the girl's flat. And I guess I have been influenced by the fact that Ruby is one of the most beautiful women I've ever seen.'

Julia wondered whether there was even the slightest possibility that she was another of the most beautiful women he had ever seen, but then dismissed the idea with an internal sigh. She had scrubbed up quite nicely tonight, and she said a quick inward prayer of thanks that she was no longer in the Primark pyjamas, but even her mother had never gone so far as to call her beautiful.

Toby carried on. 'I think the thing about Ruby was that she was so different from me. I'm Mr Sensible, with my shiny shoes and my health insurance and my pension plan, and I feel that I'm already middle-aged. My parents seem much younger than me sometimes. When I was with Ruby I felt like I wasn't so boring after all.'

'Is it past tense then? Have you and Ruby split up, or do you want to carry on going out together, take it more slowly?'

Toby seemed horrified. 'God, no, we've definitely split up. We had a huge fight and, to be honest, I'm not sure she even really wants to be in a relationship, let alone get married. I suppose you're right, it works both ways. If I was as much in love with Ruby as I thought I was, then I'd want to work at it and give her some space. But truthfully, I never want to see her again.'

Julia's heart leapt. That was the right answer anyway.

Toby looked at Julia as she knelt at his feet, arms around him, big green eyes gazing up at him, and felt a vast wave of affection, accompanied by an almost irresistible desire to kiss her. She didn't have Ruby's traffic-stopping beauty, but her sparkly eyes framed by long dark lashes, her softly rounded cheeks and her slightly quizzical mouth were all heart-stoppingly familiar, and her cleavage, of which he had an excellent view, was spectacular.

'What are you thinking?' she asked softly, still in concerned friend mode.

Toby took a deep breath and threw caution to the wind for the second time that night. 'I was thinking that I want to kiss you.'

The air was suddenly electric, the sexual tension palpable.

'Don't joke, Tobes.' They could both hear her voice shaking.

'I'm not.'

Suddenly his arms were tight round her, and his mouth had come down hard on hers.

Julia had always had a particular hatred for James Joyce's writing, after a more than usually traumatic tutorial at university when her tutor had suggested that when it came to interpreting *Ulysses*, she had the critical insight of a Teletubby. However, at this point her internal monologue owed a certain something to Molly Bloom, insofar as any attempt at coherent sentence structure was abandoned.

Bad idea rebound I don't even fancy Toby actually maybe I do how the hell did this happen what am I doing I really need to stop this thank God I put on nice knickers no I can't even be contemplating having sex with Toby it's *Toby* for fuck's sake oh my God that feels nice oh sod it I'm sick of being sensible let's just see what happens no

I mustn't Toby's been hurt it's up to me to be responsible
I'm sick of being responsible why shouldn't I enjoy myself
it feels soooo nice why have we never done this before I
don't care I'm doing it mmmmm

5

Toby woke up first in the morning. Once he had realised that he wasn't at home, wasn't alone, and was in fact in his best friend's bed with her naked leg entwined with his naked leg, he started to review the events of the previous evening. First he replayed the scene in the restaurant with Ruby and was astonished to find that, although he still felt embarrassed, he didn't feel remotely broken-hearted. In fact he felt satisfied. Pleased with himself. Content. At one with the world.

He had sensed when he arrived at Julia's the previous evening that something had changed in her attitude towards him. He had fancied her straight away, as she wiggled around in her tight skirt, giving tantalising glimpses of skin through her partially transparent blouse. But then, he was a bloke. He quite often fancied women he spent time with. Not in an I-want-to-fuck-you-now kind of way, but in a generally appreciative I-wouldn't-say-no-given-half-a-chance way. And for the first time ever with Julia, last night, some subtle change in her body language had led him to think that he might just have that half a chance.

That had felt like just what his ego needed. He hadn't intended to use Julia, exactly. Hadn't really rationalised it

39

at all. But when he kissed her and she responded, the uppermost thought in his mind had been 'I deserve this'. He winced slightly. Nice. But then it had been amazing. Julia was so soft and warm, and really, really into it. They'd had amazing sex, twice. Then he must have fallen asleep in her arms, which he never did in new relationships, or with his occasional one-night stands. Insomnia was never far away for Toby, and sharing a bed, for the whole night, had always been something more to be endured than enjoyed, but even after the trauma of his day he had felt so completely relaxed with Julia that her presence had helped rather than hindered him in drifting off.

Now, as her silky-smooth leg moved against his, he could feel himself getting hard again. He pressed into her slightly and, only half awake, she pushed back against him. Maybe further analysis could wait.

Julia had been lying half awake for a little while, trying to contain her natural impatience and let Toby make the first move, hoping that this would give her some indication of how he felt about what had happened. If it hadn't been for wanting to keep still, Julia would have hugged herself. Last night had been delicious. A complete revelation. If she had known how good it would be, she reflected, she would have gone to bed with Toby years ago. She knew that she should be feeling guilty, or anxious, or both, but the deep physical contentment left by two blindingly good orgasms had left her temporarily unable to rationalise.

When she felt him pressing into her leg, obviously after a repeat performance, she decided to let her sensible self remain on vacation and indulge once again in pure (or decidedly impure) sensuous pleasure.

Now both wide awake, and slicked with sweat, they lay in each other's arms. Julia was the first to break the silence.

'Do you feel weird?'

'No. In fact, the weirdest thing is how completely unweird I feel.'

'I *know*!' Julia scooched round so that she could look at him. 'I just can't believe we haven't done that before. Why haven't we?'

'Not for want of trying on my part.'

'Not really. I mean, I know we had a couple of snogs at uni, but it's not like you've spent the last ten years trying to get into my knickers.'

'No, not exactly, but only because I thought you'd made it abundantly clear that wasn't what you wanted, and I felt like I'd had enough rejection. Not a view Ruby shared, clearly.'

Ruby. The name fell like a brick rather than a gemstone into Julia's post-coital bliss. Bugger. Rebound. She remembered some small, rational part of her brain last night warning her that Toby's sudden desire was far more to do with Ruby's rejection than any exponential increase in her own sex appeal, but overall, logic – and, in fact, her mind – had been largely off duty.

'Now I feel a bit weird, Tobes. Like last night I was some kind of Ruby substitute.'

'No!' Toby sat up, and pulled Julia up too. 'Listen to me, Julia, this is so important. What happened between us last night, and this morning, is nothing to do with Ruby. I honestly feel like the Ruby chapter is over. You're my best friend, the person I love being with more than anyone else in the world. The person who knows me best. The person, it turns out, I just had mind-blowingly good sex with. I'm not sure what that means for us – I can't exactly ask you for your number and take you out for dinner – but you've got to believe me that I'm not in your bed now to make myself feel better about Ruby turning me down.'

A warm glow spread through Julia as she realised that she did believe him, implicitly. With good reason as well; Toby had never lied to her. Sometimes he was far too honest for her own good ('Have I put weight on?' 'Yes, you do look a bit chubbier than usual'), but he never pulled any punches. Considering matters, she realised that she felt the same as Toby did. He was pretty much her favourite person in the world, and the sex had been some of the best she'd ever had, but she wasn't sure what it all meant either.

'I believe you. And I think I feel the same. But what does that mean we do now?'

'Now?' Toby grinned at her. 'Right now you get your-self out of bed and make us some breakfast, and then we decide what we want to do with the rest of this bright and sunny Saturday.'

Julia hit him playfully, but the sun was indeed stream-ing through the white voile curtains at the window, and feeling a bubble of happiness and energy welling up inside her she decided to ignore Toby's deliberately provocative sexism. She jumped out of bed, pulled on her waffle robe and practically skipped downstairs. As she went, she heard Toby turn on the shower, and then the familiar sounds of Radio 4 floated down from the bathroom. Normally Julia was just as addicted to the *Today* programme as Toby, but this morning she tuned into a local cheesy pop station and danced round her kitchen as she tried to come up with something a bit more inspirational than Special K for their breakfast.

A little over half an hour later, encouraged by the beautiful sunshine, Julia and Toby were sitting at the little white wrought-iron table on Julia's patio, tucking into large mugs of milky coffee and very freshly made banana chocolate-chip muffins. They were acting, Julia thought, like a couple of teenagers, feeding each other, licking melted chocolate sensuously off fingers and arguing playfully about what they should do for the day. The radio in the kitchen was still tuned to the local station, and just then the intro to the weather forecast could be heard through the open French windows.

'Shh, listen, let's see if this weather's going to last.'

'. . . Good news for those of you who don't have to work weekends – London and the south-east are going to be enjoying particularly warm weather over the next couple of days. Temperatures will be reaching thirty degrees in London and along the south coast, so for once it really will feel like summer . . .'

'Ooh!' Julia almost squealed with excitement. 'I know what we should do. Let's go to Brighton for the day!'

A slow smile spread across Toby's face. 'That's an absolutely genius idea!'

Both of them knew Brighton pretty well; Julia had a friend from school who was now a teacher and lived there with her boyfriend, and Toby's colleague and good friend Mark braved the daily commute from Brighton to London, but they had only ever been there together once, ten years ago as students. They'd had hardly any money, but had gone with a large group of friends, laughed themselves nearly sick on the funfair at the end of the pier, and then bought sausages, baguettes, cider and a throwaway barbecue and taken them down to the beach. They had sat for hours eating, drinking, talking, flirting and laughing till long after the sun went down, and then all huddled together to get what illusory warmth they could from the dying embers of the barbecue before making a mad dash to the station to catch the last train. It had been an absolutely golden day, and they both felt excited at the thought of recreating it, albeit with slightly less emphasis on cheap cider.

Toby had eaten breakfast wrapped in Julia's luckily voluminous bathrobe, but neither that nor an Armani suit seemed particularly appropriate for a day by the seaside. His house was only about two miles from Julia's, but somehow, although they couldn't put it into words, neither of them wanted Toby to risk breaking the magic fragility of the bubble around them by going home to get changed.

'Hey, I've just remembered!' Julia exclaimed. 'My brother left some stuff here last time he stayed, I washed it and put it away till I next saw him, and you're probably about the same size.'

When they checked, Harry had helpfully forgotten a pair of jeans and a stripy t-shirt, which weren't too out of place with the brown Patrick Cox loafers Toby had been wearing the previous evening. With an attention to cleanliness Julia had not noticed in many of her boyfriends, Toby rinsed his boxer shorts and socks through in the shower, and they dried in the warm sunshine and light breeze while Julia was showering and getting dressed. Julia decided to make the possibly unwise choice of trusting the local weather forecast and put on her favourite sundress – crisp white cotton with yellow polka dots – along with a little white cardie and flip-flops. Underneath she wore underwear which she mentally classed as 'hopefully expectant' rather than obvious – a white broderie anglaise bra and pants set – and she put on just a touch of mascara to highlight the startlingly green eyes everyone said were her best feature, and a dab of blusher to counteract the three days post-mortem effect of her natural pallor. The overall effect was cute rather than glamorous, but she knew that the dress suited her, and it also seemed to suit the glorious weather and her sunshiny mood.

Then, giggling a little at the easy unfamiliarity, they set off hand in hand to the tube station.

6

Getting off the train at Brighton always lifted Julia's spirits, and being in a good mood to start with she was practically flying as they headed off to the Lanes. They had sat snuggled together on the train, reading the *Guardian* – Toby taking the main section, *Work* and *Money*, and Julia the magazine, *Review* and *Family*. As they read they had drawn each other's attention to things which struck them as interesting or amusing, all easy and companionable and not substantially different from the way in which they had spent countless Saturdays together, but this time punctuated by a soft kiss on the lips here and a squeeze on the waist there.

'Right, we absolutely *have* to go to Choccywoccydoodah, it's my favourite café ever.'

'We have to go *where*?' Toby looked at Julia in complete bewilderment. 'Ju, I would have hoped that after last night this wouldn't come as a complete shock to you, but not only am I a man, I'm a straight man, and I'm afraid that I can't possibly compromise my masculinity by entering a retail establishment going by the improbable name of "Choccywoccydoodah".'

'You need to embrace your metrosexuality, my friend. And honestly, when you've tasted the hot chocolate at

47

this place you'd compromise any damn thing you like to go back. Trust me; if there's one thing I understand, it's chocolate.'

They shared a large mug of liquid dark chocolate, and dipped pieces of strawberry and banana into molten white chocolate and fed them to each other, and Toby was forced to concede that Julia was right – the compromise of his masculinity was a small price to pay for such deliciousness.

Then they embarked upon a day which Julia felt could have been a montage scene in a film, probably accompanied by a soundtrack playing something obvious like 'Perfect Day'. They went on the rollercoasters and waltzers and clung to each other in terror and exhilaration. They window-shopped in the Lanes, Toby buying Julia a beautiful antique turquoise and silver necklace she fell in love with. They ate king prawns cooked with garlic and chilli and white wine, served with crusty bread, salad and a bottle of crisp fresh Chablis, at an outdoor table of a darling little café in a darling little square. They paid an eye-watering sum to peek at the eccentric Regency splendour of the Pavilion, allowing Julia to spend a few moments imagining herself as a heroine in a Georgette Heyer novel. They contemplated a traditional cream tea, but decided that they were simply too full. They walked along the beach, licking ice creams and contemplated paddling.

'I wish we had swimming things with us, Tobes.'

Toby laughed. 'You're getting old, darling. I seem to remember that as students we went in wearing our underwear, and just ran round to get dry afterwards.'

'Yep, I am getting old. Which means that if I go swimming, in the sea, in Britain, which would probably mean I was slightly mad anyway, the very least I require is a proper bikini, a large fluffy towel and some clean, dry clothes to put on afterwards.'

'We could always go and buy some stuff, if you'd really like to swim.'

'Nah. Not worth it. Listen, by the time we've walked back up to town, gone to the shops, bought stuff, come back, swum, it'll be practically time to go home. And I probably am too old to sit all gritty and sandy and damp on the train home.'

A mischievous and excited smile lit Toby's face. 'No, come on, Julia, I refuse to let you get old and boring. We're going to march up to town and buy what you need to swim in comfort, and then we're going to come back here and bloody well swim. How often do you get a day like this? We're being serendipitous.'

'Oh, okay.' Julia groaned, but was secretly delighted by Toby's enthusiasm and zest for life. He had always had that, but the hours he worked and the responsibility of his job seemed to have drained him of it a little bit recently.

In the end they set each other the £10 Primark challenge and, as an expert cheap shop shopper, Julia managed to buy herself a bright turquoise bikini, a pack of three pairs of pink-and-white candy-striped cotton knickers and a chaotically flowered beach towel. Toby's choice was somewhat more sedate: navy blue swim shorts and a plain red towel. They were becoming increasingly giggly as they raced back towards the beach.

Julia wiggled into her bikini under the beach towel and then enjoyed the feeling of Toby's eyes raking over her. Usually bikinis were her worst nightmare, requiring weeks of yo-yo dieting and close analysis of any magazine promising 'The most flattering beach wear EVER' or '7 days to a flat stomach'. Now, though, she felt sexy, sensuous, feminine, her whole body warmed by the lustful appreciation in Toby's eyes. He looked pretty good too, she admitted to herself. A year ago he had joined the gym near work and went religiously three mornings a week, and his deliciously toned abs and biceps seemed to suggest that his efforts had paid off.

Holding hands, they ran down to the water, wincing at the stones under their bare feet. Unsurprisingly for Britain, even in June, the water was bitingly cold as they inched their way in, toes, then feet, then calves, then—

'Eeoogghh! I can't do this! I can't believe you're trying to make me do this, you sadistic bastard!'

'Excuse me, it was you who wanted to swim, Madam, I just facilitated your desires. As I am only too happy to do in all areas.'

'You'll be bloody lucky! After this, you won't be facilitating any desires anywhere near me.'

'Oh won't I?' Toby suddenly lunged at Julia and scooped her up in his arms. His breath was hot on her skin as he gently sucked and nibbled her neck, and despite herself her eyes closed and she felt herself melting, pressing into him. Then without any warning Toby plunged forward, immersing them both in the icy water.

They shrieked simultaneously, and Julia beat her hands against Toby's back, in mock anger at first, and then just because she was enjoying the feeling of the muscle definition under his skin.

'See, it's not so bad once we're in, is it?'

Julia snorted. 'Oh no, positively tropical. I've no idea why people bother travelling all that way to get to the Maldives.'

To herself, though, she admitted that it wasn't so bad, and messing around in the water with Toby, chasing and swimming, pushing, pulling, ducking, kissing, sliding surreptitious hands down bikini top or up shorts, was both fun and sexy. It was still England, though, and after a while they both began to feel tired and chilly.

They struggled damply and saltily into their clothes, and then Toby said, 'It's nearly seven o'clock, shall we go and get a cocktail to warm us up?'

Julia sighed. 'I could murder a cocktail, but look at me.' She gestured at the salt-encrusted hair dripping down her back, and the mascara smudges she knew were under her eyes. 'I'm hardly in any state for Saturday night in a cool bar in Brighton. We could find a little pub, maybe.'

Toby's eyes gleamed. 'You look beautiful. I love that dress. All you need is to be able to have a shower and freshen up, and you could go anywhere.'

'Well yes, maybe, but small problem, Tobes. My shower is sixty miles away in East London.'

'No, my darling.' He put his hand in his pocket and pulled out a key. 'Your shower for tonight is approximately sixty yards away.' He gestured up towards the promenade. 'While you were mooching about doing whatever it is that girls do in the Cath Kidston shop, I sneaked off and booked us a room in what is apparently the finest boutique hotel in Brighton.'

'Eek!' Julia skipped about on the pebbles excitedly. 'You're an angel! That's the best idea ever. Wow. God, we're having a proper, traditional dirty weekend. Is it incredibly expensive?'

'It's going to be completely worth it, I promise you.'

Fifteen minutes later Julia was running a deep, hot bubble bath and gazing around, entranced. From the huge seven-foot bed, the pile of snowy white towels and bathrobes, the free-standing bath with views over the sea, to the bottle of champagne Toby had just ordered from room service, it was perfect. It was hotel fantasy land. Stripping off her clothes and sinking into the blissfully warm water, Julia giggled at the contrast between what she was doing now and what she had been doing at the same time the previous evening – lying prostrate on the sofa in ancient pyjamas with a glass of supermarket plonk.

Toby joined her in what was a completely new experience for her – sharing a bath in a way which was completely comfortable for both parties. It was the most perfectly romantic and intimate time, drinking the champagne, massaging each other and watching a spectacular sunset over the sea. Julia felt transported to another world; it was all completely blissful, but somewhat unreal. After a while the gentle massage of each other's backs and shoulders took on a more urgent quality, and their bodies slipped and slid sensuously as they made love in the warm water. As Toby came inside her, Julia felt tears welling up in her eyes and held him closer, burying her face in his shoulder, grateful that sex in the bath meant a few additional drops of water were unlikely to be noticed.

After a while, Julia washed and conditioned her hair and got out of the bath to slather herself in body lotion, taking full advantage of the delicious-smelling Molton Brown products provided. By the time she had blow-dried her hair, reapplied her make-up and re-dressed herself she felt relatively content with her appearance. Still not glamorous, but a considerable improvement on the dishevelled girl who had walked into the hotel earlier that evening. And it was hard not to feel confident in herself when Toby was so physically and vocally appreciative.

The bar in the hotel was lit only with tea lights. Toby watched the flames playing on Julia's face, creating a garnet glow of her Kir Royale, and felt his insides clench with desire, protectiveness, an urge to squeeze her so tightly she was absorbed into him. Looking just as she did now with her golden brown hair smooth over her shoulders and her face lightly freckled from a day in the sunshine, he wanted to put her into a glass case and keep her there, keep her safe, keep this moment. Sensing his mood, she put out a hand and squeezed his tightly.

'What are we doing, Tobes?'

He didn't pretend not to understand. 'I don't know. I've never felt anything like this before. The person I want to fuck more than anyone else has never been the person I want to spend time with more than anyone else.'

'Not even Ruby?'

'No, not even then. I really, really, really fancied her—'

'One "really" would have sufficed, you know.'

'Sorry. But I did. But given a straight choice of an evening spent with you or an evening spent with her, I think I would always have chosen you.'

'Bloody hell, Toby! I'm not an expert, but even I know that isn't a good basis for marriage.'

'I know. I think perhaps it was a classic case of thinking with my dick. I can't help being a man. But I've told you what I'm thinking. What about you? What do you think we're doing?'

Julia looked at him. His dark brown eyes were fixed on hers and his hand was still gripping hers slightly more tightly than was comfortable. She was clinging to the edge of an emotional precipice. Toby had been honest with her, but he hadn't said the words she had been half hoping, half terrified to hear. But then what *did* it mean if you wanted to have sex with someone all the time, and liked them more than anyone else? Surely that *was* falling in love, wasn't it? And when you combined that with the fact that this was someone she had loved and cared for platonically her entire adult life, then perhaps she wasn't exaggerating to think that she was falling in love with Toby. But then, he hadn't used those words, and the golden rule that all single girls knew was that you mustn't say them first. Sexual liberation meant that you could ask a guy out, be the one to call him first, hell, you could drag him off to the toilets of a nightclub and perform expert oral sex on him before you had even exchanged names, but never, ever, under any circumstances should you say you loved him before he said it to you. However, rules, surely, were made to be broken.

'This is really scary to think, Toby, let alone to say, but I think I might be falling in love with you. It's not just this last twenty-four hours. I think when you told me that you were going to propose to Ruby I suddenly saw sense and I've been in such a state all week, thinking that I'd lost you, I suppose. Then when you came round yesterday evening I guess I just wanted to grab my chance. But also I'm worried that whatever you think now, it's just a rebound thing for you.'

Toby let his breath out, scarcely aware that he had been holding it. 'Well, that's just bloody great!'

She frowned at him, puzzled and a little worried.

'The problem with you, Julia, is that you're so bloody slow. Twelve years it's taken you to get round to this. If you'd realised a little earlier, think of the money I could have saved. God! All those expensive first dates. Paying for my own house when I could have been sharing with you. New clothes to try and impress new girls. Honestly!'

With sufficiently flushed cheeks and heaving bosom to equip any Mills and Boon heroine, Julia gave Toby's arm an unladylike and fairly forceful whack. 'You bastard! I'm being serious, laying my heart on the line for you, and you start taking the piss. Well, I take it all back. I find, Mr Fenton, that I have been mistaken in my feelings.'

Toby rubbed his bruised arm and grinned. 'Oh no, you don't get out of it that easily. I heard what you said quite clearly.' The tone of his voice changed. 'And Julia, I'm so in love with you too. I know it seems the most ridiculous thing to say when yesterday I was asking another woman to marry me, but it's true. You're everything, Julia, and you always have been. You're warm and loving and funny and kind and sexy and clever and an amazing friend and an even more amazing cook. You're all I want.'

Julia felt her eyes welling up with tears again and blinked furiously. This was it. The moment. Possibly what she had been waiting for her entire life. Whatever she said next was of crucial importance to her future happiness.

'You're all those things too. Other than being an amazing cook. But speaking of food, now we've got all this sorted out, can we have some dinner? I'm absolutely starving, and the smell of the steak frites from that table over there is killing me.'

7

Rose Harley-Jamieson sighed deeply as she bent down to pick up yet another piece of brightly coloured plastic. It was 7 p.m. on a Sunday evening. Pre-Sebastian she would probably have been in the pub now, moaning about the fact that another Monday morning was fast approaching. If someone had told her twenty-five-year-old self that one day she would be living in a nice house in beautiful countryside, married to a handsome man whose executive salary was such that she would have no need to do any work other than looking after her adorable two-year-old son, she wouldn't have been able to believe that she could possibly be so lucky. She would certainly never have believed that she could experience a moment's unhappiness while cocooned in such an existence.

And she was happy, she told herself repeatedly. Just a little tired, sometimes. And occasionally bored. And maybe a touch lonely every so often. She adored Sebastian more passionately than she would have believed possible. It was just that being a full-time mum was just that, full time. Not full time in the way that her work as a press officer had been – hard work at times, sure, but only starting at 9.30 a.m. and finishing at 6 p.m., and involving the odd sneaky liquid lunch, or an extended loo break which just happened to take in a few chocolate Hobnobs and some office gossip in the kitchenette area. Then there were the obligatory Friday-after-work drinks. And the weekend. The bliss of knowing that every week from 5.30 on Friday to 9.30 on Monday she was a completely free agent, responsible to no one, able to do whatever she took it into her head to do. Looking back, Rose couldn't understand why she hadn't made better use of that freedom. Where had the spontaneous last-minute weekend breaks to trendy Baltic capitals been? The all-night clubbing? The classes to learn Italian, or philosophy, or life-drawing? Why had she never been to the British Museum, or to Tate Britain, or to the ballet, or to a burlesque show?

Now the weekend meant that her husband Graeme was home, and to 'help out' he was putting Sebastian to bed. Which meant that her only jobs for this evening were to scrub encrusted fish fingers and baked beans off the kitchen table, put on a load of laundry, tidy up Sebastian's body weight in discarded toys, and begin preparing supper for two. When she had been young, free, single and living in London, Rose knew now that she had not made the most of it. Now, even her attempts to live vicariously through her closest friend Julia were being frustrated by Julia's ludicrous stubbornness. Anyone with half a brain could see that Julia was more than half in love with her friend Toby, and he with her, and during the time that Toby had been dating some girl who was a model or dancer or something, Rose had watched Julia's *joie de vivre*, and in fact her desire to leave the house, shrivel away. She wanted to yell at her that now was the time, now she could do anything, be anyone, and that before she knew it she would be tied down by marriage and children and her chances of living her life just for herself would be gone for ever. But of course, as good old reliable Rose she never actually said that, and just had to listen in smilingly acquiescent silence as Julia, and everyone else in fact, told her how lucky she was to have met Graeme, to have had Sebastian.

As Rose was half under the sofa searching for the final piece of a jigsaw, the phone rang, making her jump. She banged her head. 'Oh goodness me, that hurt!' she exclaimed, before realising that her self-censored language was unnecessary as Sebastian was safely upstairs with Graeme. Typical. Motherhood meant she couldn't even swear properly any more. Fuck.

'Hello?' she snapped into the phone.

'Hi, Rosie, it's me. Is it a bad time?'

Rose listened. Sebastian was still splashing and shouting happily in the bath; it would be a good twenty minutes before Graeme got him into bed. She sank guiltily onto the sofa, promising herself just fifteen minutes of gossip and chat before she had to go and start supper. 'It's as good as any, I suppose.'

'Excellent. I have so much to tell you! You are never going to believe the weekend I've had! It started on Friday night, Toby suddenly turned up on my doorstep . . .'

Rose twisted the bottom of her t-shirt round and round her index finger as she listened to Julia's excited, animated voice. She felt flat. Rationally she was delighted for Julia. Toby was a total sweetheart, she had always thought so – tall and unthreateningly good looking, with a dry sense of humour and vibrant, infectious enthusiasm, and he and Julia were ideally well suited in her opinion. But somehow she couldn't feel the warmth and happiness she wanted to.

'. . . So he's gone back to his to get some clean clothes and his laptop and stuff for work, and I'm here making dinner for when he gets back. How domestic is that?'

'Well, making supper for you and Toby on a Sunday night isn't exactly new for you.'

'Well, no.'

Julia sounded slightly hurt, Rose thought. But then her tone brightened as she said mischievously, 'But cooking dinner for him after two nights of red-hot sex and a passionate declaration of love is something of a change for me. I feel you've missed the salient points of my story, Rose!'

'Ha bloody ha. What I meant really was that you two have always been a couple, you just wouldn't admit it to yourselves, let alone to each other. I'm so happy for you, Julia. Honestly.'

A few minutes later, grinding garlic, ginger, chilli and lemongrass in her pestle and mortar as she prepared a Thai curry, Julia smiled to herself. Bless Rose, she was such a sweetie, it had almost sounded like she was crying because she was so happy for her. For so long Julia had been jealous of Rose. She had tried not to be, and she still loved her friend, but an adoring husband and a gorgeous baby were everything Julia wanted and at times felt she would never have. Now, as she pottered happily round her kitchen amongst mouth-watering cooking smells, creating a delicious meal for the man she was madly in love with, suddenly the fantasy life Rose lived didn't seem quite such a distant dream after all.

Toby was in his bedroom, wondering how many work shirts to take back to Julia's. More than one seemed presumptuous, but on the other hand he couldn't imagine wanting to spend his nights anywhere other than in Julia's bed from now on, and it would be a pain to have to keep dragging himself back here to collect stuff. He grinned as he remembered the joke his (gay) friend Lisa had told him. 'What does a lesbian take on a first date? A suitcase.'

Would he freak Julia out if he turned up with a suitcase? It was meant to be men who were commitment phobic, but he had sensed that Julia seemed to be holding back slightly more than him, possibly because despite all his reassurances she was still worried that this was a rebound thing for him.

As if on cue, his phone beeped to announce the arrival of a text message. It was from Ruby.

Cn u come round? We need 2 tlk.

He had never been able to stand the text abbreviations she always used. His own text messages were as perfectly grammatically constructed and spelt as every other form of written communication he used. That didn't mean he had to be expansive though.

No. Sorry. There's nothing to say.

There was no reply for a few minutes, during which time Toby convinced himself that Julia wouldn't be at all freaked out by him taking five shirts. Although just to be absolutely sure, and to avoid the suitcase cliché, he was meticulously rolling his shirts into bundles small enough to be stuffed into his laptop case. As he squeezed the last one in, the phone beeped shrilly into life again. This time the spelling and grammar were perfect, but the content was such that Toby barely noticed.

Yes there is. I'm pregnant.

The world seemed literally to wobble on its axis. Toby felt a surge of overwhelming panic. The rollercoaster of emotions he had experienced in the last forty-eight hours threatened to catch up with him, and his knees went weak as he sank down on the edge of his bed. How was it that two days ago this would have seemed like the best, most exciting news in the world, and now it was close to being the worst? For ten minutes he sat there, paralysed. Then, slowly, his normal energetic and decisive self snapped back to life and he reached for his phone. Two texts.

OK. I'll be round in half an hour.

Darling Julia, so, so, so sorry, something's come up at work so don't think I'll be able to make it back to yours this evening. I'll call you. I love you. T xx

Julia grabbed at her phone as she heard the text come through. Toby had already been longer than she had expected. The curry was simmering fragrantly on the stove, the Sauvignon Blanc was in the fridge, and she was rooting around in the back of a cupboard trying to find some candles.

The pang of disappointment as she read the message was sharper than she would have believed possible. She had been so looking forward to their evening. More disquietingly, something about the text struck her as not quite ringing true. It was hard to put a finger on, and she knew that Toby's job was ludicrously demanding, but a sixth sense told her that wasn't the whole story. Her heart sank. Was Toby already having second thoughts? Things had moved so ridiculously quickly over the weekend, she couldn't quite believe it herself. And men were notoriously commitment shy. Maybe she had blown it by assuming he would stay over that night and sending him home to get his work things? But he had seemed so enthusiastic. Now was not the time to ask for reassurance, though. She had to play it cool.

Oh no, poor you, not on a Sun night! Think I'll have a hot bath and an early night though, so don't worry about phoning later. J x

Curled up on the sofa with a double portion of red Thai chicken curry (she had contemplated doing the sensible thing and freezing Toby's half, but decided that comfort eating was what was required, again), half watching *Midsomer Murders*, she reflected that it was only a week since Toby had told her that he was going to ask Ruby to marry him. She shuddered at how close she had come to losing him before he had ever been hers to lose, and wished that she could get rid of the unnerving sense that between Toby kissing her goodbye earlier that evening and sending his text message just now, something significant had changed.

8

Toby looked round the room. Thick pile carpet. Beautifully polished wooden furniture. Tastefully upholstered comfortable chairs. It seemed a bizarre place to come to end your child's life, but apparently that's what you did. Or that's what you did if you were wealthy enough to afford the £1,500 it cost to terminate a pregnancy here. He wondered if he would be paying the bill. It felt odd to do so, like he was a cad who had got Tess of the d'Urbervilles into trouble and was buying her off. It wasn't as though Ruby, or rather Ruby's parents, couldn't afford it. Although it might be a bit tricky for her to explain this little expense to Mummy and Daddy. And maybe it would be the gentlemanly thing to do. Toby shook himself. What was wrong with him? His ex-girlfriend was in there having his child aborted, and he was conducting an internal debate on the etiquette of who should pick up the bill. Surely his thoughts should be deeper and more meaningful than that?

Shamefully though, his overwhelming feeling at that moment, other than the vague, nauseous claustrophobia any medical establishment, however tastefully disguised, always aroused in him, was an overwhelming sense of relief. When he had received the message from Ruby last night, he had been forced to contemplate the hideous possibility of losing Julia before ever really having her, or the equally unthinkable alternative of abandoning Ruby to have his child alone. When Ruby had told him that she had already booked an appointment to have a termination and just needed his moral (or should that be immoral) support, he had felt that he had been given a second lease of life, a real reprieve. He just had to bluff his way through a couple of days of not seeing Julia while Ruby got things sorted and he took care of her afterwards, and then he could pick up where he had left off.

'You know I'm not ready for children, Toby,' Ruby had said to him last night. 'In fact I don't know if I ever want them. I don't know how this happened, it must have been the antibiotics I took interfering with the Pill.'

Toby hadn't even remembered her taking antibiotics; he certainly didn't know they could counteract the Pill. But he wouldn't have cared then anyway; he would have loved to have made Ruby pregnant, would have hoped it might make her calmer and more domesticated. More, he now realised, like Julia.

'So anyway, when I realised yesterday I was late I took a test, and as soon as I saw it was positive I got on the phone to this clinic that my friend went to last year, and I've got an appointment for tomorrow morning. I thought I'd be okay on my own, but then I realised that they won't let you home on your own, and also,' her voice had wobbled slightly, 'also, I think I probably do need someone with me. You know how squeamish I am about needles.'

Toby had thought she sounded hard and cold as she talked about a procedure which surely most women still saw as a last resort. He realised, though, that this was sheer hypocrisy – he wanted this baby's life to be ended before it had even begun because it would make it easier for him to continue his relationship with a new girlfriend. Had he not been so caught up in his own moral dilemma, Toby might have applied his usual perception and sensitivity to the situation and realised that Ruby's detached response was the only way she could cope. Having decided that an abortion was the right option, she couldn't allow herself any chink of emotion in case it clouded the rational decision. Similarly, while he sat there feeling tense and guilty and relieved and lovesick for Julia, Toby couldn't allow himself to attribute any warmth or feeling to Ruby in case his carefully constructed web of justifications began to unravel.

The noise of a door opening broke into Toby's train of thought. A nurse in a crisp white uniform came over to him. 'Mr Fenton?'

'Yes. Is everything okay?'

'Ms Anstey asked me to come and get you. Would you like to come through with me, please.'

'What's the matter? Is Ruby all right? Did something go wrong?'

'Don't worry, there's no medical problem.'

They walked through another set of double doors, and the pretence that this was a luxurious drawing room rather than a clinic was suddenly over. Here everything was gleaming white or steel. Ruby was sitting on a white chair in a small curtained-off area. Her head was in her hands and she was crying uncontrollably, great racking sobs which shook her whole body. Another nurse was standing beside her, patting her shoulder rather ineffectually, and when this woman glanced up and saw Toby an expression of intense and unmistakeable relief passed over her professionally impassive countenance. As far as she was concerned, the cavalry had arrived. Toby had never before felt so out of his emotional depth.

The nurse who had brought him through pulled up another chair beside Ruby's and motioned for him to sit down. Both nurses then tactfully withdrew and pulled the curtains closed behind them. As they did so Toby had a momentary feeling that his options were being closed off with them. He put a tentative arm around Ruby, and she surprised him by turning and burying her head in his shoulder, still sobbing as though her heart would break.

'Ruby, what is it? Does something hurt? Is there a problem?'

She gazed up at him, almost unrecognisable with her eyes swollen and red, her make-up streaked, her face blotchy. She seemed smaller and younger, dressed simply in skinny jeans, floral print pumps and a plain, pale pink fitted t-shirt, her dark hair pulled back in a ponytail with wisps escaping messily around her face. Normally she was so sophisticated that Toby scarcely noticed the six years between them. Now, he felt every one.

'I can't do it, Toby.'

'Can't? You mean . . . you mean, you can't . . .?'

'You see, you can't even *say* it! I mean I can't have an abortion. They sat me down here and told me about what would happen, and the risks, and the possible side-effects, and it was all so calm and clinical – God, you don't even have to have an anaesthetic at this stage, you can take some tablets, have a slightly heavy period, and then that's it, job done. And it was like something snapped and I absolutely knew that there was no way I could go through with it.'

'So . . . you mean, you want to have the baby?'

'No! That's just it, that's why I'm in this state. I don't want to have a baby *at all*. It feels like the end of everything. But I somehow know that if I do this it really *will* be the end of everything. I simply can't cope with making that decision.'

Toby felt a rising tide of panic and tried to suppress it. Of all times, this was the moment in his life when he had to remain calm and clear-headed. If this was a business meeting, how would he deal with it, how would he go about getting the outcome he wanted? Rational, logical, reasoned argument.

'Look, Ruby, I'm not going to pretend I understand how you feel. How can I? It's your body. But do you think that maybe you're putting too much guilt on yourself here? I mean, I'm sure I read somewhere that one in four pregnancies ends in miscarriage anyway. This isn't a baby at the moment, just a little bundle of cells. It's your body, and you do absolutely and categorically have the right to decide whether you want to continue with the pregnancy or not.'

'But that's just it, Toby. That's why I can't do it. Because it's only *my* decision. Because no one else can make it for me. Because whatever you, or my friends, or the doctors and nurses think, it is only *me* at the end of the day, and I'll carry the weight of it for the rest of my life, and I can't. I just can't do it again.' Her voice broke on the last word, and she collapsed in another paroxysm of crying.

Toby held her, rubbing her back and murmuring to her as though she were a child herself, trying to ignore the tendrils of icy dread creeping through him. As her sobs subsided he asked quietly, 'What do you mean, "again"?'

'No one except my mother knows this. But when I was fifteen, I had an abortion. I was about four months pregnant. Classic teenage thing, I hid it for a while, hoping it would just go away, then Mummy noticed something was wrong. I told her. She said I had to have an abortion. I knew she was right. She took me to a clinic a lot like this one. I had it done. I was back at school a couple of days later. I didn't really think about it for years. Then when I was in my first year at uni—'

'Hang on, I didn't even know you had a degree!'

She looked at him. 'I don't. This is why. When I was in my first year, Daisy told me she was pregnant.'

Toby nodded. He had met Daisy, Ruby's older sister, on several occasions. She now had three little girls aged five, three, and six months.

'She was so excited, and everyone was so pleased, and I suddenly thought about what I'd done, and how when I got pregnant it was a messy visit to a clinic, hushed up, not spoken about. To this day I don't even know if my father knows about it. Then when Daisy got pregnant my mother literally cried with joy at the news. I felt so . . . worthless, I suppose.'

Toby swallowed hard. He had thought he was out of his depth before, but now . . . As he searched for the right words, Ruby continued.

'Then when Maisie was born, it was even worse. She was beautiful, and tiny, and vulnerable, and Daisy and Max were terrified of doing something wrong, of hurting her, but actually you could tell that they loved her so much that they just couldn't do anything wrong, they were so protective and nurturing. And that's when I realised that the response I'd had to my own tiny vulnerable baby had been to have some doctor knock me out so they could scoop out my insides and kill it. I hated myself so much I practically stopped eating; my weight dropped by two stone. Punishing myself, the psychology textbooks would tell you. I dropped out of uni. I was a mess. It took a couple of years and some very expensive therapy for me to sort myself out, to stop thinking of myself primarily as a baby-killer.'

'Ruby, that's ridiculous. You were fifteen, a child yourself. You did the only thing you could have done under the circumstances. Of *course* it was different for Daisy – she must have been about twenty-five, she was married, she had her own home. She's a lovely mum, and one day, when the circumstances are right for you, you'll be a lovely mum too.' But not now, he screamed silently. Not now, not with me.

Ruby looked him full in the face, responding to the statement he hadn't made out loud. 'But if not now, when, Toby?' she asked softly. 'I'm pretty much the same age Daisy was when she got pregnant with Maisie. This baby was conceived in a committed relationship, you've got a good job, we've got somewhere nice to live. I know you've always wanted children. If it won't work now, then when would it? I can't cope with letting it not work again.

At the weekend I thought I could, but coming here this morning and everything being so familiar, I knew I couldn't. I can't.'

There were a few moments of intensely awkward silence which Toby found himself utterly unable to fill. Then Ruby spoke again.

'The thing is, Toby, I still don't feel ready. I couldn't do this without you. I never admit to needing people, but I do need you now.' She took a deep breath. 'And, about what you said on Friday night, well, I've changed my mind. I would like to marry you.'

9

As she came out of the tube at Walthamstow Central, Julia checked her mobile phone yet again. Nothing at all from Toby since that text the previous evening. She sighed as she negotiated her way through the viciously unwelcoming series of traffic lights and pedestrian crossings outside the station and made her way to the relative tranquillity of St Mary's Road.

Normally her walk home from the station was one of the best bits of her day. She had the choice of walking straight up St Mary's Road, then Church Path, which was a narrow little lane of charming rural cottages complete with roses round the door, which had somehow taken a wrong turn in its Home Counties village and stumbled into Zone Three by mistake. Or she could walk up Orford Road, Walthamstow Village's small but vibrant high street, and shop for organic Himalayan pink rock salt in what had to be the classiest Spar in the country. Tonight she was torn. After a day filled with nervous tension she would appreciate a little bit of quasi-rural tranquillity, but she was also ravenous, having worked late in the hope that Toby would phone and suggest meeting up in town, and what she really fancied was a pizza from the fantastic takeaway pizzeria in the Village. Greed won, but as she watched the pizza chef kneading and stretching the dough, she decided that this was also quite therapeutic.

Back at home she savoured every mouthful of the delectably crisp base, creamy mozzarella, richly garlicky tomato sauce and spicy salami, trying to ignore her growing sense of unease. After she had finished eating she pulled her laptop towards her, thinking she may as well indulge in a little bit of internet-related displacement activity. Generally the only things which got into her Hotmail inbox were a series of not-so-special offers, but she checked automatically, and was astounded to see Toby's name pop up in her inbox.

To: Julia_Upton81@hotmail.com
From: tobymarcusfenton@googlemail.org

To my darling Julia
    Forgive the cliché, but this is literally the hardest thing I have ever had to do. I guess I've had a very sheltered life – amazing parents, academic success, well-paid job, and maybe this is the first time it doesn't look as though things are working out the way I would have wanted them to.
    I know I should be having this conversation with you face to face, but I don't think I'm strong enough to do that. The thing is, what I need to tell you is that we can't see each other any more. Definitely not in a romantic way, and, given how strongly I feel about you, I rather think that means not at all for the foreseeable future.

When I cancelled on Sunday, it was because I'd had a text message from Ruby telling me that she was pregnant. After what was a really difficult process for her, she has decided that she wants to continue with the pregnancy. And I just don't feel that I have any choice but to support her in any way I can, which means trying to make a go of the relationship.

I meant everything I said to you this weekend, and I can't imagine a time when I won't love you, but Ruby is an amazing person too, and it wouldn't be fair to her, or to the baby, my baby, if I followed my own selfish inclinations and left them to fend for themselves. You are the most incredible, beautiful, warm and loving woman I have ever met, and you're going to make some lucky, undeserving bastard very happy some day. I hope you meet the person who can make you happy too.

I know we'll probably bump into each other through mutual friends etc., and that's obviously going to be awkward to say the least, but I also know that I can trust you not to do anything to hurt Ruby, and I am more sorry than I can say that I am hurting you.

All my love

Toby

Julia read, then re-read the email before slamming the lid down on the laptop. She had an urge to throw it out of the window, to get it out of her sight, as though somehow that would mean that the message had never existed. A twenty-first-century version of shooting the messenger, she thought ironically. She could feel the pizza she had eaten solidifying and congealing in her stomach, and the once-appetising savoury aroma wafting from the discarded box made her feel nauseous.

She had a heartbreak routine. Of course she did, she was a thirty-year-old single woman. It involved wrapping herself in her duvet and listening to 'Nothing Compares 2 U' by Sinéad O'Connor and 'I'll Sail This Ship Alone' by The Beautiful South and a few other maudlin classics, on repeat. Then getting Rose round to do the same thing accompanied by vast quantities of wine, spirits and Dairy Milk. Then going home for a weekend of restorative roast dinners and chicken casseroles made the way only her dad could, and chocolate fudge cake made the way only her mum could. Occasionally, cooler friends had convinced her that an evening of drinking in random bars and snogging random men was the final essential stage to get through, but that had long since started to lose its appeal. Through all this, even when she was genuinely sad, there was always a small part of her revelling in the theatricality.

This time, though, she couldn't even muster the energy to go and get her duvet. She curled into the foetal position on the sofa, unable even to cry. Twenty-four to forty-eight hours earlier she had been experiencing the most intense happiness of her life. The pieces were falling into place, she could see a future which filled her with delighted anticipation, she had felt as if she was actually living her own life rather than existing on the fringes of other people's. If this were a real bereavement, if she had just had a message to say that he had been killed in a car crash, then she would be able to ring her parents, ring

Rose, phone into work sick, benefit from a ready supply of loving sympathy. But although Toby had killed not only their fledgling love affair but also their twelve-year friendship, this wasn't something she could share. In the eyes of the world Toby having a baby with his fiancée would be a cause for joy and celebration. A baby. She let out an animalistic cry of pain and the tears began to flow. Not only had she just lost the man she loved, and her best friend, but another woman, a woman who didn't really want him, was having his baby. Toby's baby, a baby Julia wanted so badly she felt the pain and longing would tear her in two.

Maybe she could phone him and beg? He loved her, not Ruby. Surely. What she had experienced in the last two heady days was so perfect and intense that surely, surely she couldn't have been experiencing it alone? Like sex, love could only reach those dizzying heights when it was a fully shared experience. Okay, so Ruby, as a result of some giant cosmic twisted joke, was pregnant, but that didn't mean Toby had to be with her. This was the twenty-first century, plenty of babies grew up without fathers. Even while formulating this line of argument Julia knew that it was useless. That wasn't who Toby was. He was sweet and kind, and had the highest ethical standards of anyone she had ever met – something she had always felt to be particularly admirable given that as an uncommitted atheist he had no expectation of any reward in a life to come, just a deeply held conviction that we all have a responsibility to live in a way which enhanced the sum of human happiness, even if it was at the expense of our own. And although, as he said in his email, he had never been tested like this before, Julia somehow knew that begging now would serve no purpose other than to eradicate the last few shreds of dignity she still possessed. Dignity. That was what was required. Before that thought could desert her, Julia grabbed the laptop, opened it and clicked 'Reply', barely able to see for crying.

To: tobymarcusfenton@googlemail.org
From: Julia_Upton81@hotmail.com

Toby
Thank you for letting me know, I appreciate your honesty, and understand why you have reached the decision you have.
Take care
Julia

'Send.'
And that was that. The end. Or actually, no. One final thing.

To: martin.kennington@stbenedicts.nhs.org
From: Julia_Upton81@hotmail.com

Hi Martin
Really sorry but I've come home from work feeling terrible. I think I've got some kind of flu bug. Going to dose myself up and go to bed now, but realistically I don't think I'm going to be in for the next couple of days. Apart from anything the pressures on the wards

are bad enough without me infecting everyone with something noxious.

Nothing major in my diary – could you get Louisa to cover Theatre 2 User Group tomorrow lunchtime?

Will ring you when my voice comes back!

Cheers

J

Amazing, and depressing, that this was all it took to unravel the suddenly fragile-seeming threads of her life. No Toby. She had spoken to Rose last night, so she wouldn't phone again for a while. Her parents were staying with Harry and Angela for a couple of nights, so they probably wouldn't call. This time, with supreme effort, Julia managed to drag herself upstairs, shed her work suit in a crumpled heap on the floor and fling herself into bed before she collapsed yet again into desolate sobs.

IO

'But why not, Toby, why *not*? I just don't understand.'

Toby didn't fully understand either. Looking at Ruby, he saw the charming, petulant face of a thwarted child. Tears hovered unshed on her long dark lashes, and she was pouting up at him. Most men would have given her anything she wanted. A few short weeks ago he would have been one of them, but now the balance of power in their relationship was very different.

'I have explained, Ruby. You told me very clearly less than a month ago that you didn't want to marry me. No, wait, don't interrupt. You said that you maybe never wanted to get married, but certainly not now, not to me. Remember that?'

'Yes, of course I remember, but I've told you, things are different now. We're having a baby. And when I tell my parents I really want to be able to tell them that we're engaged as well. They worry about me. They like you, they'll worry so much less about this baby if they know I'm marrying you. Plus, I'm not showing at all yet. If we get married in the next few weeks, I'll still be able to fit into a nice dress before I look like a whale.'

Toby sighed. Suddenly his role as Ruby's boyfriend felt like excellent preparation for fatherhood. 'I don't think anyone should get married just to please their parents and get to wear a nice dress, Ruby.'

'Well, that's why most people I know get married!'

'Well, maybe that's why one in three marriages end in divorce!'

They glared at each other. Then Ruby took a deep breath and softened her voice. 'What about for the baby? You know it's best for a baby to have two parents. Surely you want the best thing for the baby?'

'Our baby is *going* to have two parents. You're moving in with me. I'll be there for everything, all the classes, the birth, we can get one of those sling thingies and I'll take it for walks. But you don't need to be married to do all that. I asked you to marry me because I wanted to make a big romantic gesture. You made it clear what you thought of the idea. I'm just not prepared to get married now, to a reluctant bride, for the sake of a baby who won't know one way or the other. And, before you say it, I'm definitely not getting married to spare your parents' blushes when they have the vicar over for tea.'

It had been a difficult few weeks for Toby. And, he dimly appreciated, for Ruby, although it was a struggle for Toby to treat Ruby with the compassion that a part of him deep down knew she deserved. He didn't think that he would ever again come so close to falling apart as he had that day at the clinic, when he had realised that there was no chance Ruby was going to have an abortion. When he had studied Philosophy and Ethics at A Level, he had relished the debates with classmates on the rights and wrongs of various situations, abortion included. And at university he and Julia and their circle of friends had enjoyed nothing more than whiling away an evening with a 'What would you do if . . .' discussion. What would you do if your girlfriend told you she had cancer just as you were about to dump her? What would you do if you discovered your father was having an affair and your mother knew nothing about it? What would you do if you found out your best friend was plagiarising their dissertation? What would you do if the woman you've just asked to marry you tells you she's pregnant the same day you realise you're actually in love with someone else? In an abstract way it was a very interesting discussion; problem was, Toby couldn't see, couldn't for the life of him see, that there was more than one ethical conclusion to be drawn.

He and Ruby had hardly spoken after they left the clinic. He had driven her home to her little studio flat, made her a cup of tea and tucked her up on the sofa. Then had rather sheepishly asked if she would mind if he went home. 'Lot to think about . . . need some time . . . work tomorrow . . .' Half-formed sentences had floated into the ether, unanchored by concrete verbs.

Ruby had been sanguine, filled with the indolent serenity which always follows an outburst of crying.

He had gone home, drunk too much whisky, smashed five plates on his patio in an orgy of anger and frustration, and then slowly, painfully, reluctantly composed an email to Julia. What else could he do? He knew that there was no alternative – he couldn't possibly abandon Ruby, vulnerable as she clearly was, along with his unborn child – and yet pressing 'Send' on that email was so much more bitter than his rejection by Ruby three days earlier.

He had cried himself then, just a little. Then he had taken a long shower, letting the warm water wash away what tension it could, made a pot of strong coffee, and sat down to write a list.

> To Do
> R to move in with me
> Ballet dancing while pregnant??? - find out
> Tell R parents
> Tell Mum and Dad
> R doctor appt
> Food to avoid??

Toby knew that he was going to have to take a lot of responsibility for planning, organising, arranging. That was very definitely not Ruby's strength, but it was his. So he had worked slowly and methodically through his original list, adding new things as they occurred to him.

> Redirect R's post
> Rent/sell R's flat?
> Hire a van for move?
> Add R's name to car insurance
> Pregnancy vits?
> Remind R about pregnancy exemption cert
> Book leave for 12-week scan

It was hard work, made harder by Ruby herself. Suddenly many of the traits he had found so endearing became a source of irritation: she was capricious, disorganised to the point of chaotic, chronically unpunctual, and took *laissez-faire* to new levels. He was the one who had to phone her GP surgery and book an appointment for her, and then enter the appointment into the calendar on her iPhone, complete with advance reminder set up. He had helped her to pack and sort her possessions into boxes he had collected from the supermarket, and then ferried them back to his house where they had erupted into the monochrome-with-blue-accents decor like a Jackson Pollock on the wall of a laboratory. He had printed out a list from the internet of foods it was inadvisable for pregnant women to eat and taped it to the fridge. It seemed that Ruby carried on as she had always done, with the addition of regular nagging as to when they would get married, when she could tell people they were engaged, what she would tell her parents.

The irony was not lost on him. Whereas he had once hoped his engagement would impress his parents with its wildly romantic spontaneity, he was now going to be a central protaganist in the clichéd farce of a shotgun wedding. Except he couldn't. Everything else, yes. Ruby had moved in. He would look after her, share a bed with her, stand by her, care for the child, but at the present time he felt utterly incapable of standing up and promising to a roomful of people that he would love her and only her for as long as they both lived.

With a final kiss, Alicia Fenton shut the door behind her son and his girlfriend and turned to her husband, eyebrows raised so far they practically disappeared into her hairline.

'Well! What do you think of that?'

Hugh Fenton smiled in wry amusement. 'I think you should wait until they're at least out of earshot before you say anything else.'

Alicia flapped her hands impatiently. 'Oh you! Don't be silly, of course they can't hear me. This is really important. Hugh, do you think Toby's happy?'

Hugh shook his head. 'No . . .' he said slowly. 'No, I wouldn't say he seemed happy. I wouldn't say Ruby did either, mind you.'

'Oh, Ruby!' Alicia dismissed the mother of her grand-child with a careless gesture. 'I don't mean to sound callous, but I don't really know Ruby well enough to worry about her. Leave that to her parents. What are they, Sir Rupert and Lady Anstey? I wonder how they feel about their daughter getting knocked up by a prole! It's Toby I'm interested in, though.'

Hugh grinned. 'But has it not occurred to you, my darling, that Toby's happiness is probably now inextrica-bly linked to Ruby's? If she isn't happy then she won't be able to make him happy.'

'You old romantic.' She kissed her husband lightly and affectionately.

'Come on then, let's do the post-mortem.' Hugh pushed Alicia gently in the direction of the sofa and poured them both a generous measure of Glenfiddich.

Alicia's eyebrows rose again. 'It's only 5.30. You are worried, aren't you?'

Hugh chose his words carefully. 'I'm puzzled. I must admit, this wasn't what I was expecting.'

'Puzzled! You can say that again. They've only been together a few minutes, and now they're moving in

86

together with a baby on the way. Our careful, cautious boy.' She shook her head, frowning.

Hugh took her hands gently. 'To be fair, sweetheart, you are always saying you wish he would be more spontaneous.'

'Yes, I know. I'm not upset about the speed of it all, *per se*. But he looks so tense and drawn. And I'm not sure that Ruby is right for him at all. She's beautiful, but she's so young, and they don't seem to have anything in common. Do you think she's got pregnant on purpose to trap him?'

'No, I don't. I don't think she seemed any happier about the situation than he did, to be honest.'

'Then in that case, *why*? I don't want to be heartless, but it's not 1950, there are ways and means of dealing with unwanted pregnancies in this day and age.'

Another thought struck her. 'And what about darling Julia? She's going to be devastated. I've always thought that she and Toby would get it together eventually.'

'I'm sure Julia already knows – she's generally the first person Toby turns to, isn't she? Maybe she's looking forward to being Auntie Julia. I mean, if she and Toby were going to make a go of things, you'd think they'd have got round to it before now. But, speaking of that, how do you feel about being Grandma?'

Alicia, pencil slim, perfectly groomed, stylish, elegant, delightfully *soignée*, and looking a good ten years younger than the sixty-odd she actually was, raised her hands to her face in horror. 'Oh my God, I hadn't thought of that! Grandma! No, I can't bear it.'

'I'm afraid you're going to have to. And more besides. If Toby is really unhappy about this, and not just adjusting to the shock, he's going to need a lot of support from us.'

'I know. The first thing we need to do is talk to him properly, without Ruby; try and find out what's really going on.'

'Well, I think both of us would be too much. Why don't you arrange to meet him for a coffee or something in the next few days and see if you can encourage him to talk? But, Ally, you can't force it. And *don't* bad-mouth Ruby, whatever you do. She's having his baby, she's going to be in our lives now for a long time to come.'

I I

Even when you felt overwhelmed, torn apart, utterly unable to go on, you still had to. Suicide had never seemed a viable option; even in the midst of the inevitable selfishness which accompanies heartbreak, Julia knew she couldn't do that to her parents. She did have scabby half-moons over the backs of her hands from where she had lain in bed digging her fingernails into her hands as hard as she could in the hope that inflicting physical pain would ease the emotional anguish. But somehow things carried on.

She spent two days off work 'sick', curled up in bed crying. She scarcely ate, wasn't able to summon the energy to have a shower, didn't speak to anyone. On the third day she knew she had either to return to work or obtain a doctor's note. Pulling on a pair of tracksuit bottoms and a t-shirt, finding some trainers and inserting her feet into them seemed to take all her energy, but somehow she managed to phone the doctor's, make an appointment and drag herself to the surgery.

Her voice was husky from lack of use and crying, and her mouth felt coated and furry – it was now Thursday, and she hadn't brushed her teeth since Monday morning. As soon as the doctor looked at her with warmth and empathy and asked what the problem was, she started crying again. The doctor listened sympathetically to her halting and confused tale, and agreed to sign her off for a week with 'viral fatigue', avoiding the dreaded 'D' word that would send alarm bells ringing with Julia's HR department.

'Now listen.' The doctor was as expansively compassionate as seven-minute appointment slots would allow. 'Are you close to your parents?'

Julia nodded, doubtfully.

'Then if I were you, I'd get yourself on a train and go home for a few days. You need some TLC, some mothering. You don't have to go into the details with your mum and dad, but you need someone to look after you for a bit.'

And Julia managed to pull herself together enough to follow the doctor's advice. Her husky voice lent credence to the story she told her mum on the phone – had flu, doctor says need a complete rest, should come home. Buying her ticket on the internet to collect from a machine at the station avoided any human contact, which she dreaded. She forced herself into the shower, brushed her teeth and flung a handful of clean t-shirts and underwear into a bag. Her mobile phone was deliberately left in a drawer at home; every moment which didn't bring a message from Toby saying that it was all a dreadful mistake was a further agony. Then she wrapped herself in a long cable-knit cardie which, she had always joked, was as near to staying in bed as you could get while leaving the house, and made the journey home.

Her parents were great. For five days they let her spend her time wrapped in her duvet, either in bed or, in rarely adventurous moments, on the sofa, re-reading her mum's Agatha Christies. These were the perfect comfort reading, low on emotion, low on romance, and all life's complications unravelled with a flourish in the final chapter. Pat and Eddie made tempting little dishes of food which she scarcely ate and, whether they believed the 'recovering from flu' line or not, most importantly they didn't ask any questions. By Tuesday, over a week since Toby had dropped his bombshell, Julia felt strong enough to get dressed and return to London.

Wednesday morning saw her back in a sharp suit (gratifyingly loose round the waist) and killer heels, ready to face work and her colleagues. Now, a few weeks later, she was managing to get through. Work helped, because it demanded every ounce of concentration she had, and because she was still good at her job and the problems which presented themselves there could generally be solved. Evenings were harder. She couldn't face going out, had largely cut herself off from social contact and, unfortunately, her earlier loss of appetite had been replaced by her more habitual response of comfort eating. So she would spend an hour on the sofa, eating and re-reading or re-watching something comforting, before heading off to bed at about 9 p.m. and crying herself to sleep.

There were embarrassing incidents when she lost control – at the checkout in the supermarket, or on the tube. One morning she went for a long-pre-arranged dental check-up, and lying there on the dentist's chair suddenly knew that she was going to cry. She tried everything to hold back the tears, but they were inexorable, and greatly to the dentist's disconcertion she sobbed throughout her check-up, and throughout the standard advice on brushing and flossing regularly, and while she paid the receptionist. She cried walking along the street, and sitting at the table in the coffee shop she went into to try and compose herself sufficiently to go back to work. What she found bitterly amusing was that throughout all of this, no one ever asked this wildly sobbing woman if she was okay. The dentist had appeared slightly alarmed, but possibly it was just a novelty for him to witness pain and suffering unrelated to his profession. These incidents were getting fewer, though, and the only remaining problem was an extreme and debilitating tiredness. Even though she was normally in bed by 9 p.m., it was still a huge struggle to get out of bed when the alarm went off at 6.30 a.m. Her feet felt weighted by cement as she trudged to the tube station, and at weekends she would sleep for twelve or fourteen hours at a stretch.

One evening, four weeks after Toby had arrived on her doorstep to tell her he wasn't engaged, she finally felt strong enough to call Rose. It was probably the longest they had ever gone without speaking, but Rose was the only person she had told about her gorgeously mad weekend with Toby, and therefore the only person she would have to tell that it was now all over, and up until now she had been completely unable to face it. They had exchanged brief functional texts, Rose's becoming chillier in tone as the weeks went by.

'Rose, it's me.'

'Oh, hello.' Rose's voice was icy. Julia felt her courage ebbing away, and was tempted to hang up.

'How are things with you?'

'Oh, you know, living my boring little life. Playgroup, and Toy Library, and trips to Waitrose. Not for all of us the heady excitement of conducting wild affairs in various seaside resorts around the country.'

'Oh, Rose.' Julia's voice broke down on a sob.

'Hey, come on, Ju, I'm only having a go cos I'm jealous. I don't mean it really.'

'There's nothing to be jealous of.'

'What do you mean?'

'There's nothing. Me and Toby are over, have been for weeks. There's nothing left.'

'Oh, Julia, honey! What happened? Tell me.'

And after all this time, there was a comfort in sinking back against the sofa cushions and confiding it all.

'So there we are,' she concluded wearily, nearly half an hour later.

'Wow. God, Julia, that's horrible for you. I don't know what to say. And poor Toby as well.'

'Poor Toby?' Julia's voice was acid. 'Poor Toby is reaping what he sowed. Lying in the bed he made. Getting what he fucking deserves.'

'Come on, Ju. That's not fair. It must have been horrendous for him. And he didn't do anything wrong, she was his girlfriend at the time, he wasn't cheating on you. In a way . . . in a way he *has* done the decent thing, you've sort of got to respect him for that.'

'Oh I know. Saint Toby. Angelic Ruby. Maybe it has been hard for him, Rose, but at the end of the day, all I can see is that Toby has ended up with a beautiful girl-friend he loved enough to want to marry. Ruby has somehow got my Toby *and* she's having a baby. And I'm still on my own, no boyfriend, no baby, and never likely to have either as far as I can see.' She started crying softly again.

'Right, that's it, I'm coming up for the weekend. We're going to have a proper girly weekend, DVDs, junk food, alcohol. I might even make you get all dressed up and we can go somewhere glam for cocktails.'

'That's really sweet of you, but what about Graeme and Seb? And I'm no fun at the moment, Rose. I'm too wiped out to go out, I'm in bed by nine most nights.'

'No, listen to me, Julia. I know you're miserable at the moment, and I totally understand why, but you have *no idea* how lucky you are being young, free and single in London. I have no social life anyway because Graeme doesn't trust babysitters, but it hardly seems worth the fight just so that I can go to the village pub quiz, or the local Brownies doing *The Wizard of Oz*. I said nothing about coming for *your* sake; I'm coming because I'm going stark staring mad here, and I need to escape!'

Julia laughed in spite of herself. 'Okay, but if you can't even manage an evening out, how are you going to get here for a weekend? You could always bring Seb, I guess. I haven't seen him for ages, and I can babysit while you go out for those cocktails.'

'Don't even think about it, lady! No, it's easy, my mum's been nagging me for ages that she doesn't see enough of Seb, so she can have him for the weekend. I'll drive up on Friday, drop him off with her, and get the train down to London. You can meet me after work. Then I'll get the train back up to Manchester on Sunday evening, stay the night at Mum's and drive me and Seb back on Monday. Graeme'll probably be thrilled to have a weekend to himself as well; it's perfect.'

Rose's enthusiasm was infectious. In spite of herself, Julia felt a big smile spread across her face. 'Oh, Rose, it would be fun. It would be so nice to see you, it's been ages.'

'Right, well, consider it a done deal. I'll text you to confirm, but expect to meet me at Euston at about seven on Friday night, and be prepared to go out and party!'

12

In the end they didn't go out on Friday night. Julia had had an exhausting week at work, culminating with medical staff shortages meaning that she had to go and cancel a Friday afternoon clinic, after all the patients had already arrived at the hospital. This wasn't a particularly unusual occurrence, but on this occasion it happened to be a colonoscopy clinic, and the patients in question had been on a liquids-only diet and strong laxatives for forty-eight hours. They were considerably less than happy to learn that it had all been for nothing and that they would have to repeat the whole thing the following week, and they were not at all reticent in sharing their displeasure with her. Plus Seb was cutting his back molars and Rose had been averaging five hours of broken sleep a night, so even the adrenaline rush of being temporarily childless and back in London couldn't compensate enough to make her feel like a night out.

They had gone home, taken off their make-up, put on their pyjamas and curled up on Julia's sofa with a Chinese banquet for four and a couple of bottles of wine. Julia couldn't help but notice, with a pang of concern, that the wine disappeared at an alarming rate, even though she wasn't drinking much. On her part, Rose noted that Julia hoovered up two thirds of the food almost before she had rolled up her first crispy duck pancake.

Rose was as concerned and sympathetic as she could manage, but found herself getting exasperated as Julia meandered on in what she could only think of as an unnecessarily self-indulgent manner. Especially as she couldn't help but feel that Julia had got herself into this mess by being so unrelentingly dense about her feelings for Toby. Julia could see that Rose was far from being entirely happy, guzzling her wine down and responding with more than a tinge of bitterness to any enquiries about Graeme, or home, or even Sebastian; and she couldn't help her irritation at such a fuss being made about what seemed like the most trivial of blots on a perfect domestic landscape.

The next day was more successful. They spent the day shopping on Kensington High Street, Julia noticing with dismay – though not surprise – that her weight loss had been short lived and that, if anything, her normal size now felt slightly tight after all the comfort eating. Rose lusted after tailored pencil skirts and subtly sexy wrap dresses, but had to settle for a couple of pairs of jeans and a pair of Converse, as she didn't feel she could justify the purchase of clothes she had no foreseeable reason to wear. As a consequence she realised she was in danger of sinking back into depression.

'Right, it's nearly cocktail o'clock!' she announced firmly. 'I'm in the mood for somewhere seriously indulgent. Oxo Tower?'

Julia flinched. She hadn't ever told Rose that had been the venue for the engagement that wasn't (or wasn't then), and she didn't want to get into another Toby discussion, but equally she knew she couldn't face it. 'No, last time I was there the service was crap. And I don't mind paying fifteen quid a cocktail if it's all fabulous, but we had to wait for ages, and when I told the waiter that it had been twenty minutes and asked where the drinks were, his response was, "I think you'll find it's only been eighteen minutes, Madam," as though that were a perfectly acceptable wait.'

Rose laughed. 'Okay then, so where? I want lethally strong cocktails beautifully presented, a lovely view, preferably some gorgeous men to flirt with, and not to feel out of place all dressed up.'

Overcome with excitement at being back in London, Rose was wearing a strappy, floaty, Ghost-esque dress and genuine Manolo Blahnik sandals. She had looked a bit out of place shopping in Gap and H&M, even the Kensington branches, and inwardly she acknowledged that wearing heels for pretty much the first time in two years, on a hot day, for a shopping trip, had not been the best of ideas, but now she had suffered this far she was determined not to end up in Pizza Express or Wagamama for the evening.

'How about Skylon at the Royal Festival Hall? It's got really yummy cocktails and river views, and we can eat there as well if we feel like it.'

'Okay, you've convinced me. And I've pinched Graeme's credit card for the weekend, so this is on me!'

A couple of hours later they were sitting at a table for two with strawberry Bellinis in front of them. A group of thirty-something men at the bar were giving them appreciative glances, and Rose sighed with satisfaction. 'This is more like it. I feel . . . I feel *alive* again.'

Julia looked anxiously at her friend. She had already slurped more than half her Bellini, while Julia had barely started hers; but then Julia hadn't really known what she wanted and had ordered the Bellini because it was her usual favourite, rather than because she particularly wanted one.

'You feel alive because you've had a drink?' she queried.

'No! Don't be silly. I'm not turning into an alcoholic on you, Ju. It's lovely to have a drink, and this is the most delicious thing I've ever tasted, and I'm definitely going to let my hair down safe in the knowledge that I won't be woken at 5.30 a.m. tomorrow, but honestly I don't drink much at all at home. Glass of wine most nights, two glasses at the weekend maybe? I'm certainly not necking down the gin at 10 a.m. every day, if that's what you're worried about.'

'No, I didn't mean to imply that. But what did you mean by saying that you feel alive again?'

Rose met Julia's gaze, assessing how honest she could be. Suddenly, maybe because of the Bellini, maybe because of how honest and vulnerable Julia had been with her, she felt that she could talk to Julia, if no one else. 'I'm so, so miserable, Julia. I just don't know what to do. I feel totally trapped. I feel as though I'm living under a great, oppressive black cloud and there's no way of escape. I feel that I'm vanishing altogether.'

'Oh my God, Rose. You've never said, I had no idea.'

'I haven't said, because you haven't wanted to hear. No one wants to hear – not you, or my mum, or the other mummies at the playgroup. I don't know if any of them feel the same and it's a great silent conspiracy that we just die quietly inside while putting on a brave face and singing "Frère Jacques", or whether they're all genuinely happy and I'm just a freak.'

'Don't be silly, of course you're not a freak. Do you mean . . . is it your relationship with Graeme that's the problem? I know that you love Seb . . .'

'Of course I adore Seb, and I do love Graeme too. But it's both of them that are the problem in a way, just the whole lifestyle. Graeme earns a lovely big salary, and he's bought a lovely big house, in lovely green countryside, and he has a lovely wife and she looks after their lovely son, and sooner rather than later there'll be another lovely baby, and then he will have his lovely little family, all complete.'

'So . . . are you pregnant?'

'No! That's part of the problem. Graeme really wants us to try for another baby. Before Seb was born we always said that we wanted two, about two years apart. You know, get the nappy stage over and done with all at the same time, and they'll be able to play together as they grow up, blah blah blah.'

Julia nodded. She may have been childless herself, but she had enough friends with children to know all about the Holy Grail of the two-year age gap.

'Anyway, we're obviously running a bit late on it. Thing is, Graeme assumed we were trying from round about Seb's first birthday, cos that's what we originally agreed, but I knew I wasn't ready then, so I just kept quietly taking the Pill.'

Julia opened her mouth as though to speak, then shut it again and blushed as a sudden thought struck her.

'Graeme wasn't bothered, it took a few months for me to fall pregnant with Seb, but we knew that there was nothing wrong with either of us, and to be honest, with a one-year-old, there aren't that many opportunities for having sex, even if you have the energy, which I never seem to. And Graeme hasn't been that keen on sex since Seb was born – he's a typical reserved public schoolboy, and I think the birth freaked him out, too much exposure to messy lady bits. Anyway, I think he just assumed we were accidentally following the rhythm method. Then round about Seb's second birthday all my mummy friends from NCT and baby massage class seemed either to be pregnant or just having their second, and he suddenly said that we had to be much more focused, and maybe buy some ovulation tests because otherwise the age gap was going to be too big.' Rose looked at Julia shamefacedly, and gestured to the waiter to bring her another cocktail. 'I know I should have told him then . . .'

'You think?' Julia asked, her voice heavy with irony, though she knew that she had no real right to criticise.

'I know, I know. But I simply felt that I couldn't explain the reasons why I didn't want another baby without opening a whole can of worms.'

'What are the worms?'

'I'll come on to that in a minute. But to cut a long story short, the inevitable happened and Graeme found my Pill packet, and went ape. And now we're barely speaking. This weekend is a break for both of us to think things over, and then we've got a "date" on Tuesday to talk things through properly.'

'Bloody hell, Rose! I had no idea about any of this. I must admit, I've kind of been expecting – dreading – you telling me that you're pregnant again, just because everyone does seem to do this two-year gap.'

'Why dreading?'

Julia shrugged. 'Let's not go there, we need to talk about you at the moment. It's only my normal thing that I really, really want a baby, and it just feels like it's going to happen for everyone except me.'

Rose patted her hand sympathetically. 'Any chance you'd like to have a baby with Graeme and get me off the hook? No, thought not. You don't want *a* baby, you want Toby's baby. But anyway, if you really don't mind, I'm going to go back to my worms, because if I don't talk now I'll probably never work up the courage again.

'I'm just so *bored*, Julia. I know it's pathetic, because I've got everything any girl could possibly want, and I do know how lucky I am. But it's a struggle to get out of bed in the morning because every day feels like fucking Groundhog Day. I make breakfast, I clear up breakfast, I have a fight to get Seb to go upstairs to get dressed. I have a fight to make him use his potty as something other than a helmet when he plays spaceships. I have a fight to wrestle him into his clothes and comb his hair and clean his teeth and wash his face. And after I've done all of that I have a fight to try and persuade him to stay in one place and not wreak havoc while I try and get myself washed and dressed.

'Also, frankly, Julia, I'm not even sure whether it's worth getting dressed some days. I might as well be in my pyjamas with greasy hair and no make-up. When you've got a young child no one looks at you as a woman, or even a person, you're just a generic mummy-blob. I get no recognition for my brains, or my personality, and so I feel like they're disappearing. I love Seb so much, Ju. Not being with him today is like a constant ache, even though I've been having a really nice time, but what no one ever tells you about children is that they're so bloody *boring* most of the time. If I haven't been with Seb for a few days, because my mum's been down or something, we have such a lovely morning together when I first get him back to myself. We finger-paint, and bake cookies, and make shapes out of playdough, and go to the swings. But by then it's only lunchtime, and we've done all that, and I still have the afternoon to fill, and then the next day, and the day after that and every other bloody day until he goes to school.

'And sometimes the only thing which keeps me going is practically counting off the days until he does start school, so the last thing I can face is the thought of going back to square one with a new baby.

'Plus, I hate where we live. It's pretty, but there's nothing whatsoever to do. It's okay for Graeme, he goes off on the train every day and gets his fix of urban life; if he wants to stay for a drink after work he can, and then he can enjoy relaxing in the countryside at the weekend. But I never get to go anywhere. I mean, seriously, a shopping trip to Waitrose and meeting a friend for coffee is a big day out for me now.'

She paused, more to draw breath than because she had finished everything she had to say. She glanced round the restaurant. Beautifully dressed beautiful people laughing and drinking and having a good time. It was what she fantasised about constantly when she was stuck at home on her own, but now she was here all she could think or talk about were Graeme and Seb and her situation.

'And you don't think Graeme has any idea how you feel?' Julia broke into her thoughts.

'No, I don't think so. I just feel so spoilt and ungrateful saying anything.'

'Whoa, stop right there! Ungrateful? You haven't got anything to feel grateful to Graeme about, Rose. I know I'm not the world expert, but even I know that marriage is a partnership, and I think that anyone, certainly anyone who's ever had anything to do with children, would agree that you're bringing just as much to the table by looking after Seb day in, day out as Graeme is in earning his big salary.'

'I know that in theory, of course. But I can't really make myself believe it deep down. And when I was pregnant, and when Seb was tiny, we both agreed that the best thing for him was to have his mum at home with him, not to be farmed out to a nursery or a childminder. I feel like I'm being lazy or disloyal if I renege on that now, and say that I want to go back to work.'

Julia breathed a sigh of relief. 'Oh, thank God for that. At least you see what the solution is!'

'Well yes, to an extent, but it's just not that simple. Thing is, I don't want to go back to working as a press officer. I loved it, most of the time, but all the really fun bits were the launches and evening things I got invited to, and the going out with colleagues, and none of that is particularly compatible with being a mother.'

Julia frowned slightly, considering. 'So do you know what you do want to do?'

'Yes.' Rose glanced down shyly. 'Yes, I want to train as an aromatherapist.'

'Okaaay. Look, Rose, maybe I'm just being thick here, but I really don't see what the problem is. Whatever you and Graeme agreed when Seb was small has got to be subject to review now he's older. I mean, for heaven's sake, when you decided not to go back to work after maternity leave you were still breastfeeding every two hours. Things have changed since then. Seb's changed. And I don't want to sound harsh, but he'd probably benefit hugely from going to nursery and mixing with other children.'

'But that would cost a fortune! I wouldn't be earning anything while I trained, in fact there'd be course fees to pay. I can't ask Graeme to do that for me.'

Julia prayed silently for patience. 'I don't want to poke my nose into your financial affairs, but can you afford nursery fees plus your course fees?'

'Well yes, technically, I suppose we could, but that's not the point—'

'Rose, that is *exactly* the point. Listen to me. Does Graeme enjoy his job?'

'I think so, yes, most of the time.'

'And would he want to stay at home and look after Sebastian all day?'

Rose shook her head adamantly. 'God, no, he'd be insane within a week.'

'Well then, he has no right to expect you to do something he wouldn't do himself. And Rose, to be fair to the poor bloke, he hasn't had a chance to have a view at all, because you haven't bloody talked to him! He thinks you're a happy stay-at-home mum trying for a second baby. He has no idea that you're actually a frustrated aromatherapist who's taking the Pill!' She paused as a thought struck her. 'Do you really not want another baby? Will Graeme find that difficult?'

'I don't necessarily *never* want another one, but I'm only thirty, I've got loads of time yet, and I'm just not ready now. I need to get my life sorted out a bit more first. Seriously, it's going to take at least another couple of years to recover from the accumulated lack of sleep.'

Julia smiled across the table. 'Well look, Rose, I'm really, really glad that you've talked to me, but the person you really need to go away and have this conversation with is Graeme.'

Rose nodded. 'I know. But thanks so much, Julia. Just vocalising it has helped so much. I'll find it easier to talk to Graeme now, I think. Anyway,' she said with a smile, 'you, my friend, have some serious catching up to do with these drinks! I'm about to start my third and you've barely sipped yours!'

Julia pulled a face. 'Hmm, I know. I don't feel very well, to be honest. I'm so tired at the moment, I seriously am always in bed by now. And for some reason I've gone off alcohol a bit recently. It seems to make me feel vaguely nauseous. I might have to take a rain check on the big night out.'

Rose looked at Julia and grinned suddenly. 'God, Ju, tired all the time, feeling sick, gone off booze ... *You're* not pregnant, are you?'

The grin faded from her face as her eyes met Julia's and she saw no answering smile.

'I don't know. I don't know, Rose. It literally only just occurred to me, while we were talking this evening, that I might be.'

13

Le Pain Quotidien in St Pancras Station wasn't, perhaps, the ideal location for an intimate mother–son chat, but it was all that Alicia had been able to persuade Toby to agree to.

They met at 6 p.m. on a Sunday evening; Toby was on his way up to Sheffield for a client meeting early the next morning and had said it was St Pancras or nothing. They had ordered a bottle of house red and some sharing plates of dips and bread, and were now sitting in somewhat uncomfortable silence. To Alicia's anxious eyes Toby looked haggard, and silence, uncomfortable or otherwise, was extremely uncharacteristic of him and of their relationship. They got on so well that normally they were both bubbling over with jokes or anecdotes they wanted to share and whenever they met the time sped by, the only challenge being how to fit everything in.

'So you went down to see Ruby's parents and tell them about the baby, then? Were they thrilled to have another grandchild on the way?'

Toby grinned ruefully. 'They were thrilled about the grandchild, I think. Less thrilled that there won't be a ring on the third finger of Ruby's left hand before its arrival.'

'Oh! Well, plenty of couples don't get married before having children these days, it's surely not a big problem, is it?'

'I think it is for them, Ally.' Toby had always called his parents by their given names, although he and his dad were the only ones who got away with using a shortened form of his mother's name. 'They're quite traditional and respectable. Not like my disreputable parents. He's a baronet, so he's basically the local squire, and there still seems to be lots of forelock tugging in the local village. And she's in the Women's Institute, and does the flowers at church, and he's the church warden, and it's all quite 1950s. For them it is definitely first comes love, then comes marriage, then comes Ruby with the baby carriage, and they're a bit disconcerted at us messing up the order.'

'Oh!' said Alicia again. Part of her was delighted that Toby was opening up a little bit, but instinct told her that she was skating on very thin ice and needed to proceed with extreme caution. Toby was usually warm, open and friendly, but she knew from bitter experience that he could shut down and become icily proud if you strayed onto conversational territory he found uncomfortable.

'But I'm sure they'll get used to the idea, darling. I mean, if marriage isn't for you, then it isn't. Anyway, there's nothing to stop you getting married once the baby arrives. Ruby will feel more like it then anyway. No fun getting married if you can't even drink at your own reception!'

Toby looked thoughtfully at his mother. Alicia had a carefully created frivolous, light-hearted, even scatty, demeanour, but it concealed a very warm, very wise woman and amongst close friends and family she was much relied upon for the perspicacity of her observations and the soundness of her advice. She and Julia had always been the first people he would turn to for advice on any romantic or personal dilemma, and as Julia was clearly out of the running on this one, Alicia was the obvious person for him to talk to. On the one hand, however, some sense of loyalty to Ruby as well as a fear of what his mother would say had been holding him back. On the other hand, he was self-aware enough to know that total repression of his feelings probably wasn't doing him any good and that actually, having someone to talk things through with might enable him to be a better boyfriend to Ruby than he was managing at the moment.

As he hesitated, caught between conflicting demands and loyalties, Alicia took the plunge. 'Is there a particular reason why you and Ruby don't want to get married?'

Toby hesitated again, then he too took the plunge. 'She does want to get married. It's me.'

'Oh, I see. Yes, that does explain why her parents might be a little sensitive, I suppose. And why don't you, darling? Fear of commitment doesn't seem very like you, and we always tease you that you're overly conventional, if anything.'

'Yes, I know. But the thing is, Ally . . .' He paused, searching for the right words. 'The thing is, I just don't feel I can marry Ruby, because I'm in love with someone else.'

Alicia exhaled slowly. So that was it. Suddenly, things which had puzzled her made a lot more sense.

'Well, you're absolutely right, darling. Being in love with Julia certainly does make marrying Ruby inadvisable, I would say.'

'Julia!' Her son's eyes were wide with amazement.

Her heart sank. Surely she wasn't wrong about this? 'I thought, I mean, I've always had my suspicions . . . Oh God, have I totally put my foot in it?'

'No! You're absolutely right, it *is* Julia. But I only worked that out myself a few weeks ago, so how the hell did *you* know?'

A couple of hours later, comfortably ensconced in the first-class carriage of a train to Sheffield, Toby had his laptop open but was gazing unseeingly at the screen. His mother had been wonderful. Insightful, sympathetic, understanding. However, a workable solution to his problem had been beyond even her scope. She had suggested, tentatively, that these days there was no need for parents to be together in order to provide stability for their child, but he could tell that she didn't really believe it in her heart. And if his mother, who had put his happiness and well-being above every other consideration for thirty years, couldn't honestly see a way out for him, then it just confirmed his miserable conviction that there simply wasn't one.

While Toby and Alicia were having their heart-to-heart in St Pancras, Julia was just down the road at Euston, waving Rose goodbye.

As she sank down into a welcome, and scarce, seat on the tube home, she reflected on the last twenty-four hours. Her dominant feeling was one of radiant, overwhelming joy. She found it impossible to believe that the aching, gnawing misery she had endured for the past few weeks could have been dispersed so suddenly.

She thought back to the previous evening. Sitting in Skylon, Rose had gazed at her in sheer open-mouthed astonishment as she had confessed that she could indeed be pregnant. Even in the heady and irresponsible days of their late teens and early twenties she had never had so much as a scare.

'If you were, would it be Toby's?'

'Yes, it would.' Julia had almost laughed at the look on Rose's face. 'I'm not a complete slapper!'

'No, you're not a slapper, but you wouldn't be the first girl to seek consolation in the arms, or bed, of another. And surely, I mean, it's a few weeks since the thing with Toby. Haven't you had a period since?'

'First, no, I haven't found any consolation elsewhere. And second, no, I feel so stupid now that I haven't put two and two together, but I'm ninety-nine per cent sure I haven't had a period since. My mind's been on other things anyway, and if I thought about it at all, it was just to think that I'm often late if I'm stressed out at work, and I've certainly been stressed out.'

'Oh my God, Julia. But hang on, don't panic. You're on the Pill, aren't you? It's very unlikely that you're pregnant. The tiredness and sickness and missed period could actually just be down to stress.'

Julia glanced guiltily at her friend. 'Umm, no, I'm not on the Pill. I came off it a few months ago because the doctor was worried about my blood pressure, and I wasn't seeing anyone, so it didn't seem to matter.'

'Okay, but you used a condom?'

Julia shook her head again.

'What!?' Rose practically shrieked, oblivious to the more than interested attention of the couple at the next table. 'But you're so sensible! Didn't you use *anything*?'

Julia paused, well aware that even her best friend was going to judge her for her stupidity and carelessness. 'No, we didn't use anything. I think Toby must have assumed, like you did, that I was on the Pill, because he never mentioned anything about contraception.'

'Bloody hell, no wonder Ruby's pregnant if he never mentions contraception!'

Julia glared at her friend. 'It's not his fault; I knew I wasn't on the Pill.'

'Well, yes, I was just coming to that point. Why on earth didn't you say anything? You're a bit old to be embarrassed, aren't you?'

'It wasn't that I was embarrassed. It's really hard to explain, but on that first evening we were both so carried away that I genuinely didn't think about contraception until it was almost too late.'

'Almost?'

'Almost. By the time it did occur to me I was terrified to say anything, because I didn't have any condoms and I was scared he wouldn't either. And I don't want to over-share, but I was at the point where I thought I would literally die if I didn't feel him inside me, and I just couldn't take the risk.'

'Couldn't take the risk of *not* having unprotected sex?' Rose gaped at Julia in disbelief. It wasn't that she found the scenario Julia had just described particularly implausible – she had been there, or somewhere very similar herself, and knew of various girlfriends who had been there too. It was just that it was so radically unlike Julia. Julia, who would pack a first aid kit for a picnic in Regent's Park. Julia, who had initialled all her CDs with permanent marker before she started university in case any got lost or stolen (although, to be fair, she had always blamed her mum for that one). Julia, who always wore a seatbelt, even in a black cab. She was a byword for cautious, sensible, always prepared. She *couldn't* have been carried away by passion to the extent that she'd had completely unprotected sex.

Half reading Rose's mind, Julia said defensively, 'I was just fed up of always being sensible. Where has it ever got me? I wanted this so, so badly.'

Rose sighed, half affectionate, half exasperated. 'Bloody hell, Ju, you chose a place to start. Couldn't you have begun gently, maybe by not using antiseptic hand gel every time you get off the tube or something?'

'If you'd seen the statistics on the likelihood of a serious flu pandemic, you'd use—' Julia stopped, realising the discussion was veering off course.

'The thing I don't understand is what you did the next day. I mean, as I recall from your technicolour descriptions, there were several more incidents of shaggage. What did you do then?'

'There were six,' Julia murmured dreamily. 'Friday night, twice. Saturday morning. Saturday night before dinner, Saturday night after dinner, and Sunday morning.'

'Okay, spare me the details. But seriously, how did you explain asking him to use condoms then, when you hadn't the first time? Oh no' – catching sight of Julia's face – 'you didn't, did you?'

Julia shook her head. 'How could I?' she asked pleadingly. 'We'd have had to have a whole discussion then about the morning-after pill and stuff, and it was all so perfect and blissful and romantic, I kept on thinking that if we let the sensible stuff intrude it would all just vanish in a puff of smoke. Then it did anyway. But also, I just thought, how many girls my age have never once taken a risk with unprotected sex? And most of them are fine. I just felt that fate owed me one.'

By this time, the couple at the next table were so engrossed in the unfolding drama that they had given up any pretence of not listening. They had both turned sideways for a better view, and their eyes were swivelling from one girl to the other, as though watching a tennis match. Julia caught the woman's eye, and she blushed.

'Well?' Julia asked the woman. 'Haven't you ever taken a risk?'

'Yes,' she admitted, 'I have.'

'And what happened?' asked Julia and Rose in unison.

'I have a five-year-old daughter! Sorry to have butted in, I just couldn't help overhearing. But seriously,' she turned to Julia, 'if I were you, I'd go and get a test.'

'My thoughts exactly,' Rose said sternly.

'Oh, come on,' Julia protested, although she was secretly burning to know. 'Where am I going to get a pregnancy test from at this time on a Saturday night?'

'That's easy, there's an all-night Boots on Piccadilly Circus. Let's go now.'

Rose put Graeme's credit card to good use, and then regretfully swapped her Manolos for some flip-flops before they set off across the Hungerford Bridge. It was just getting dark and London looked at its spectacular best, with the lights reflected in the river, and the floodlit splendour of the Houses of Parliament to the left and St Paul's to the right. Neither woman was in the mood for architectural appreciation, though. Rose was haranguing Julia for her carelessness, and Julia was letting the words wash over her as she tried to suppress the bubble of queasily nervous excitement that was welling up inside her.

Up Villiers Street to Trafalgar Square, up Haymarket, past the bustling theatre-goers and crowded restaurants. Then into Piccadilly Circus, usually one of Julia's favourite places in London. Growing up in Manchester, she had considered London to be the most romantic, exciting city in the world. Her parents had fed that passion when they brought her and her brother for a weekend break in the capital when she was about thirteen. Pat and Eddie had grumbled about the overcrowding and the overpricing; her brother had only been interested in going to the Science Museum, a geek in the making, but she had been completely enchanted by every element. The noise, the crowds, the skyline, the shops, the history, the sense of purpose and busyness and being at the centre of things. And Piccadilly Circus had epitomised that for her. She remembered standing, squashed between a lot of other tourists, next to Eros, gazing at the bright lights and the Routemaster buses swinging past, and thinking, '*This* is it, *this* is where I belong.' Her conviction about this had never really altered; seventeen years later, even with the advantage of now also having visited Paris, Rome, New York and Istanbul, she still found London to be the most romantic, exciting city in the world, and every time she passed through Piccadilly Circus she still experienced some of the wonder of her thirteen-year-old self. Not tonight, however. Tonight she and Rose walked purposefully, ignoring the traffic lights and tutting at the lingering tourists who impeded their progress. Tonight Julia walked straight into Boots without even so much as a glance at the Sanyo advert, and purchased her first-ever pregnancy test.

She peed on the fateful stick in the toilets of Waterstones Piccadilly, not far down the road. Rose waited for her in the coffee bar and she sat in the cubicle by herself, timing the two minutes on her mobile phone, superstitiously refusing to allow herself even to glance at the stick in her hand until the full time was up. Then she looked down, pulse racing, hands clammy, mouth dry, to see the blue line which would change her life for ever. She felt an immediate surge of pure euphoria. The only feeling which remotely compared was Toby telling her that he loved her, and she pushed that thought out of her mind as quickly as it had popped in.

She wrapped the test stick carefully in toilet paper and ran down the stairs, two at a time, tiredness forgotten. She flung her arms around Rose, incoherent with excitement.

'Oh Julia, thank God! You're not, it's negative,' Rose exclaimed.

Julia paused, incredulous. 'No, it's positive! It's positive, Rose. I'm having a baby, I'm having a *baby*!'

14

Ruby couldn't help it. As she stood in front of the mirror, tugging at a zip which clearly wasn't going to budge, she felt hysterical sobs welling up and a loud, frustrated, almost guttural moan emerging.

'Tobyyy!' she wailed.

He came running as fast as he could, panicked by the anguish in her tone. 'What is it, what's the matter?'

'I can't fit into any of my clothes, not even my fat trousers! What am I going to do? I'm so sick of this, everything is ruined.'

Caught between relief that there was nothing wrong with the baby, and irritation at Ruby's melodramatics, Toby gathered his internal resources to reply calmly.

'Well, buy some maternity clothes.'

'But I need something to wear *now*! Anyway, I might be huge, but I'm not big enough for those monstrous tents.'

Toby looked at her as she stood there, naked apart from a thong. She certainly wasn't huge; even at seventeen weeks pregnant most women would still envy her figure, and most men would have a much baser reaction. Her breasts were larger and the nipples darker, a fact which repulsed Ruby, and when she stood sideways you

121

could see that her tummy bulged very slightly, but they were the only visible changes. Other than her hair and nails, of course, growing thicker and more lustrous than ever, and her skin having taken on an almost iridescent hue. The emotional manifestations of her pregnancy were more extreme. She, and by extension Toby, was suffering from horrendous mood swings. Every minor setback was a drama; every genuine problem a major crisis. Toby had read the pregnancy book (which he had bought, and which Ruby had not yet opened) and knew that 'mood swings are common, and you may feel emotionally vulnerable', and that he ought to be patient and supportive of this aspect of pregnancy-related discomfort. It was just that he couldn't help wishing that Ruby had suffered from morning sickness or cravings instead, as he felt that holding her hair back as she vomited, or bringing her ginger tea and dry biscuits in bed, or running out to the 24-hour Tesco at 2 a.m. to buy pickles would be a lot easier than continual alternation between being screamed at, berated, cold-shouldered or wept on.

However, what he had learnt was that arguing or attempting to thwart her in any way only made things worse and that complete indulgence of her whims was generally the quickest way to a peaceful resolution. Plus, in this case, he was feeling quite turned on, and so dissent was certainly not going to do him any favours. They had not had sex since Ruby told him she was pregnant. Ruby hadn't seemed keen and Toby felt, in some obscure way, that it would be disloyal to Julia. However, it had been nearly three months, one of the longest periods of chastity in his adult life, and there was no denying that Ruby was enough to tempt a gay monk.

He walked over to her, and lightly traced his fingers down her spine.

'You're not huge at all, Ruby, you're absolutely gorgeous.'

His fingers moved down, across her buttocks, cupping and squeezing them, and then pulling her in towards him so that he could bend down and lick her nipples. For a moment it seemed as though she was going to resist, but then she sighed in sensuous acquiescence and began to undo his jeans, easing the pressure on his groin, and then ground her still tiny hips into him.

Holding her tightly in his arms afterwards, Toby felt closer to contentment than he had done for a long time. There was a niggling guilt about Julia, but rationally he knew that living with and having a baby with Ruby rather rendered celibacy redundant as an act of fidelity. Ruby seemed content too, her breathing so slow and even that he thought she had gone to sleep, until she gasped and put her hand on her tummy.

'What? What is it?' he asked, alarmed again.

'I just felt a sort of . . . flutter. Oh God, there it is again. I think it must be the baby!'

Toby immediately placed his hand on her tummy as well.

'Silly! You won't be able to feel it yet! You're the one who's read the books.'

'I know, but I just want to feel the connection.'

They had made love over a hundred times. They had each proposed marriage to the other. They had lived together for three months. They had conceived a child together. But to Toby, this felt like a moment of unprecedented intimacy. Just as he was revelling in it, Ruby leapt up.

'Oh my God, I'm going to be late!'

'Late for what, darling? It's a Saturday afternoon.'

'For the meeting with Jeanette and . . . everyone, about the choreography project. That's what I was trying to get dressed for. Oh shite! I still haven't got anything to wear, and now I'm going to be late as well.'

The decision had been taken by her employers that, within a very few weeks, it would no longer be desirable for Ruby to dance professionally until after the baby arrived. She had been devastated by this and partially consoled only by the suggestion that she could get involved with some choreography for a new ballet which the company was developing.

Toby had been about to suggest a late lunch and a walk round Wanstead Park: couple time to reinforce the fledgling closeness which seemed to be developing. However, her meeting was clearly important. Racking his brains to remember the conversations he had been forced to listen to between two of his colleagues who had been pregnant at the same time earlier that year, he suggested that Ruby might be able to fit into a wrap dress. He helped her to find one in the depths of her (his) wardrobe, plain black and clinging, which accentuated her fabulous cleavage and disguised her baby bump. Ruby then accessorised it in her own inimitable fashion: a Pucci print silk scarf holding her hair back from her face, bandanna style, a vintage charm bracelet, some snakeskin stilettos and her trademark red lipstick. As he courteously helped her into the taxi he had ordered, Toby reflected that with post-coital and pregnancy glow she had never looked sexier, but he also felt that their few moments of closeness had evaporated, and when he returned to the house it felt bigger and emptier than it had ever done when he lived alone.

While Ruby resented almost every aspect of her preg-nancy – its effect on her body, her career, her living arrangements, and most of all the fact that it would culminate in a baby for whom she was responsible – the baby was the only thing which kept Toby going. Perhaps logically he should have resented the baby too; after all, its existence had ended his chance of happiness with the woman he had loved since he was eighteen. However, his coping strategy had been to throw himself into all things baby, and to see it as the only thing which would make sense of a senseless episode.

He had bought Ruby a 'pregnancy bible' which she barely glanced at, but which had taken up permanent residence on his bedside table. After Ruby left he went upstairs and opened it on the page for Week 17. Entranced, he discovered that his baby was now nearly five inches long and that s/he already had eyelashes, eyebrows and fingernails. Reading that the baby could hear sounds from outside the mother's body made him even more determined to broach the subject of him reading out loud to it with Ruby. After the twelve-week scan had confirmed that everything was all right, he had gone out and bought a full set of Paddington Bear books, his favourite early childhood reading. Of course it would be years before the baby was old enough to read them, but somehow it seemed to make it more real and exciting. Then he had read an article saying that babies can recognise voices they have heard from inside the womb, and recommending that fathers read to their unborn children to increase the closeness of their bond. This seemed like an excellent idea to him, and the Paddington books would be perfect, but the snag with this antenatal book club was that the mother was pretty much compelled to participate as well, and Toby had a sneaking feeling that Ruby would find the idea of lying on the sofa while he recounted Paddington's adventures to her stomach either hilariously funny or insufferably boring. Of the two he felt that being laughed at would be more painful, and he had been considering how to raise the subject in a way which would minimise the chance of embarrassment.

In a desperate moment he had even considered reading to the baby while Ruby was asleep. The problem with that was, despite the fact that they officially lived together, he and Ruby actually very rarely slept under the same roof. She had point blank refused either to sell or rent out her studio apartment, and he knew that she had left quite a lot of stuff there. Very shortly after moving in she had suggested that to avoid them disturbing each other unnecessarily – as he often had to get up extremely early for work and as she was rarely home before 1 a.m. after performances – she should sleep at the apartment on those nights. 'Those' nights had turned out to be most week-nights, and the occasional weekend as well. Toby knew that this wasn't healthy, but felt powerless to change it, and was equally unconvinced as to how much he wanted to. Without Ruby's presence in the house he could carry on with his work and social life very much as before, with one aching omission.

Now he was no longer in love with Ruby, Toby could see with agonising clarity that they had very little in common. In fact, they each only understood about fifty per cent of what the other said. Toby's interest in the performing arts was moderate at best, and Ruby's interest in modern management techniques was non-existent. In one sense Toby felt he should be worried about this, but in another he was pinning his hopes on things changing radically once the baby actually arrived. Every woman he knew who had children, even the most career-focused, had been besotted by their newborn to the exclusion of almost everything else. In fact, several of Toby's male friends who had children had complained to him that while they loved their baby, they hated the feeling of being pushed into second place, of no longer having first claim on their partner's time or affection. This was a problem Toby was more than confident he and Ruby would circumnavigate. After all, he had never been used to being number one in her affections, possibly at best coming a poor fourth to her dancing, her friends and her clothes. The arrival of a tiny perfect person for whom they shared an enormous love would surely create a new and lasting bond between them. Toby checked himself at this point, aware that using the phrase 'tiny perfect person', even in his own thoughts, was putting his status as a bloke in severe jeopardy. Probably for the moment counterbalanced by having recently shagged a beautiful woman he wasn't in love with, but still.

He gave himself a mental shake and decided to fill the Saturday afternoon space, which still seemed Julia-shaped despite Ruby's absent presence, in the most time-honoured bloke fashion. Call a mate; meet at the pub.

15

Julia gazed dolefully at her reflection in the bathroom mirror. Blooming pregnancy was so far proving to be a gigantic myth. She had washed her hair only the evening before, but it now hung limply and greasily round her face. Her skin had developed an extraordinary sensitivity, even to products she had used for years, and so was a fetching combination of hives, pimples and scaly dry patches. Although she was only three months' pregnant she had already abandoned her normal clothes and purchased some size 18 leggings and tunic tops. It wasn't that she had a bump, exactly; yes, her stomach was bigger, but then so were her hips, and her bum, and her thighs, and her upper arms. Despite this, and despite the fact that her boobs felt as though they had been used as punch bags, and that her favourite foods, Thai, Indian, Mexican, Moroccan, were now a distant memory as she could only stomach the blandest of carbohydrates, Julia was loving every second of her pregnancy. It was possible that the enthusiasm with which she had thrown herself into eating vast quantities of foods she had barely tasted since childhood – Rice Krispies, sliced white toast and butter, Mr Kipling's Fondant Fancies, milkshakes, fish fingers, Heinz Spaghetti Hoops – was in part responsible for her weight gain. But she didn't care. For the first time since she was thirteen Julia had no interest in attracting male attention; she had tried that, it hadn't worked, and her role now was to nurture her baby. And if her baby required half a loaf of toasted Warburtons as an afternoon snack, then Julia was happy to oblige. She was downing Pregnacare vitamins to assuage the vague pangs of guilt that came when she considered that, far from eating five portions of fruit and veg a day, she was averaging about one. And that was only if you counted banana milkshakes as a portion.

This morning, though, Julia's stomach was churning with something besides morning sickness. She had her twelve-week scan today, a major pregnancy milestone. When she'd had the date through a few weeks earlier, Rose had instantly offered to find a babysitter and come up to London for the day to be with her. Julia had dismissed the idea; how hard could it be? She wanted to save any offers of support for the labour ward. Now she was very glad that Rose had ignored her protests and insisted on coming anyway. She was experiencing a mixture of nerves and excitement she hadn't felt since taking the pregnancy test, and she was realising that her silent prayer, 'Please God, let me be pregnant, I'll never ask for anything again,' had been a complete lie. She now understood that she was going to be constantly imploring a higher power she wasn't even sure she believed in to keep her baby safe, and according to Rose this would only increase when the baby was actually born.

She looked at her watch: 10 a.m. She had only just woken up, taking advantage of the fact that she had booked a whole day off work for the scan. She and Rose were going to have lunch afterwards, and then Julia thought she might return home for another little nap. The tiredness of pregnancy was like nothing she had ever experienced. Waves of sleep would wash over her, she could try to surface in response to her alarm clock, but more often than not the tidal currents of exhaustion would win, dragging her back to depths where nothing, not work, nor telephones, nor deadlines, seemed as important as succumbing to the weight of her eyelids. Now, though, she had to rush to get ready for her 11 a.m. appointment. The hospital (not, thankfully, the one where she worked) was normally only a ten-minute walk from her house, but she knew she had slowed down over the past couple of months and today it would probably take her more like twenty. Presumably by the end of her pregnancy it would be taking her a good hour. Or perhaps at that point she would give in and book a cab.

Julia jumped into the shower, gave in to the inevitable and washed her hair again, then pulled on black leggings, her favourite ditsy-patterned floral tunic and ballet pumps. On the one hand there didn't seem to be much point putting make-up on, but actually she didn't want Rose to think that she had lost the plot completely. She compromised with a quick sweep of mascara and the all-important Touche Eclat in an attempt to disguise the bags-for-life under her eyes. Freshly blow-dried, she knew that her hair would last for around three hours before it collapsed again.

The weather was sunny and warm with just a hint of crispness to indicate that this was September and not

July. Despite the ever-present lethargy, Julia still felt that she could skip as she set off to the hospital. Autumn was her absolute favourite time of year. Toby had always teased her for having a morbid streak because her favourite season was autumn and her favourite time of day was twilight. The autumn thing wasn't morbid, though. Autumn seemed to represent a fresh start so much more potently than spring. Everything was crisp and expectant; it was the season of newly sharpened pencils and unblemished erasers, the season of excited anticipation of Halloween, Bonfire Night and Christmas. Autumn suited pregnancy. By Christmas she would have a proper big baby bump, and then only a couple of months before her baby arrived some time in the middle of March.

Rose was already waiting for her in the main entrance lobby of the hospital when she arrived. She gave her a big warm hug, and Julia was dismayed to feel tears prickle against her eyelids. Bloody hormones. The waiting room was, unsurprisingly, filled with women at various stages of pregnancy. Julia almost caught herself in her usual pang of jealousy before realising that this time it was okay, she too was pregnant. Or hopefully she was. Suddenly the nerves really kicked in, and she rushed to the toilet. Kneeling on the hard tiled floor, throwing her guts up into the chemical blue of an NHS toilet, which at least bore reassuring signs of having been recently cleaned, with Rose holding her hair back from her face, Julia reflected contentedly that this wasn't normal. This surely confirmed those miraculous blue lines; this surely wasn't a dream. She rinsed her mouth out and then, back in the waiting room, sipped the water and nibbled the ginger biscuit which Rose gave her. Time ticked by with agonising slowness, but eventually she heard 'Julia Upton' and went through, clutching Rose's arm as her legs had turned to water.

It wasn't magical in the way she had expected. To her untutored eye it was definitely more blob than baby, but what the blob did have was a little blinking cursor, right in its centre. A cursor which, the sonographer informed her, was her baby's heart. The somersaults, waves and hiccups she had heard about from various friends and acquaintances must have been complete lies, she concluded. This was just a blob, but it was her blob, and it was a blob with a heartbeat. Julia started crying again, not delicate tears sliding down her nose in a ladylike fashion, but huge gasping sobs which made her nose and eyes run so much that she soon soaked the tissue she had, and was getting through the blue paper roll used to give women as much modesty as can be obtained from a piece of tissue paper when you're naked from the waist down under fluorescent strip-lighting. All the misery about Toby and the anxiety about the baby leached away from her in those tears, and by the time she had stopped crying and given her nose a final blow on the soggy blue paper, she felt physically lighter, as though it was that volume of saltwater which had been weighing her down.

Everything was fine. Her due date was confirmed as 12 March, and she was told that as far as they could tell at this stage, everything seemed normal and the baby was developing nicely. An hour later she and Rose were sitting in Mondragone, the family-run neighbourhood Italian in Walthamstow Village. Despite the ginger biscuits, Julia was ravenous and could feel saliva welling up in her mouth as she scanned the menu.

'Wow, Rose, I really, really, really want penne all'arrabbiata!'

'So what's new? You've eaten penne all'arrabbiata at pretty much every Italian restaurant we've been to for the last fifteen years.'

'Yes, but not recently I haven't. For the last few weeks even the thought of a chilli has made me want to throw up, but now I feel like my tastebuds are back. Maybe being sick at the hospital was my last bout of morning sickness? After all, I'm nearly thirteen weeks now, isn't it meant to pass in your second trimester?'

Rose, veteran of one completed pregnancy, raised her eyebrows in sceptical amusement, but declined to burst Julia's bubble. That bubble, anyway. Once they both had steaming bowls of pasta and a mountain of garlic bread in front of them, Rose looked sternly across at Julia.

'Right, you.'

Julia glanced up, surprised, an oily slick of red around her mouth, but didn't pause from shovelling pasta.

'What?'

'Don't you think it's time you sorted a few things out?'

'I don't know what you mean.' Julia refused to make eye contact.

'Yes, you do. Come on, Julia, you're not stupid, don't pretend to be naïve with me. You are pregnant, by a man with whom you had what was practically a one-night stand, who is, as far as we know, engaged to another woman who also happens to be having his child. You are single. You live two hundred miles away from your parents and forty miles away from me. You have a very big mortgage on a very small house. You are, to use the technical description, in the shit. And you don't seem to be in the least bit interested in coming to terms with that, or in making any practical plans.'

'If by practical plans you're meaning abortion again—'

'No, calm down. I got the message on that one. And I would hardly have come to the scan with you if I was still trying to persuade you that was a good idea.'

Rose and Julia had come close to a major row when, during an early oh-my-god-you're-pregnant phone call, Rose had hinted that Julia should have a termination. Her arguments had been similar to the ones she had just outlined; Julia didn't have the resources, either financially, emotionally or practically, to support a child. Julia, seeing her pregnancy as a lifeline, the thing which was giving her a reason to get up in the morning once more, the thing which would for ever more connect her to Toby, however invisible the links, saw this suggestion as positively evil.

'Good, because I love this baby, and I'm having this baby, and I'll manage. Women in worse positions than me have managed.'

'Yes, granted they have. But that doesn't mean it's been easy for them, Julia, and it won't be easy for you, especially if you won't face facts and start making plans.'

'I've got plenty of time! Six whole months – I think that's enough time to buy a few babygros and paint the spare room.'

'Julia, are you being deliberately obtuse? Now, listen to me. I don't particularly like being in the position of having to lecture you like this—'

'Liar,' muttered Julia, 'you love it.'

Rose smiled, despite herself. 'Okay, so I'm bossy. But I'm also right. I'm not talking about buying things for the baby, although that is important, I'm talking about all the other stuff. When are you going to tell Toby, for a start?'

Julia pretended to fumble in her handbag for her diary, and her voice was laden with sarcasm as she replied, 'Oh, right, hang on. Let me check. When would be a good date for telling my "one-night stand", as you put it, that he's knocked up his bit on the side? I'm going with never!'

'Julia!' Rose really was shocked now. 'Julia, you have to tell him, it's his right to know that he's going to be a father.'

Julia's voice was bitter. 'Except that he already knows, doesn't he? He's already well aware of the fact that he's having a baby with Ruby. That, in case you'd forgotten, is the reason why we are not a couple.'

Rose leant forward to emphasise her point. 'But that's *because* he wanted to stand by Ruby, to be a father to the baby.'

Julia nodded vehemently. '*Exactly!* But he can't fucking well stand by both of us, can he? Come on, Rose. Let's compare, shall we? In the red corner we have Ruby: beautiful beyond men's wildest dreams, only woman Toby has ever wanted to marry, stylish and slim and graceful and talented and from a wealthy, aristocratic background. Oh yes, and just happens to be carrying his child. In the blue corner, I give you Julia. Julia, who only passes as pretty on a very good day, and at the moment could fry chips with the oil from her face and hair, and by the looks of her waistline has been doing just exactly that,

and eating the results with indecent regularity. Not graceful, not especially talented, and certainly not rich or posh.
Woman Toby has known for twelve years but only had
sex with after being temporarily dumped by our friend in
the red corner. Oh yes, and just happens to be carrying
his child. I have to tell you, Rose, from where I'm sitting
it's not looking good for the lady in the blue corner. And
frankly, even if I was prepared to ignore the only request
Toby made, which was not to upset Ruby, I'm damned if
I'm going to put myself through the rejection and humiliation of turning up as the fallen woman the young master
"got into trouble".' Julia concluded her polemic slightly
breathlessly.

Rose was silent for a moment.

'See?' cried Julia, darkly triumphant. 'See what I
mean?'

Rose nodded slowly, and Julia felt her heart sink. There
was, she realised, a small part of her which had been
hoping Rose would argue with her, would tell her that of
course Toby loved her and would come back to her and
the baby, and it would all be okay.

'I can see that it would be very difficult for you to tell
him,' Rose conceded. 'Personally, I still think you should;
apart from anything else, you could do with the financial
support. But—' raising her voice to drown out Julia's
protests, 'but, if you won't, that certainly doesn't mean
you don't have any planning to do. The opposite, in fact.
You have a lot to think about, and you need to start this
afternoon.'

16

'So, no Ruby then?' Alicia raised her eyebrows enquiringly as she opened the front door and ushered Toby through.

'No,' Toby responded curtly. He contemplated making an excuse, and then decided that he was just too tired to be bothered.

'That's a shame, darling. Your father and I have been looking forward to getting to know her a little better. That is, if you're still, I mean . . .' Her voice trailed off in sudden embarrassment.

'You mean, if I'm still in a relationship with the mother of my child?'

Alicia hadn't actually seen Toby since their meeting at St Pancras Station, now nearly three months ago. This in itself wasn't unusual; she and Hugh now employed a full-time manager as well as several part-time assistants in their gallery, and that gave them a good deal of freedom to travel, mixing business with pleasure as they checked out galleries in cities across the world and, occasionally, found a promising young artist they could tempt with London exhibition space. Toby also travelled extensively for work, so months could easily go by without them seeing each other, but the difference this time was that they had barely spoken on the phone either. She was worried that he had thought the better of confiding in her and was using avoidance tactics as a consequence.

The truth was more layered than that. Toby was embarrassed at having admitted his feelings for Julia so openly, and he felt guilty that the feelings were there to admit to. What he had really hated, though, was the realisation that his mother was unable to solve this particular problem for him; perhaps the discovery that there are things our parents cannot resolve for us is the real coming-of-age experience, and it was all the more potent for coming to Toby so comparatively late in life. He had avoided Ally because it hurt that she couldn't help him. Then, however, he felt guilty about that too, and so when she had invited him and Ruby over to Sunday lunch he had accepted. His childhood had not been particularly conventional, but Alicia had always insisted that family Sunday lunch was a ritual they upheld, and he knew it would be womb-like in its comforting familiarity. He had felt relieved when Ruby had said she wasn't coming, even though he had been irritated by the manner of her refusal.

'You are joking, darling?' she had said. 'Sunday lunch with your parents? Terribly bourgeois, don't you think?'

'I don't know what you mean, Ruby. I'm damned sure your parents sit down to roast beef and Yorkshire pudding at 1 p.m. sharp, every Sunday.'

'They certainly do, but it may have escaped your notice that I do *not* join them. Not my scene, *at all.* To be honest, wouldn't have thought it was *Ally's* scene either.'

He debated whether or not to pick her up on the tone of scornful derision in her voice and trigger yet another row, or whether to let it go. Recently he had been ignoring a lot of barbed comments or jibes which once upon a time would have infuriated him. It made life easier. And usually, just when he had got to the point where he didn't feel he could cope with much more, she would turn to him, defenceless as a child suddenly, and sob that she would never be able to manage without him, that she needed him, that he must never leave her. Not, he noticed, that she loved him, but then he hadn't said that to her either since that far-distant day five months ago when he had proposed. This comment felt different, though. He could put up with her scorn directed at him – he was boring, he was a money-grubber, he worked too hard, his clothes weren't cool, he wasn't cool, his friends weren't cool, his worrying about and planning for the baby wasn't cool – but he drew the line at her insulting his parents.

'What do you mean, you wouldn't have thought it was *Ally's* scene, in that tone of voice?'

'I mean that I wouldn't have thought the kind of woman who is so self-consciously bohemian she keeps those dreadful photos on her wall would be the kind to get so hung up over Sunday lunch.'

'She's hardly hung up on it, Ruby, she just asked if we'd like to go. Which I would, as it happens. And I don't know what disgusting photos you mean.'

'The ones of her pregnant, all gross and deformed. It's sickening, frankly.'

Realisation dawned on Toby at that point. His father was a photographer and throughout Ally's pregnancy with Toby he had photographed his wife, naked, on the same date each month, so they had nine photos recording her changing body. These photos, tasteful as they were, in black and white, with his mother's long hair hiding her breasts and her hands placed protectively and concealingly underneath her growing bump, had caused Toby acute embarrassment as a teenager when his friends came round and saw them displayed in a row in the hall. As an adult, however, he was rather proud of them, displaying as they did his father's talent, his mother's beauty, and their joint pride and delight in him.

'I don't think the photos are disgusting,' he replied carefully.

'Well, I do,' she responded vehemently. 'It's bad enough knowing that I'm becoming hideously deformed like that, and it's only going to get worse, without having to see photographic evidence of it all over the place.'

Indeed, Toby had noticed that she completely refused to look at the section in the pregnancy book headed 'Your Changing Body'.

Bringing himself back to the present with an effort, Toby met Alicia's concerned gaze. 'Don't worry, Ally, I'm not getting at you. I'm sorry Ruby's not here, but she's busy with work, and we're not getting on that well at the moment, to be honest.'

Alicia was a notoriously awful cook, and Toby had spent most of his childhood dreading her deciding to make anything. She could just about manage fish fingers and baked beans without disaster, but anything else would be tasteless at best and downright disgusting at worst. His worst memory was of the time she had mistaken Nescafé granules for Bisto, a mistake which had not been discovered until the results were poured all

over everyone's (desiccated) beef. His father's favourite
story was of when, overly ambitious for a dinner party,
she had attempted Duck à l'Orange but had forgotten to
buy oranges, and so had substituted the low-calorie
orange squash she had found in the cupboard. The
Fentons' culinary life had taken a marked turn for the
better when they began earning enough money to afford
M&S ready meals, and an even more dramatic upturn a
few years previously when Hugh had decided to learn to
cook, had attended a week-long residential course, and
discovered a surprising talent.

That had been too late for Toby to benefit from while
living at home, but it did mean that a meal at his parents'
home could now be pleasurably anticipated for something other than the company. Today he was especially
looking forward to it, as, deprived of Julia's cooking, he
was existing almost entirely on microwave meals whenever he ate at home. Hugh didn't disappoint. Instead of
the traditional roast, they had butterflied chicken breasts
marinated with lemon juice, olive oil, garlic and chilli,
then pan-fried, served with couscous, roasted vegetables
and thick Greek yoghurt speckled with fresh mint.

It was delicious, and Ally and Hugh were as warm,
loving and interesting as ever, but throughout the course
of the meal (the chicken being followed by homemade
steamed syrup sponge and custard), he found himself
getting more and more depressed. Somehow, here in his
parents' flat, he missed Julia more than ever. She got on
so well with his mum and dad, and they both adored her.
She usually joined him whenever he went to lunch there,
and in his mind's eye Toby could see her helping his

father in the big open-plan kitchen, chopping, dicing and gently flirting, while he and Alicia lolled on the cream sofa, gossiping and teasing and demanding that the food be hurried up. She made his parents laugh until they almost cried sometimes with tales of hospital life and her impressions of Call-Me-Holy-Trinity (God alone being not quite good enough), the impossibly arrogant surgeon and Medical Director with whom she had a love-hate working relationship.

Sunk in these thoughts, Toby was unaware that his parents were exchanging increasingly troubled glances and frenetic eyebrow signals. The result of this was that Hugh put his spoon down, pushed back his chair and announced, 'Right, Ally. I've done all the hard work shopping and cooking. I think it's only fair that you do your bit by loading the dishwasher and I get to go for a walk with my son on the Heath, and maybe a quick pint in the Holly Bush afterwards.'

Alicia made a token protest for form's sake, but was inwardly thrilled when Toby agreed. Toby felt it was against his better judgement; a walk on the Heath was another activity he closely associated with Julia, but suddenly the thought of being outside in the fresh autumn air was irresistible.

They stomped along in companionable silence for a while. Hugh was wondering if he ought to make enquiries into the state of Toby's emotional health; Toby was wondering if there was any point talking to his dad when no one could really help him. In the end, inevitably, they both spoke at once.

'So, have you decided—?'

'Can I ask you something?'

Hugh broke off. 'Of course, ask me anything you want. You know you can.'

'Before I was born, did you really want a baby? I mean, was I planned?'

Hugh hesitated for a moment. 'You were most definitely planned. I have to say, though, that it was more your mother's idea than mine. I was about the same age as you, and we were having so much fun as a couple, I thought there was plenty of time to worry about children, even though I knew I wanted them eventually. But Ally suddenly got broody. And although it's only thirty years ago, things were different. She was about thirty-two or thirty-three, I suppose, and that was considered quite old then, for a first baby, so she wanted to get on with it. I suppose I just loved her so much that I was willing to do whatever would make her happy. And then, as soon as we knew she was pregnant, I felt completely different about it. I was like a kid before Christmas, I literally couldn't wait for you to arrive. In fact, ironically, it was your mum who had bigger doubts then.'

Toby's face lit up. 'Really? Ally didn't like being pregnant?'

'Well, I wouldn't say that, exactly. She got very nervous about the birth, I think, and worried in case anything went wrong with you. She was worried that I'd stop fancying her, too – in fact, that's one of the reasons why I took those photos, because I wanted to show her just how beautiful she was.'

Toby sighed. He didn't know exactly what he had been hoping for. Some indication that Ruby's behaviour was normal, that it wasn't a problem for a pregnant woman to refuse to discuss her pregnancy, or the baby's birth and its care afterwards, or to look at pictures of pregnant women, or to treat her partner with scarcely veiled hostility alternated by brief fits of clinging neurosis. But it didn't sound like his parents had anything to offer there. Bloke not sure he wants to give up his freedom, but excited when pregnancy actually happens. Woman really wants a baby, but a bit nervous about the birth. It didn't really seem to fit on the same spectrum as Ruby. But then, everything his father had said seemed to centre around how much he and his mother loved each other. That struck a chord with him very strongly, but was reminiscent of his feelings for Julia, not Ruby. He groaned aloud.

'Look, Toby. No secret that your mother and I talk. She told me that this pregnancy wasn't planned, and that, to put it bluntly, if it hadn't happened, you were going to try and make a go of things with Julia. Is that still what's troubling you?'

'Yes, to an extent. I do love Julia, and I miss her so much, but I think I might be able to cope with that. I'm really excited about the baby, you see, and although the fact that Ruby's having a baby is the reason I'm not with Julia, having a baby to look forward to actually makes it easier to manage, if that makes sense.'

Hugh nodded, doubtfully.

'But it's Ruby, really. She just doesn't seem to want the baby, at all. She won't talk about it, or plan, or engage with the pregnancy, and she gets really irritated with me when I talk about it.'

Hugh glanced thoughtfully at his son. 'Can I ask, in those circumstances, why she decided to go ahead with the pregnancy?'

Toby considered for a minute, and then decided that his dad was one of the most discreet people he had ever met.

'Look, don't even tell Ally this, but she had an abortion when she was a teenager, and it sent her off the rails a bit and she felt too guilty to do it again. I think she somehow saw this baby as a chance to make things right, to make amends to the other baby, though that doesn't seem to be how it's working out so far. But the thing is, I'm trapped. Every time I get to the point where I feel I can't carry on, she gets in a state and tells me how much she needs me, and I've got a responsibility to her and the baby. I can't just bale out now.'

Hugh stopped walking, and turned to face Toby. 'No,' he agreed, 'you can't just bale out. But you've got to think long term. For the child, if not for yourself. If you and Ruby both carry on like you are, you're not still going to be together when this baby gets to eighteen, and heaven knows what damage you'll have done in the meantime. You need to think very carefully about that, Toby.'

17

Pat Upton glared at her daughter. 'The thing is, Julia, I just don't think you have the faintest idea of how difficult it is to care for a new baby and bring up a child, and that's difficult enough for any new mother, let alone one who doesn't have any support from the father. It's really hard work. And this house . . .' She glanced round the room. 'It's so small. I don't see how you'll manage.'

Julia glared right back, hoping a burst of anger would subdue the tears she could feel prickling behind her eyelids. 'If it's so horrible having a baby, I'm surprised you had two!' Even to her own ears her voice sounded childishly petulant; why did having an argument with her mother automatically mean that she regressed fifteen years?

'I didn't say it was horrible, I said it was hard work. Although it's interesting you consider the two to be synonymous. The point I'm trying to make is that when I had you and Harry I was happily married, you were both planned and wanted, I had a nice home, I didn't need to go back to work until Harry started school. My circum-stances were very different from yours, and I struggled at times. I simply don't see how you're going to cope.'

This time Julia did feel a surge of white-hot anger, although treacherously the tears started to spill out as well. Her voice was choked as she replied. 'Okay, first of all, and most importantly, this baby may not have been planned but it is most certainly very much wanted – by its mother, even if not by its grandmother. Second, I think I do have some concept of hard work. Can I remind you that my job isn't exactly a walk in the park. I have responsibility for over sixty staff, and a multi-million-pound budget, to say nothing of ensuring that patients at one of London's largest teaching hospitals get treated as quickly and effectively as possible. So don't bloody patronise me. Third, I think I do have a very nice home, even if you don't like it. Fourth, nearly half of marriages end in divorce, and at least I won't be putting my baby through that trauma. He or she will just have a very loving mother. And fifth—' She paused. Damn. She'd forgotten fifth. 'Oh yes, and fifth, Rose has stayed at home with Sebastian and is going mad with boredom. So it's probably better all round that I'll be going back to work.'

With a huge effort Julia prevented herself from concluding her impassioned speech by saying 'So there!' She then flung herself out of the front door and slammed it behind her.

Pat winced as the bang from the door reverberated around the small house, and then buried her head in her hands.

'Come on, love.' Her husband Eddie crossed the room and put a supportive arm around her shoulders.

'Oh, Eddie, I just don't know what to do for the best. I'm so angry with her for being so stupid, and at her age as well – you'd think she'd know better. But I want to help her too. It's just that every time I open my mouth I seem to rub her up the wrong way.'

'I know. The two of you have always been a bit like that, to be honest, haven't you? Plus her hormones won't be helping – you had such a short fuse when you were expecting our two, and I reckon Ju's just the same.'

'Oh, you're probably right. But how am I going to help her prepare for the baby if we can't even have a civilised conversation? I just want her to be safe, and comfortable, and to be as happy as I've been. I mean, look at this house. It's tiny. Where's she going to put a baby? Also, I've been researching the prices of nurseries and childminders round here, and believe me, by the time she's paid her mortgage and her childcare, she'll barely have anything to live on. I just want to try and convince her that the best thing to do would be for her to sell up and move back to Manchester. She could get a bigger house for half the money and I could take care of the baby for her when she goes back to work. And we'd see more of her and the little one.'

'Pat, listen.' Eddie crouched down and took both her hands in his. 'We've got to be careful here. I know what you mean. I'd love her to come back home and I can't see what she gets out of living down here, but it's not about what *we* want, is it? Julia loves it here, she's got her friends, she likes her job, and it's a bloody good one. Just tread carefully, that's all I'm saying.'

Outside in the street a light yet pervasive drizzle was falling. Julia reflected forlornly that there were huge disadvantages in storming out of the house after an argument when it was your own house, you didn't have your hand-bag with you – therefore no keys, Oyster card, phone or money – it was cold and wet and you didn't have a coat. Still, there was no way she was swallowing her pride and ringing the doorbell for her mum to let her back in and probably use this as just another example of her unfitness to be a mother herself.

She set off towards the centre of the Village. Although it was getting dark and felt later, when she checked her watch she saw that it was only 4.30 p.m. Her spirits lifted slightly. The Deli Café would still be open; maybe she could blag a free drink.

Luckily for Julia, Simone, her favourite waitress, was on duty and smiled warmly at Julia when she came in. 'Hiya, hun, how are you and the bump?'

'Cold. And wet. And miserable. I've just had a huge row with my mum and stormed out of my own house without even bringing my handbag with me. Don't suppose I could have a cup of tea and owe you the money, could I?'

'I think I can trust you,' laughed Simone. 'Tell you what . . .' She glanced round the little café. Only a couple of tables were occupied. 'We're not busy. How about you sit down and I'll get us both a drink? Then you can tell me all about it.'

She came over a few minutes later with two mugs of hot chocolate and a plate of chocolate-chip shortbread. 'On the house!' she winked.

Julia was staring morosely out of the window. It was raining harder now and the streets were gleaming wetly under the street lamps. Although it was cosy and warm in the café, the weather suddenly made Julia feel vulnerable and exposed; perhaps her mother's criticisms were having an effect at a subliminal level because she was suddenly inordinately conscious of the baby, and how she and she alone had the responsibility of keeping it safe for the next twenty years or so.

'So, what are you fighting with your mam about?'

Simone had been waitressing at the Deli Café for the last couple of years. Since Julia went in at least twice a week for coffee on her way to work, or for a slice of cake or a panini lunch at the weekend, and as Simone was extremely gregarious and talkative, Julia knew a good deal about her life, although she didn't feel they had ever quite crossed the invisible barrier which would take them from being acquaintances to friends. She knew, though, that Simone was Liverpudlian (anyone who had heard more than one or two words pass from her lips knew that), and that she was mixed race – her dad a black American, her mum white and born and bred in Belfast. She knew that her mum had brought her up as a single parent, the relationship with her father having been a holiday romance which fizzled out. She knew that Simone was now a mum herself to five-year-old twin boys. She knew that she was studying Psychology at university part time, and waitressing to supplement her musician boyfriend's relatively meagre income. She knew that they all lived in a flat above one of the other shops in the Orford Road parade. All these facts, gleaned in a thousand light-hearted exchanges, flew through Julia's head now and she wondered what Simone knew, or surmised, about her.

Had she, for example, noticed that Julia was nearly always alone when she came in to eat now, whereas previously she had normally been with Toby? Did she wonder how Julia had got herself pregnant when she hadn't ever seen her with a boyfriend? Or had she put two and two together and realised that the timing of Toby's visits to Walthamstow coming to an end coincided quite remarkably neatly with Julia suddenly declaring that she couldn't face coffee and developing a sudden passion for hitherto-despised herbal teas?

Simone was still sitting, head tilted at a sympathetic angle, waiting for Julia's response.

'Oh, usual thing, I guess. You've probably realised that this baby doesn't have a father on the scene, and my mum's found that really hard to cope with, I think. She just won't quit nagging me about how difficult I'm going to find motherhood, how expensive, how much room babies take up, etc., etc. But she seems really contradictory as well; like one minute she's telling me that babies need their mothers at home and it's a shame I'll have to go back to work after six months, and the next minute she's telling me that babies are really expensive and that I'll need a bigger place to live. I despair, I really do.'

Simone looked thoughtfully at Julia for a few minutes. 'She's bound to be worried about you, Julia. She's your mam, and she can't help wanting what's best for you. No parent wants to see their child struggling, and I have to say, single parents do struggle sometimes.'

'Oh God, Simone, don't you start too. I know that your mum brought you up on your own and you didn't know your dad, and you've always said how close it made you and your mum – more like sisters.'

'Yes, we are. But that doesn't mean it was always easy for her, not by any means. I knew that we didn't have much money, but I know now that Mam protected me from the reality of how little we had and what that really meant. I know that, because I do the same now for my boys.'

Julia started to speak, but Simone hushed her and carried on. 'When my boys were born – two weeks after – Matt and the band went on tour for six weeks. They couldn't turn down the opportunity; it was as a support act for Arctic Monkeys, so a really big deal, and we certainly couldn't afford to say no to the money. But it meant that I was pretty much a single parent myself for the first few weeks of the boys' lives. And honestly, Julia, I could not have done it without my mam. She was a life-saver. Don't know if it was my life or theirs she saved, but I do know she was essential. You can't afford to fall out with your mam, Julia, cos you're going to need her big time in a few months.'

Seeing that Julia appeared even more crestfallen, Simone flashed her a warmly reassuring smile. 'But you'll make it up with her, no worries. You'll have mates to help as well. In fact, listen, I've got loads of baby stuff the twins have grown out of, you can have some of that if it'd be any use. Save a few pennies.'

'Oh yeah, that would be great! My best friend's offered to lend me a few things, but her husband wants them to have another baby soon, so I don't think it would be very tactful to walk off with all of it.'

Simone laughed. 'Well, every now and again Matt does say that he'd love a little girl, but believe me, twin boys are more than enough. Especially in a two-bedroom flat! You're very welcome to anything you can use.'

At this point, one of the other customers signalled that they wanted another coffee, and almost simultaneously the door opened and Eddie Upton came in. Julia looked up, surprised.

'Hiya, Dad.'

Simone slipped away and Eddie took her vacated seat. 'Hello, pet. You all right?'

'I'm sorry I ran off like that, Dad. Mum was just really getting to me.'

'She just w—'

'I know, I know, she just worries about me.' Julia smiled ruefully. 'I just wish it didn't always come out like criticism.'

'That's just her way, love. Look, I thought I'd better come and find you so we could have a little chat, and I remembered you said you came here a lot so I thought I'd pop round and see. Your mum thinks I've come out for milk.'

Julia smiled. 'Thanks, Dad. I'd say that I'd get you a drink, but I didn't bring any money with me!'

Eddie was scanning the prices on the menu, and visibly paled. 'No, it's all right, I had a cup of tea before I came out. I can't pay *two pounds* for another one!'

Julia smiled again. 'That's London prices for you, I'm afraid.'

'Yes. Well. That's why I wanted to talk to you. The reason your mum's been going on a bit about how hard it will be for you is that she's building up to persuading you to move back up to Manchester.'

Julia stared at him in horror. 'You. Are. Not. Serious.'

'I knew you'd react like that. Look, what she's thinking, and I do agree with her, is that it would be easier for you. You'd have a lot more money because the house prices are so much cheaper, and we'd help you as much as we could with the baby. You would be able to get another job. We do have hospitals "Oop North", you know.'

'I know, Dad. But it's not what I want to do. It's not that I hate Manchester or anything. It's a great city and I'm proud of coming from there, but this is where I live now. I love my job and my little house. I love that I know the people around the Village. I feel I've got the best of both worlds: twenty minutes to Oxford Circus on the tube, but a real little community to live in here. And it'll be a great place to have a baby; there's loads of groups – Baby Sensory, Baby Yoga, Baby Massage . . .'

Eddie nodded, sadly. 'I know. I knew you'd say that. I do understand. And I think deep down, *very* deep down maybe, your mum does too.' He paused, half wondering if he should seek enlightenment on just how, and why, babies do yoga, but resisted the temptation offered by this tangent. He then said a little awkwardly, 'Plus, of course, being so near Toby will be a big thing, too.'

Julia felt her face flame with colour. 'What? What do you mean? Why should I care whether I'm near Toby or not?'

Her father looked her, then nodded again. 'I thought so.'

'What? What did you think?' Julia's voice was shrill and panicked.

Eddie reached out and patted her arm. 'Toby's the father, isn't he?'

Julia's colour ebbed as quickly as it had risen, and she felt the room beginning to spin.

'Oh goodness, pet, I didn't mean to upset you. Here, have some of your drink.'

Eddie's voice seemed to be coming from a long way away, and she felt a wave of the nausea she had escaped for the past few weeks.

'Why do you say that?' she asked faintly.

'Well, I'm not completely stupid. First, your mum and I have always thought that you had more than a soft spot for Toby, and that you'd make a lovely couple. Second, there was obviously something more than flu wrong with you when you came up to stay in the summer, and then next thing you tell us you're pregnant. Then round about the same time you completely stop talking about Toby and cut us off if we ever ask after him. Finally, I know you, Julia. You're not the kind of girl to get yourself pregnant by someone you hardly know, even if that's what you'd have us believe. You haven't had a boyfriend for a while and you're just not the kind of girl to have one-night stands.'

Blushing guiltily as she recalled a couple of youthful indiscretions her father was thankfully unaware of, Julia had to concede that his reasoning was spot on.

'Oh God! Does Mum know too?'

'Not as far as I know. I certainly haven't said anything. But I think you should tell her, Julia. Apart from anything, she'll be so relieved that it wasn't a one-night stand. I don't suppose—' He hesitated. 'Toby's such a nice young man, I can't understand why he's not . . . not, erm . . . more . . . involved, I suppose.'

Julia took a deep breath. 'He's not involved because I got pregnant while he was on a break from his long-term girlfriend. She then discovered she was pregnant, and Toby decided he wanted to make a go of it with her. I haven't seen him since, but I assume they're getting married. He doesn't know about my baby, and I intend to keep it that way. And believe me, Dad . . .' Her voice was shaking with the intensity of her feelings. 'If you and Mum want to have a relationship with your grandchild, you will forget *any* idea of contacting him yourselves.'

Eddie threw up his hands in a gesture of surrender. 'All right, all right! I promise we won't. It all sounds too complicated for me, pet. Listen, I've brought an umbrella for you. Let's walk back. I think you and your mum should make an effort to have a proper talk this time.'

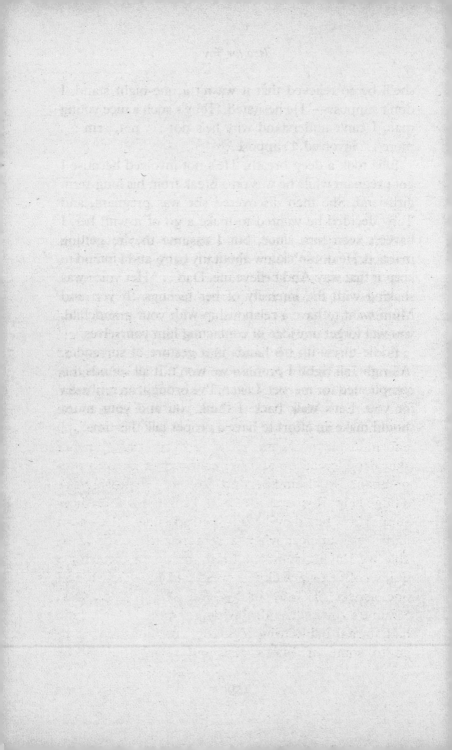

18

'Right, let's do this.' Julia opened her notebook at a clean, fresh page and looked expectantly at Simone, who was sitting opposite her at the kitchen table.

'Wow, a list! You really are quite anal, aren't you?' Simone laughed, but in a way which felt friendly and teasing rather than critical. Since their chat in the café a few weeks earlier, Julia and Simone had become good friends. It was now late November, but as the weather outside had worsened, Julia felt herself becoming more and more positive. It seemed that she had entered the blooming phase of her pregnancy at last; she was still enormous all over, and growing by the day, but her skin had cleared up and her energy had risen to pre-pregnancy levels and beyond. Simone's friendship was a huge help; Rose was lovely, and still being incredibly supportive, but they hadn't met up since Julia's scan and it was unclear when they were next going to be able to. Having someone local she could meet for a quick coffee or a walk felt great, and replaced at least one aspect of Toby in her life. Aaron and Zack, Simone's sons, were absolutely adorable as well. Julia had started babysitting regularly, enabling Simone to go to some of Matt's gigs and giving Julia some childcare practice, as well as repaying some of Simone's kindness.

This Saturday morning, however, Matt had taken the boys to the park to work off some of their apparently limitless energy, and Simone had come round to Julia's to advise her on what she needed to do to get the house ready for the baby.

Simone pushed back her chair, and stood up. 'Right, let's walk round then. You said space was one of your main worries?'

'Yes. Well, no. *My* main worry is that I'll never sleep again. My friend Rose's main worry is that I won't be able to afford to pay the mortgage. My mum's main worry is that my house is too small, and completely unsuitable for a baby. Whatever that means. So I don't expect you to solve the first or second problems – although if you want to that's fine! – but I was hoping that you could give me some pointers on how to customise the space to make it more family friendly.'

'Well, I'm certainly the expert on that! And at least you haven't got a boyfriend with three different guitars and a full-sized electronic keyboard to accommodate.'

Seeing the shadow that passed across Julia's face when she mentioned a boyfriend, she hurried on.

'Right, anyway. So obviously the kitchen is lovely!' She scanned round and took in the spacious, airy room. It was the largest room in Julia's house, big enough for a table and four chairs in the middle, a huge, retro duck-egg blue fridge-freezer, two long work surfaces and an old-fashioned dresser at one end.

The cupboards were painted cream and the worktops were maple, butcher-block style. Patio doors led out into the small courtyard garden, which was fairly drab in November but would obviously be a riot of colour in the summer.

'Thank you. It's my favourite room – I love cooking, and I've tried to make it nice. The size was one of the things which attracted me to this house.'

'Okay, well, you'll probably spend a lot of time in here when the baby arrives as well, so maybe put the bouncy chair in here. With a bit of luck that will keep Baba quiet for a bit while you do some jobs.'

Julia scribbled on her list, and they moved out of the kitchen into the narrow hall.

'Hmm. Well, you either need to get a very small pram, or one that folds up easily. I'm afraid you won't fit an all-singing, all-dancing off-roader in here. I can't help you there, cos I had a double buggy and that's the last thing you need.'

They turned into the living room. This was tiny, all the space on the ground floor having gone into the kitchen. There was a small open fireplace, and Julia said immediately and defensively, 'I know I'll need to get a fire guard.'

Simone looked amused. 'Well yes, eventually. But not for a while. And being totally honest, Ju, you're probably not going to feel much like the hassle of open fires for a bit. All that building it up, and nursing it to get it going, then having to clear the sodding grate afterwards – you're just not going to have time, and if you do have time, that's not what you'll want to do with it.'

Julia gulped, taking a slight reality check as her vision of sitting breastfeeding her baby by firelight, while IQ-enhancing classical music filled the room, receded slightly.

It was the same as they carried on through the house. Simone was full of sensible and practical advice – use baskets for storage, safety catches for cupboards, no need for a changing table – as well as generous offers of loans of various bits of baby kit. Julia diligently made notes, but found herself getting more and more depressed as the reality of life as a single mother started to dawn on her.

Finally Simone noticed that Julia was starting to hunch over with tension and misery. 'What on earth is the matter, hun? I don't feel I've been very helpful; you're in a worse state now than you were when I came. Come on, let's go and have a cuppa.'

A few minutes later they were back at Julia's kitchen table with steaming cups of tea and some homemade oatmeal raisin cookies.

'So what's the matter, then?'

'Oh, I don't know. I think I've been so excited about having a baby, how I felt about it emotionally, that I just haven't let myself consider the practical implications, even though everyone's been nagging me to. Now I've started, I just feel really depressed. This house *is* too small for a child, and money *is* going to be incredibly tight.'

'You'll manage, don't worry. I've always been in the same boat; we've got no space, and no cash. I just try and hang on to the fact that kids don't really care about the material stuff, they just need loving parents—' She stopped, aware that she had been tactless and hoping that Julia hadn't noticed. Unfortunately, she had.

'That's another thing I can't give my baby. They're never going to have a father, so I've got to provide all the love, as well.'

Simone was torn. Did she go for the warm hug and reassuring platitudes? Or did she use this as an attempt to try and satisfy her curiosity? She decided on the latter, consoling her conscience with the thought that it would probably do Julia good to talk about it.

'So what's the deal with the dad then? Was it a one-night stand or a sperm bank or what?'

Julia was amused at Simone's bluntness. Funnily enough, since her father had guessed about Toby and she had plucked up the courage to tell her mum what had happened, she found talking about it much easier. Both her parents had been supportive, and her mum far less critical than she had feared. In fact, she got the impression that they were both relieved that the father was someone they knew and liked, although she hoped that she had managed to persuade them once and for all that there was absolutely no chance of a reconciliation and a game of Happy Families.

'Do you remember my friend Toby? He used to come into the café with me sometimes.'

'Tall, dark hair, broad shoulders? Oh my God! Is he the dad? Wow! I never could work out whether you were a couple or not. I never saw you holding hands or anything, but there was a real chemistry between you.'

Julia felt her heart leap, and cursed herself. After all that had passed, the one thing she was relatively sure of was that there *had* been real chemistry between her and Toby. Affirmation of this from a third party didn't really help her situation now, however.

'Yes, he's the dad. But we weren't really in a relationship.' Julia carefully explained the circumstances which had led to her pregnancy, scanning Simone's face as she did so for signs of disapproval. There were none. She just seemed interested and sympathetic.

As Julia concluded her story, Simone came round the table and hugged her. 'You poor thing. It must have all been absolutely horrendous for you.'

Julia managed a watery smile, and nodded. 'It's certainly had its moments.'

'Are you still in love with him?'

Julia's smile wobbled as a montage of images flooded her mind. Toby's smile. His shoulders. The feel of his arms around her. The warmth in his eyes when he had looked at her. Their long conversations which segued from teasing to serious to satirical and back again. She nodded, almost imperceptibly.

Simone gave her shoulders a quick squeeze and then sat back down again. Julia absent-mindedly reached for another cookie.

'Did you always fancy him? All the time you were friends? How long have you known him, anyway?'

Julia considered how best to answer. It was a question she asked herself time and time again as she lay unable to sleep, and she still wasn't sure what the truth was. She cast her mind back to their time together in Oxford; three of the most perfect years of her life, with Toby an integral part of all those memories.

She had met him very early on in her first term – he was on the same course as the girl who lived next door to her – and a big group of them used to get together in the college bar, drinking and philosophising and generally pretending to be grown up, hoping that no one would guess it was all a bluff. She had fancied Toby at the beginning; he was tall, dark and handsome, and his enthusiasm and confidence were incredibly attractive. She was shy, though, and hid her attraction behind sarcastic witticisms, suspecting that he fancied Amanda, who was beautiful, thin, posh, clever and more self-confident than any eighteen-year-old had a right to be. (In fact, Amanda had more than a little in common with Ruby, which was perhaps why she had taken such a strong dislike to her at their first meeting.) By the time that Amanda, inevitably, started dating the captain of the men's First Eight and Toby realised that sharp, funny, curvaceous Julia might actually be far more what he was looking for, Julia's efforts to convince herself that she didn't care about Toby had paid off and she was deep in the throes of a crush on an American graduate student called Trey.

When Toby kissed her at the Christmas Ball at the end of her first term, she relaxed into the kiss for a moment, amazed at how good it felt, before remembering a distinctly promising flirtatious conversation with Trey earlier and pulling away, in case he was watching and thought she was already spoken for.

She had a brief fling with Trey, but he was way out of her – non-Ivy – league, and a few weeks into Hilary term she was single, decidedly opposed to transatlantic alliances, and remembering how much she had enjoyed that brief kiss with Toby. When he came round to her room late one night with a bottle of cheap wine, she was fully prepared for the evening to end with them in bed together. Unfortunately he had come round to confess that he fancied Elinor, a girl on her course, and to ask her to try and find out whether she liked him too.

And so it went on. Although they became best friends and were almost constantly together through all the drunken rituals of an Oxford education – May Mornings, balls and formal halls, punts, parties and Pimm's, and the traumas of 2 a.m. essay crises, Mods and Finals – they never became a couple. Occasionally Julia would look at Toby and feel a shiver of something far from platonic, but always when he was going out with someone else, and she was never sure whether he was still attracted to her. Not, that is, until the day they finished Finals.

Julia's last exam was in the morning, Toby's in the afternoon, so she went to meet him, still wearing her academic gown which was obligatory for formal exams, and the red carnation which traditionally denoted someone sitting their last paper. She took party poppers and champagne and, with a large group of friends, they spent the rest of the sleepy, sun-kissed golden afternoon getting absolutely blind drunk. It was a curious feeling. Elation that the sleepless nights and nervous tension of Finals were at an end. Sadness and nostalgia for the last three years, but excitement that 'real life' was about to begin. It was probably around two in the morning, the temperature now pleasantly balmy after the sultry heat of the day, and she and Toby were lying on their backs on the green velvet lawn in Fellows Garden, gazing at the stars.

Suddenly she felt his mouth on hers, slow and tentative at first, but then parting her lips with his tongue and creating waves of desire which rippled through her. Senses both heightened and dulled by champagne, she sank into the kiss without questioning. Only at the point when one of Toby's hands was inside her bra and the other snaking up the inside of her thigh did she reluctantly pull away. Although they were a little way away from their friends, they were not alone in the garden, and she was not sufficiently drunk either not to know what would happen if they carried on, or not to mind such a public display of rather more than affection.

Taking his hand, she pulled Toby in the direction of her room, and they stood in the arched medieval stone doorway while he began unbuttoning her blouse and she fumbled for her key.

Then she felt his breath hot in her ear, murmuring, 'Julia, I think I love you. Oh God, Julia, I really think I do.'

Somehow the words broke the spell and produced the effect of a cold shower. She was now aware that the wall she was pressed up against was damp and digging uncomfortably into her lower spine. The after-effects of the champagne were starting to make her feel queasy. She had been operating in an emotional vacuum where only her erogenous zones seemed to matter, but now her brain was engaged. She was leaving the following week to go inter-railing round Europe for three months with Rose – her last taste of freedom before she started as an

NHS graduate trainee in the autumn – and Toby was heading off to the States as a counsellor for Camp America. No way did she want to break her best friend's heart, or her own, and somehow she knew that sleeping with Toby that night would, could, only end in one or the other.

She tried to explain this to Toby, but although he said he understood, she always sensed that he had felt personally rejected. But by the time summer ended, she'd had flings with a Jean-Paul, a Carlos and a Marco, and Toby had a preppy East Coast girlfriend called Serena, with whom he maintained an on-off long-distance relationship for almost a year.

The platonic nature of their friendship was never questioned again, until that life-changing weekend in June.

Remembering all this, Julia felt her face moving into a more natural and totally involuntary smile.

Simone laughed across at her. 'Okay, given the cat that got the cream expression on your face, I'm guessing that there have been, shall we say, "romantic interludes" in the past?'

Julia dropped her eyes demurely. 'You may say that, but I couldn't possibly comment.'

Simone laughed again, but then her expression took on an unwonted severity. 'You are making a serious mistake. Not telling him about the baby, I mean. Apart from anything else, he's got a right to know. And what about your baby? They've got a right to meet their father, surely. Plus, *you're* the one he loves. He should be with you!'

Julia shook her head adamantly. 'No. I've no evidence he loves me, and I don't want him in my life out of pity. I couldn't stand that. At least at the moment I can let myself think that maybe he did love me, but if I tell him and he stays with Ruby then I don't even have that to fall back on. Trust me, Simone, there's no way on earth I'll let him know that I'm pregnant.'

19

Rose looked glumly out of the window at the rain beating against the glass, and then back into the living room at the sofa cushions piled up in the middle of the room with her son bouncing up and down on them. The weather had been unrelentingly bleak for the last three days – rainy, windy, cold and foggy – and she and Sebastian had been almost entirely confined to the house. She was mentally composing the case for suing under the Trade Descriptions Act her husband, the estate agent and sundry well-meaning friends and relatives who had told her that the countryside was the perfect place to bring up children. They were all bloody liars.

The countryside was a perfectly acceptable place to bring up children between May and September. From October through to April it was a living hell. The three sources of pre-school entertainment available to her were the (admittedly large) back garden, the playground on the village green, and the mothers and toddlers group which met for two hours every Tuesday morning in term time only. Rose thought wistfully of conversations she'd had with friends living in London who had small children. She had heard so much about the children's facilities at the Science Museum, the Museum of London, the

Museum of Docklands, the Museum of Childhood, the Tate Modern. There was a plethora of music groups, dancing groups, story sessions and craft sessions in almost every London neighbourhood. Although Sebastian had the time of his life in the summer, in and out of the paddling pool in the back garden and spending hours on the swing his father had rigged up on the big apple tree, Rose couldn't even feel that smug then because her friends and their offspring had easy access to Richmond Park, Hampstead Heath, Hyde Park, Regent's Park, Green Park, St James's Park, Clapham Common . . . to name but a few.

An enormous crash, followed by a series of earsplitting wails, interrupted her train of thought. She spun round. Oh God. While she had gazed mournfully out of the window it looked as though her son had attempted to climb the free-standing bookcase, but had succeeded only in toppling it over. After she had ascertained that Sebastian was scared rather than hurt, Rose turned her attention to the chaos that was her living room. The bookcase was splintered in several places, and books were scattered everywhere. Many had fallen open and she could see that the pages were crushed and torn, the spines bent. The large glass vase which had contained roses had smashed, and the rather dirty and distinctly malodorous water had spilt everywhere, soaking into her rug and ruining several more books. The floor was now a lethal carpet of shards of broken glass and rose thorns.

She had picked Sebastian up to comfort him, and now his sobs had subsided he had nestled his head into her shoulder. She buried her face in it, relishing the comforting scent of Johnson's baby shampoo and small boy. Then from nowhere a great racking sob emerged and tears began pouring down her face, soaking into her son's hair. He looked up, alarmed.

'Mummy? Why is Mummy crying?'

Rose fought for composure. She knew she was frightening Sebastian, but even that knowledge didn't seem able to stop her. 'It's okay, darling,' she managed between sobs. 'The big bang just gave Mummy a bit of a fright like it gave you.'

Sebastian's face crumpled again in sympathy. 'I'm sorry, Mummy. I didn't mean to do it.'

Rose felt an even sharper pang of guilt. This was all her fault for not supervising Seb properly; he could have been killed. Not only had her world shrunk to the four walls of the house and the care of one small child, she couldn't even do that properly.

She forgot her own tears in her renewed efforts to soothe her son, but ten minutes later when they were both sitting in the kitchen, Seb with a consolatory beaker of milk and a biscuit, she with a cup of tea which she desperately wished was something a good deal stronger, she realised that she just couldn't do it any more. She just didn't think she was capable, mentally or physically, of going back into the living room, clearing up the mess, finding something to keep Seb occupied and safe while she did it, and then finding ways to keep him occupied and safe for the next eight hours until he went to bed. For the sake of her sanity, something had to change.

Suddenly galvanised, she reached for her mobile and called Julia.

'Hey, it's me, can you talk?'

'Erm, it's not a great time for a long chat, but I've got a minute before my next meeting. Are you okay?'

'No, not really. I mean, I'm fine, we all are, but I need to escape. Can Seb and I come and stay for a few days?'

Forty-odd miles away, Julia gulped, and hoped guiltily that the gulp hadn't been audible. Rose was such a good friend to her, and she wanted to return the favour. Really, she did. It's just that Seb, in common with most toddlers, was a one-man destruction unit, she didn't have a lot of space at the best of times, and being nearly six months pregnant and working full time, plus commuting halfway across London for two hours a day, plus trying to sort out her life to accommodate a baby, wasn't exactly the best of times. However . . .

'Yes, of course you can! When where you thinking?'

'Erm, well, now. I mean, this afternoon. After I've got some stuff together and driven up, really.'

Julia gulped again. 'That's fine, except that I'm probably not going to be home before seven at the absolute earliest, and I just can't get out of the stuff I've got on this afternoon.'

'That's all right. I've still got your spare key from last time I stayed, so if you don't mind, I could just let us in.'

Julia's mind spun as she tried to compute what state she had left the kitchen in, where they would all sleep, whether she had any clean bedding or towels and finally, why on earth Rose was running away from home. Seeing her secretary frantically signalling to her that she was running late for her next meeting, though, all she said was, 'Yes, of course, that's fine. Sorry if it's a mess, do whatever you need to do. I'll see you later, and we can have a proper catch-up.'

Her place of refuge organised, Rose became frighteningly efficient. As the mother of a small child, running away from home was slightly more complicated than it looked in films – throwing a handful of clothes and a toothbrush into an oversized yet chic shoulder bag simply wasn't an option. Sebastian was parked in front of the television in the playroom with his favourite *Thomas the Tank Engine* DVD while Rose ran upstairs to undertake the packing marathon which even one night away from home required. She threw into a bag a pair of clean jeans, a sweater and some underwear for herself, and then went into Sebastian's room. This bit was more difficult. There was Teddy, and Giraffe, as well as the three or four additional soft toys who were this week's indispensable favourites. There was the baby monitor, and the nappies and wipes (potty training had been a total failure so far), the travel cot and all the bedding, a selection of picture books, and that was all before the five different outfits, vests, socks and pyjamas which were necessary for any stay of more than a night or two. In the bathroom she grabbed both their toothbrushes, her moisturiser and a range of *Gruffalo*-branded toiletries.

She flung the bag into the boot of the car and chucked the travel cot, which he was almost-but-thankfully-not-quite too small for, and the pushchair in after it. She checked that Seb was still absorbed in the world of Sodor Island, and then headed to the kitchen to prepare a selection of wholesome and nutritious snacks for the journey.

Almost as an afterthought she grabbed a pad of paper and a pen and scribbled a note for Graeme.

Graeme,
   Sorry about the short notice, but I'm taking Seb up to London for a few days to stay with Julia. Have got mobile if you need me. There's a lasagne, some bol sauce and chicken curry in the freezer.
   Rose

She paused for a moment, and then added a solitary kiss after her name.

Once they were on their way, Seb securely strapped into his car seat and listening to one of the CDs she kept in the car for him, she let her mind wander back over the last few months and reflected on how she had let her life get to this point.

After her stay in London with Julia back in the summer she had returned home fired with enthusiasm for having an open and honest discussion with her husband about their family, her career and the future. To say that it had not gone well would be an understatement. She had completely underestimated the scale of Graeme's sense of hurt and betrayal. All around the world women were tricking men into getting them pregnant and men were doing their utmost to evade responsibility. If you considered the situation critically, even Julia had come very close to doing that. Trust her to be stuck in the role-reversal relationship. Trust her to find the only *man* whose biological clock started ticking as he approached thirty-five.

She had honestly felt that her relationship was teetering on the brink. And because she wanted what was best for Seb, and because she did feel genuinely guilty about the illicit Pill-taking (for most people this would have involved Ecstasy, for her it was Ovranette), and because at the end of the day she did realise that somewhere, deep down, under all the layers of boredom and resentment and frustration, she probably did love Graeme, she agreed to stop using contraception. She didn't mention anything about Sebastian going to nursery while she retrained as an aromatherapist. She still had no desire to get pregnant, and decided she would follow a homemade rhythm method. It had taken a few months for her to get pregnant with Seb, so she knew her body quite well and was perfectly aware of when she was ovulating. Avoiding sex for a week or so around that time seemed a fairly easy and relatively foolproof option. Especially as their sex life had dwindled into the once-a-fortnight-if-we're-not-too-tired-and-there's-nothing-good-on-telly variety and Graeme didn't seem particularly interested in reinvigorating it, even to assist the conception of the child he claimed to want so badly.

Unfortunately her self-sacrifice had not really improved the state of her marriage. Maybe Graeme could sense that her heart wasn't in it. When they had been trying to conceive their first child, the arrival of her period had been a shared source of regret; in fact, at that time she probably felt it more than Graeme did, because failure to fall pregnant on her honeymoon as they had planned shook her confidence in her own fecundity. This time, though, Graeme could probably sense the relief coming off her in waves as she reached for the Tampax, and when she saw his hurt puppy-dog eyes she was torn between a sense of remorse and a strong desire to slap him. These disparate and conflicting emotions were building a wall between them which she didn't feel she had the energy to climb. Meanwhile, she was still stuck at home with a child whom she loved to the ends of the earth and beyond, but in a lifestyle which bored her rigid.

Rather appositely, Seb began to whinge at this point and glancing at the clock on the dashboard she realised that it was past his lunchtime. She pulled over into the next set of services, intending to park, let Seb eat the nutritious and well-balanced picnic meal she had brought for him and maybe grab herself a coffee. And then for the second time that day, she felt as though something snapped inside her. The windows of the service station were brightly lit, and it looked warm and cosy compared to the driving rain outside. Without really thinking she unsnapped Seb from his car seat, wrapped her big water-proof jacket round both of them and raced for the doors. Inside there was a steamy fug which smelt absolutely delicious. Still moving in a sort of daze, Rose found herself ordering a lunch which was the polar opposite of the organic, low-GI, high-super-nutrient diet they normally ate. Fried egg, chips, beans, a full-fat Coke for herself, a chocolate milkshake for Sebastian, and an iced bun to share for dessert. It tasted like heaven.

On the way back to the car they passed an M&S Simply Food, and she popped in to get some child-friendly supplies to take to Julia's. She did buy milk, yoghurt, cheese and fruit as she had intended, but they comprised rather a small percentage of her purchases compared to the pizzas, dips, crisps, chocolate and wine which seemed also to have found their way into her basket.

Arriving at Julia's house, she was startled by all the changes which had taken place since she was there for her friend's twelve-week scan. The rather poky room which had once been Julia's seldom-used office had been cleared out completely. The walls were now a soft white and the paintwork a vibrant buttercup yellow, with yellow gingham curtains to match, and it felt at least twice the size. Other than a polka-dot spotty rug, there was no furniture at all. Well, at least that solved the problem of where Sebastian was going to sleep. The sofa in Julia's living room converted to a double bed but took up most of the available room in doing so, and, if Sebastian's travel cot were in there, would also mean that the room would be inaccessible after 7 p.m. With a sigh of relief Rose assembled the travel cot, arranged the changing mat in the corner, Seb's teddies in the cot, and folded his clothes and put them in the corner in a cardboard box she had found lying around. It now looked a very cosy space for a little boy and she smiled, thinking how excited Julia would be to see the room being used for that purpose.

It was 7.45 before Rose heard Julia's key in the lock. She had cooked Sebastian's tea, bathed him and tucked him up in bed, loaded the dishwasher and given Julia's kitchen a cursory clean. So far, so normal evening. Now, though, she was curled up on the sofa with a large glass of wine, a packet of tortilla chips and a tub of guacamole. Since meeting Graeme, Rose had been on a pretty much permanent diet. First of all it was Atkins, in a desperate attempt to achieve and maintain the size 8–10 figure which seemed compulsory for a banker's WAG. Then it was the pre-wedding crash diet. Then it was the high-micro-nutrient diet meant to prepare her body for pregnancy and aid conception. Then it was a pregnancy and breastfeeding diet in which every portion of carefully washed fruit and veg, mono-unsaturated fat and oily fish was prescribed to the last gram. Recently it had been a low-GI diet, keeping her figure but setting a good example of balanced eating for Sebastian. Everything was organic, free range, wholemeal and unprocessed, so seeing Rose halfway through a packet of M&S's best convenience food caused Julia's eyebrows to rise sharply in surprise as she came into the room.

Rose jumped up to hug her friend. 'Get you with your big bump!' she exclaimed.

'Thanks, hun, I love you too!' Julia returned her hug warmly.

'You know what I mean. You're properly pregnant now, it's so exciting.'

'I am really excited. Getting more scared as well, though.' She gestured at her bump. 'You do realise that this huge thing has got to come out of me? How does that work?'

Rose laughed. 'It's fine, honestly. I mean total agony, zero dignity, but so worth it. And the rush of hormones afterwards, my God, if they could put that in a pill there'd be no need for any illegal drugs.'

'Really?' Julia was interested.

'Definitely! You know I tore really badly when I had Seb?'

Julia winced and nodded. She did remember Rose going on about something like that, and sitting on a rubber ring for ten days afterwards, but it had all sounded completely disgusting and she had rather passed it over in favour of cooing at the milky, sleepy little bundle that was Seb, and the darling little booties, scratch mittens and sleepsuits which covered every surface in Rose's house. Now, though, such topics had taken on a new immediacy.

'Yeah, it was horrible, really, really, really hurt. Then they had to inject local anaesthetic into my bits and stitch me up, and I could hear the doctor saying to the midwife, "Ooh, nasty one this, she's torn right across there. Wouldn't be surprised if it was internal too. Going to need quite a few stitches." And normally, as you know, I faint at the idea of putting a plaster on a blister, but here I was, legs akimbo in stirrups with the world and his wife between my legs, and some seventeen-year-old junior doctor giving a running commentary on the mangled mess that was my genitals, and I was floating in a cloud of bliss. Everything else seemed to be coming from miles away, almost like it was happening to someone else, and I just kept gazing at Seb, and smelling him and watching him rooting for my boob, and I have literally never been happier.' She smiled reminiscently.

Julia stared at her with an expression of mingled horror and awe. 'Oh my God, Rosie. That sounds horrific!'

'I know, it does, but the bizarre thing is, it really wasn't.'

Julia shuddered, and then collected herself. 'Oh God, sorry, Rose! Here you are, fleeing to me in distress, and I'm blathering on about pregnancy stuff. Listen, come into the kitchen while I see about making us some supper and tell me all about it. I might even have a splash of that wine with my fizzy water tonight; I don't think the bump will mind too much.'

'I've bought some M&S pizzas, if you fancy those for dinner?'

'Brilliant, you're an angel. Come into the kitchen anyway. I'll stick them in the oven and throw a salad together while we talk.'

20

'Fuck, fuck, fuck.' Ruby tore herself away from what she was doing and looked at her boss in some distress.

'What on earth's the matter with you?'

'I've just remembered, I'm meant to be meeting Toby tonight. I'm going to be late.'

'Ruby, darling, you're late for everything. Toby must surely be used to that?'

'Yes, but this is a special meal he's booked for us.' She bit her lip self-consciously. 'He said we need to make more of an effort to spend quality time together before the baby comes.'

'Really? How touchingly romantic of Toby. I'm sure you must be looking forward to that.'

Ruby glared at him. 'Don't be so fucking sarcastic.'

He raised a sardonic eyebrow. 'Well, you'd better get yourself sorted and go, hadn't you? That is, if you really want to continue in that farce of a relationship.'

'I've told you before, I don't have any choice. I don't want a baby at all, I'm damned if I'm going to do the whole thing by myself. And honestly, Toby is going to make a brilliant dad. He's so excited.'

'Hmm.' Paul remained sceptical, but refrained from further comment. 'Well, off you go, my dear, I'll see you in the morning. It seems a bit late to tell you to be good, but Ruby . . .' His voice was suddenly serious. 'Do be careful.'

In the end Ruby was only a few minutes late, and she and Toby arrived at almost exactly the same time. It was a cosy, intimate little French restaurant in Covent Garden, full of nooks, crannies and alcoves, with crisp white table-cloths, twinkling candles and attentive waiters who made Ruby, a beautiful and heavily pregnant woman, a source of much Gallic chivalry and charm. Ruby wondered ruefully to herself when the only male attention she could rely on had become middle-aged waiters. Once upon a time, a night out would have been cocktails in a stylish bar, followed by dinner in a trendy restaurant, followed by dancing at a hip club, possibly followed by some wildly gymnastic sex. Now it was an early dinner at a quiet restaurant, and the early night which would surely follow would be strictly for sleep alone, as she and Toby had made love only once since she had discovered she was pregnant. She knew what had changed everything of course. It was the moment when she bottled out at the abortion clinic. Every problem in her life felt as if it could be traced back to that decision. She sighed deeply, and Toby looked across at her in concern.

'Tired, darling? We can always give dinner a miss and go straight home for an early night if you want.'

Ruby would have laughed at the accuracy of her prediction, had she not felt like crying. 'No, I'm fine.' She made a huge effort. 'It'll be nice to spend some time together properly.'

Toby was rather startled, as over the last few months Ruby had given absolutely no indication whatsoever that she wanted to spend time with him. After his conversation with his father on Hampstead Heath he had given a good deal of thought to his relationship with Ruby and his now non-existent relationship with Julia. There was no doubt that somewhere along the line he had made a total mess of things.

Part of him knew that things weren't working with Ruby; maybe their relationship would never have stood the test of time anyway, but it certainly couldn't withstand the two-pronged assault of an unplanned pregnancy and him falling in love with someone else. Equally, though, she was having his child and he didn't think his relationship with the unborn baby would be able to survive an acrimonious break-up with the mother before it was even born. Fathers who had been happily married for years with close, positive relationships with their children frequently had difficulty with custody arrangements after a divorce, so he didn't hold out much hope for his far more precarious situation. He had therefore remained almost entirely passive, and had simply withdrawn emotionally from the relationship. To all intents and purposes he and Ruby were flatmates who occasionally (platonically) shared a bed, and had a joint project in common. He had ceased to question where she was, who she was with, why she was working the hours she did, and had simply thrown himself deeper into his work, hoping, despite the disastrous economic climate, to be able to secure both a generous bonus and some paternity leave when the baby arrived.

They chatted in a desultory manner as they flicked through the menu. Toby couldn't help reminiscing about the mesmerisingly beautiful girl he had taken to bed a year ago, and wondering how, why and when she had transformed into the sulky and withdrawn woman sitting opposite him now. Several of his deliberately bland conversation openers had resulted in her snapping at him, and he was desperately searching for an uncontroversial topic of conversation when the waiter arrived. Toby greeted him with the fervour usually reserved for a long-lost sibling, and placed his order.

'Prawns Provençale and then steak Béarnaise, rare, please.'

Ruby shot Toby a quickly provocative glance which he missed, and declared, 'Same for me, please.'

'Umm, Ruby?'

'What?' she snapped.

'You're not meant to have prawns, or rare meat, because of the baby. Risk of listeria, remember?'

'But they're my favourites! And you're having them. It's not fair!'

Toby sighed. Had she always sounded so petulant, or was it another side-effect of the pregnancy? 'Well, I'll choose something else to keep you company, if you like.'

She pouted. 'That's not the point. It's just the whole pregnancy thing getting me down. I feel like I always come second to the baby. Everything I love is either impossible or frowned upon when you're pregnant, and it's like you just see me as a womb on a stick, not as a woman any more.'

Toby felt a tide of exasperation rise within him. It galled him beyond belief to hear Ruby whingeing about what she had to give up for the baby when he had lost the love of his life for it. For once he felt unable to muster the soothing response which had become second nature, and he snapped back at her.

'Oh for heaven's sake, Ruby, it's not for ever. You just need to be a little bit more mature and responsible about it all.'

She glared at him, her eyes welling with tears. 'That is *so* unfair. If you knew ... if you had any idea what I'm giving up for this baby ...' Her voice became choked, and before he knew what she was doing she had pushed her chair back, knocking her glass to the floor in a shower of gleaming fragments.

He rolled his eyes. 'Great. Nice way to demonstrate your maturity, Ruby.'

She didn't even bother to reply, just got rather laboriously to her feet and stormed to the door. Toby looked up at the waiter and shrugged embarrassedly.

The waiter was gazing after Ruby with naked admiration all over his face. '*Mon dieu*, she is a passionate woman! You are a lucky man, my friend.'

Toby stared at him incredulously. *Lucky?*

The waiter patted him paternally. 'You go after her, apologise, and then take her home to bed. We will see you both another time.'

Toby felt thoroughly fed up. He was British. He had none of the Gallic appreciation for a passionate scene; as far as he was concerned, he and Ruby had had enough arguments in restaurants to last a lifetime. He had no desire whatsoever to go and tramp the cold streets in search of her, and contrary to the waiter's expectations, he knew that there would be no passionate reunion if he did. Just more tears and recriminations. What he wanted was to sit here in peace and quiet and enjoy a tasty steak and several glasses – possibly several bottles – of very good red wine. However, that seemed impossible. Reluctantly he stood up, thanked the waiter, and left the restaurant.

Ruby hadn't gone far. It had started to rain and she was struggling across the slippery cobbles in her high heels, her once-graceful gait now hampered by the heaviness of late pregnancy. Toby watched her for a moment, feeling weariness seep into his very bones. Then summoning what little energy he possessed, he broke into a run and caught up with her. She was crying. His heart smote him a little at the sight of her tears, but he had endured so much over the past seven months that he still wasn't deterred from his original purpose.

He drew her under the arches of the Piazza so that they were sheltered from the rain. Her shoulders were hunched with misery, and he put his hand under her chin and gently lifted her face so that they could see each other. There was a depth of unhappiness in her beautiful eyes which surprised him. He had got so into the habit, the self-pitying habit, of considering all that *he* had lost – Julia, a warm, loving relationship, the chance to have children with a woman who entered into all his excited anticipation – and all Ruby's iniquities – absence, mood swings, carelessness – that he had long since stopped considering her feelings at all.

'Look, Ruby. This isn't working, is it? You and me? We're not really having a relationship, and I don't think the pretence that we are is really working for either of us.'

Her eyes widened in panic. 'No! You can't dump me, Toby! I'm pregnant, I need you. I *can't* do this on my own.'

'Shh, shh. You don't have to do it on your own. I'm still going to be here for you, Ruby. I'm still going to be here for the baby. You can live with me, if you want to – there's space for you to have your own room. I'll still come to the classes. I'll still be there for the birth, if you want me. But I don't think I can carry on pretending that we're a couple when I don't think, if we're honest, we've really felt like that about each other for months now.'

He had his hands lightly on her upper arms, and he could feel the tension in her.

'What do you mean, you don't think we feel like that about each other? We're engaged, for God's sake.'

He shook his head, firmly. 'No, we're not engaged.'

She tried to interrupt and he talked over her.

'I know you want to get married, or claim to want to, but I've never agreed to it and you know that. You're not in love with me, are you?'

Slowly, almost imperceptibly, she shook her head.

'I've known that for ages, really. And the thing is, Ruby, I'm not in love with you any more either. But that doesn't mean we can't still be good parents, and it doesn't mean you have to do all this on your own.'

'You say that now, but before long you'll meet some-one else, and they won't want you hanging around your ex-girlfriend all the time, and before I know it, you'll see the baby for a couple of hours on a Saturday afternoon, and the whole of my fucking life will still be ruined and you can just move on. All men are just the same.'

She was almost screaming now, and passers-by were giving interested glances at the beautiful, distraught pregnant woman, and disapproving glances at the man who was causing her such distress. Toby drew a deep breath. He could feel the disapproving glances like knife blows, and being subjected to several of his least favourite things – public embarrassment, raised voices, hysteria – made it difficult to keep calm, but he knew he had to. He still felt incredibly guilty, but having deliberated for months he now felt an overwhelming clarity that this was the right thing to do. He searched for a way to make this all right, to make Ruby stop crying and screaming, and then hit upon it.

'I won't meet anyone else.'

'Yeah, yeah.'

'No, Ruby, I mean it. I promise. I solemnly promise that I won't date anyone else while you're pregnant, or when the baby is still small. I'll still be completely there for you both; we just have to stop this pretence that we're in a relationship.'

She leant against him, burying her face in his shoulder, and he felt her whole body heaving with sobs, but it seemed as though some of the tension had left her. For the first time since receiving her text message all those months earlier, he felt himself metaphorically start to exhale. Maybe, just maybe, this would work out after all.

21

It was the weekend following Rose's hasty retreat to London, and she and Julia were in the local playground watching as Sebastian charged round, up and down the slide, on and off the roundabout, performing hair-raising stunts on the climbing frame and generally expending the ridiculous amounts of energy that an almost three-year-old boy seemed to accumulate.

It was only a couple of weeks before Christmas, and the weather had changed from cold and wet to very cold and crisp. Both women were wrapped up, Julia in a huge poncho her mum had crocheted for her as none of her coats fitted over her bump, and Seb was barely visible at all under the layers of woollens which enveloped him.

'Have you spoken to Graeme?'

They had been chatting lightly about Christmas and Seb's presents, and speculating on whether the baby would be a boy or a girl, so Julia's question fell with a leaden thump into the froth which preceded it.

'No. Not spoken to him. I've texted him a couple of times.'

Julia took a deep breath. Time for the tough love. 'Well, you need to. Look, Rose, I'm no expert, God knows, but even I can see that you can't carry on like this. What are you hoping to achieve?'

Rose shrugged miserably. She had been asking herself the same question, but no coherent answer had emerged. 'I don't know. When I came to London I wasn't intending to leave Graeme or anything like that, it was just an impulse because I was having such a shitty day, or such a succession of shitty days, and I needed a break. I wanted to see you, and have some company, and have some fun. And maybe I thought that having some time apart would make Graeme appreciate me a bit more, and I could try talking to him again about not having another baby just yet, and me going back to work, or retraining.'

'Well, that sounds like a plan,' Julia responded encouragingly.

'Ye-es.' Rose was dubious. 'Do you think it's a problem that I don't miss Graeme? That I feel happier this last couple of days than I have done for the past eighteen months?'

Julia regarded her friend and shrugged. 'I don't know. It doesn't sound like your marriage is particularly healthy at the moment, but like I said, what do I know? Thing is . . .' Her voice trailed off apprehensively.

Rose narrowed her eyes suspiciously. '*What's* the thing?'

'I phoned Graeme and asked him to come round this afternoon. I thought I could look after Seb and give you and him a chance to talk properly.'

'Bloody hell, Ju! You are an interfering cow, aren't you?'

But Rose wasn't angry, not really. She knew deep down that she couldn't continue living in this state of limbo, and after a break and several long talks with Julia, she felt much better and more confident in herself and in the reasonableness of what she was asking.

They headed back, gave Sebastian his lunch, and then Julia took him off to Simone's to play with Zack and Aaron while Rose prepared herself to see Graeme. He had told Julia he would be there at 2 p.m. and, true to form, at 1.59 precisely the doorbell rang. Rose was sitting in the living room, trying to quell the butterflies in her tummy, telling herself it would be all right. If only, when she saw him, he would fling his arms round her, tell her it would all be all right, that they would do whatever it took to make her happy. Such overtly romantic statements had never been Graeme's style, but that fact was easier to ignore when she hadn't seen him for nearly a week.

'Hi.'

'Hello, Rose.'

He stood on the doorstep, and they stared at each other. Neither of them made any move for physical contact. After a moment, Rose took a step backwards and asked him to come in.

They went through to the kitchen and Rose busied herself putting on the kettle, making tea, finding biscuits, anything she could think of which would act as a displacement activity. Graeme remained completely silent while she fussed around, until she finally ran out of excuses and came to sit opposite him at the table.

She offered him the plate of biscuits. He shook his head, and absent-mindedly she began to crunch one herself.

'You don't normally eat biscuits,' he remarked accusingly.

Instantly all her resolutions for a calm and reasoned discussion evaporated and she felt a sudden surge of anger. How could he? After all the problems they had been having, after not seeing her for five days, with really important issues to discuss, all she got was a reprimand for not sticking to her diet.

'I don't think I'm going to put on that much weight after a couple of biscuits, Graeme.' Her voice was icily controlled.

'I didn't mean that,' he blustered, although, to be fair, he had meant exactly that. 'I just meant that you don't want to set Sebastian a bad example.'

That did it. Her remaining self-control vanished.

'You're a fine one to talk about setting a good example, Graeme. Sebastian never sees you because you work all the hours God sends, so you don't set any kind of an example at all.'

'That's not fair! I work "all the hours God sends", as you so emotively put it, so that you don't have to work, so that we can have a nice house and holidays, so that you're free to be able to make a home for our child – our children, hopefully.'

Rose resisted the temptation to scream, or to shout that the endless weekends spent on the golf course were nothing to do with making a life for her and Seb. Or to remind Graeme that, despite his repeated assertions that he wanted at least two children and a full and happy family life, actually he was rarely there, and even if he was physically present he never seemed mentally present. He didn't really seem to enjoy Seb's company; after half an hour's play he would be bored and his hands, and attention, would wander to his BlackBerry. She knew, though, from experience, that these accusations wouldn't help and that she needed to stay calm and focused.

'I do appreciate how hard you work, I really do. But our lifestyle at the moment just isn't working for me, Graeme. I'm not happy, and I haven't been for a while now.'

'I know, darling.' He reached across the table, and covered her hand with his. At last some physical contact, although it seemed more paternalistic than anything. 'But when we have another baby everything will change. You loved being pregnant with Seb, remember?'

She did remember. She remembered the delighted anticipation they had shared, how cherished she had felt when he carried her bag, or made her endless cups of ginger tea, or gently rubbed her back to help lull her to sleep. The problem was, she also remembered how this had changed completely once they were confronted with the reality of a tiny bundle of colic that never seemed to sleep for longer than ninety minutes consecutively, day or night. She had been exhausted and sore from the birth, and while overwhelmed with love for the baby, totally unprepared for the havoc that would be wrought on her life and sleep patterns. From feeling feminine and cherished she had gone to feeling bovine and ignored. Very early on, Graeme had stated that because he had to get up for work he should sleep in the spare room, with ear plugs, because she had all the following day to catch up on sleep. To be fair, he had offered to pay for a maternity nurse, but even from the depths of sleep deprivation Rose had been determined that she would care for her baby herself, and as she couldn't cope with him being out of her sight – even five minutes while she had a shower would leave her edgy, tense and paranoid – she couldn't see that a maternity nurse would really help.

Looking back, she wondered if she'd had mild postnatal depression, but at the time she had been too exhausted to even consider the possibility, let alone ask for help.

'I do remember. I loved – love – having Seb. But it's not easy, Graeme. I know you work hard, but I do too – twelve-hour days, permanently on call, no time off at weekends.'

She smiled, but Graeme didn't.

'I'm sorry, Graeme, but I'm just not ready to do it all again. I need to do something for me first. I've been thinking about it a lot. That's one of the reasons why I came to stay with Julia for a few days, just to give myself some time and space, and I think what I'd like to do is go back to work. Maybe retrain. Possibly just part time to start with. Seb could go to nursery. I think he'd really like it now . . .'

Graeme remained silent, and she felt compelled to continue talking to fill the gap.

'I've been thinking about training as an aromatherapist. I know it's a complete change, but I've always been interested in alternative therapies. And I was talking to Mum's friend Jean, you know she had breast cancer, and she was telling me that her local hospital has an aromatherapist and she found it really helped with the side-effects of her chemo, and I just thought that would be an amazing thing to do. Then when I was trained it would be really family friendly – I could do consultations at home, and just work the hours I chose if I was working for myself. But it would give me something for me, something other than just being a wife and mum. Not that I don't like being a wife and mum, but I could do with a change sometimes. I know you want another baby, darling, and I'm not saying that I don't *ever*, but I don't feel ready at the moment. In a couple of years, maybe. Also, I was reading this thing which said that five or six years is actually a really good age gap, much less jealousy that way.'

She ground to a halt, not sure whether the torrent of words was making things better or worse.

Graeme looked at her, and she felt quite intimidated by the anger in his eyes. 'Have you carried on taking the Pill?' he asked, in dangerously quiet tones.

'No, I swear I haven't. But probably not trying very hard to get pregnant either.'

He glared at her. 'Do you know what the rumours in my office are? That I'm firing blanks. How do you think that makes me feel?'

Rose gasped. The irrelevance of his response was astounding. 'Come on, Graeme. Office gossip! What does it matter? People are always saying something.'

He jumped up and began pacing about the room. 'You know nothing about it!' he almost spat at her. 'Office gossip can ruin a career, ruin your life, if you don't take steps to sort it out.'

Rose tried to take deep steadying breaths. The conversation seemed to have gone off in a disconcertingly unexpected direction, and she was unsure how to bring it back to what she felt was the central topic of their relationship.

'You're surely not suggesting we have a second baby to stop office gossip, Graeme! Anyone who knows anything about it knows that you're not infertile – we've got a child, for fuck's sake. What does it matter anyway? It's none of anyone else's business. For heaven's sake! It would be like a rumour going round that you're gay, so you go out and marry the first girl you see, or—'

She stopped as the colour drained from Graeme's face. Time seemed to stand still. She grasped the edge of the table to try and steady herself. Suddenly a number of things which had always been slightly puzzling seemed to slot into place. The speed with which Graeme had proposed. The shortness of their engagement. His insistence that they have children as soon as possible. The paucity of their sex life. Then, sickeningly, something else. The time, not long after they first got together, when she had gone to check something on his laptop and had found some pretty explicit gay porn. His explanation was that a friend had sent it to him as a joke, and at the time she had accepted that – after all, this was the period in their relationship when he was bombarding her with flowers, phone calls, presents; it had never even occurred to her that he might be gay. Now though, as he stood statue still, with that sickly pallor, she forced herself to ask, 'Graeme, are you gay?'

'Of course I'm not gay! I'm married, for God's sake, we have a baby, I want another one. How could I possibly be gay?'

She tried a slightly different line. 'Have you ever had sex with a man?'

He turned from white to red. 'No, of course not!'

'Tell me the truth, Graeme!' Her voice was icy.

'Well, you know, I'm a public schoolboy.' He gave a self-deprecating shrug. 'We all messed around a bit at school.'

'What about later? University?'

Silence.

'Graeme, *tell me*!'

'It was just fooling about. Kids' stuff. Loads of young men experiment, it doesn't mean anything.'

'What about after university? Did something happen at work?'

'No, not really. We were just drunk. You know what it's like when a deal comes off.'

She nodded. She did indeed know that in the intensely macho world of investment banking it was *de rigueur* to go out and drink champagne to oblivion when a deal was signed off.

'But then the thing was, this man – he was an intern – put in a complaint. Completely ridiculous, we were drunk, we just got a little bit carried away. Stuff like that happens all the time. But because he was an intern I got a rap over the knuckles from HR, and then there was all this gossip.'

He came back to the table and sank his head into his hands. 'It was horrible, Rose. Whispers, sniggers, people stopping talking when I came into a room. I couldn't stand it.'

Rose felt sick, but she knew that whatever else happened now, she had to get at the facts once and for all. 'When did this . . . incident . . . happen?'

He met her eyes, agonised. '2008.'

Oh God. They had met in 2008, at a friend's Christmas party. Engaged in the spring of 2009; married that summer. Sebastian was born in January 2011.

'Graeme, I need you to be honest with me. Did you marry me to stop rumours at work that you were gay?'

'No, it wasn't like that.' He stopped to think, to try and find the words to explain how it had been, how it was. 'I've never been very good with women, I suppose. All boys' school. All men's college at Oxford. No sisters, so I never really learnt how to talk to girls. But obviously, you know, I wanted sex, and I was always surrounded by men and boys. And it was easy, and I enjoyed it.' His voice was barely a whisper now. 'But I didn't think I was gay. I mean, I'm not gay. I don't want to *marry* a man, or anything like that. I always knew that I wanted to meet a nice girl and settle down and have children.'

He cast his mind back to how things had been in his twenties. He had taken girls on dates and slept with one or two of them, but it never really went anywhere, and always seemed strangely difficult and unsuccessful compared to his sexual encounters with men at university. So he had entered a sort of Jekyll and Hyde existence, dating girls – the nicely brought up, Home Counties girls who were the daughters of his mother's friends, or the secretaries at work – and then every so often getting drunk and visiting gay bars where he would pick up random men. He always told himself that this meant nothing. Loads of men visited strip clubs, even slept with call-girls, this was no different. It only happened when he was drunk. Then Matthew had started his internship, and Graeme was mesmerised. Suddenly the gay bars were strangely unsatisfying, the dates with girls even more so. He found himself alone at home of an evening, masturbating miserably as he watched porn on his laptop, imagining Matthew's face on the bodies of the men he saw, not daring to think what these feelings meant. That disastrous night, he had found himself next to Matthew in the bar, both of them drunk. Matthew had said he was going outside for a fag, Graeme had gone with him, and somehow they had found themselves kissing. Down a little alley next to the bar it had gone much further than kissing, but not as far as Graeme wanted it to. Then they had seen their director at the entrance to the alley, gazing at them in disgust.

Graeme knew that if it had been a female intern the director would – metaphorically at least – have looked the other way. As it was, they were both in big trouble. Graeme always told himself that Matthew had complained of sexual harassment simply to protect his career; he *knew* the attraction between them had been mutual. But either way, Graeme had a real problem. He was on a warning at work and the office gossip was becoming intolerable, when he met Rose. Tiny, lively, vivacious and warm, with a mass of red curls, she was the polar opposite of the identikit Sloanes he had been dating. She had a completely different background from him: northern comprehensive, red-brick university, now a poky flat-share in Brixton. And because she wasn't playing according to *The Rules*, hoping to bag herself a rich banker husband, she had no concept of waiting for him to make the first move. She was dancing when he first saw her, and when she caught his eye she just extended her arms, grabbed him and pulled him into her circle of friends on the dance floor. He was entranced. There was no awkwardness with her. She laughed when she was amused, cried when something made her sad, shouted at him when he pissed her off. She shopped in Topshop and Dorothy Perkins rather than Joseph and Selfridges, and somehow she made him feel normal and relaxed. He could picture spending the rest of his life with this girl, and knew that she would be a brilliant mother. So he pursued her, using every lesson he could learn from romantic films, overheard conversations at work or articles in the lifestyle sections of the weekend papers. Rose seemed the solution to all his problems – gossip at work would be completely stopped if he got engaged, then married, then had children. He could have the life in the countryside he had always dreamt of. Best of all, when he was with Rose he no longer felt quite so desolate at the thought of Matthew.

It got harder, though. He loved it when Rose was pregnant. She was too sick, and then too uncomfortable, to want sex, and he loved the feeling of nurturing her as she nurtured their baby. But then the birth was a nightmare, and he found breastfeeding repellent. Rose's breasts grew huge with the milk, a complete contrast to her usually boyish figure, and he felt completely superfluous. Rose was continually snappish with tiredness, and so the emotional support he had come to rely on from her was to some extent withdrawn. He hoped that another baby would bring back some of the closeness of the first pregnancy, and felt cheated and betrayed by her obvious reluctance.

'I loved you, Rose, I *do* love you. The timing helped, after the thing at work, but I would have wanted to marry you anyway.'

Rose gazed at this stranger who had shared her bed for nearly five years. 'Could I have caught anything? Have you put me at risk? Oh my God, Sebastian! Babies can catch things through breast milk . . .'

He was shaking his head. 'Calm down, it's okay. I got tested before we slept together, and I've never cheated on you. I promise, you don't need to worry.'

Rose's palms were still sweaty, her heart still racing, but she did believe him.

She looked up at the kitchen clock. Only half past three. Less than two hours since he had arrived, and she had thought the biggest thing they would have to discuss would be whether Sebastian went to nursery or had a nanny. Part of her wanted to scream at her husband, throw him out, ban him from ever coming near her again. She felt more betrayed than she would have believed possible, but she knew that for her son's sake she had to try and sort something out, and she also knew that feeling as numb as she did at the moment was a good thing because it would enable her to have a calm and rational discussion before the tears started later. Julia had promised to keep Seb with her until Rose phoned, and she had hours yet before his bedtime. She got up. 'I think I need something stronger than tea. What about you?'

He nodded gratefully, and she mixed two strong gin and tonics.

'Do you still want to be married to me?' she asked, barely knowing herself what she wanted the answer to be.

He looked as though she had slapped him. 'Yes, of course I do. I love you. I love Sebastian. Being part of a family like that is all I've ever wanted.'

'That's not true, though, is it, Graeme? You also want to have sex with men.'

He shook his head in disbelief. 'Rose, I've never cheated on you, I swear. I had a few youthful indiscretions, so what? You'd had lots of boyfriends before you met me, and that's not a problem, never has been. I wouldn't care if you'd had a fling with a couple of girls before we were married either. Surely it's what we've done since which counts.'

'I couldn't agree more. That's the problem, though, we're not happy now. I've felt for ages that there was something missing from my life, from our marriage, and I've thought it was that I'm not happy as a stay-at-home mum. And that is part of it, a big part of it. But what I've realised this afternoon is that those feelings are also rooted in you being half absent from our marriage, and you trying to persuade me into being something that I'm not in order to live out your little happy families charade. You might scarcely be aware that you're doing it, but you're trying to box me off like you've boxed yourself off.'

'I don't believe I'm hearing this. I thought you prided yourself on being so open-minded. You've got loads of gay friends.'

Rose spoke slowly, enunciating each syllable, as she did when she was trying to convey something important to Sebastian. 'Yes. I have got a lot of friends who are gay, and I have absolutely no problem whatsoever with homosexuality. But it's actually quite a leap from that to discovering that your husband is gay and accepting that as a matter of course! I think even Peter Tatchell might cut me a bit of slack on that one.'

'I'm not fucking gay! I'm married!'

'Will you *stop* saying that as though they were mutually exclusive? You've had sundry relationships with men since you were a teenager, you married me on the rebound from an affair with a male colleague in order to stop office gossip, you have withdrawn emotionally and physically from our marriage for the last two years, and I've caught you with gay porn on your computer. Maybe that doesn't add up to being gay in your book, but it sure as hell does in mine, and I think even you will agree that it doesn't exactly make ideal husband material! Can you honestly tell me you haven't looked at gay porn since we were married?'

Rose paused, more because she had run out of breath than because she had run out of things to say. Anger and adrenaline were breaking over her in waves now. She couldn't believe that while she had been made to feel guilty about her reluctance to have a second child, her whole relationship was based on a lie. Then, thinking about the mess they had got into, and the effect that this was undoubtedly going to have on Sebastian, she felt the anger drain away as abruptly as it had come, leaving her feeling washed out and exhausted.

Graeme was refusing to meet her eyes, and she noted that he hadn't denied looking at porn.

'Look, Graeme.' She spoke more gently now. 'This has been one hell of a shock for me, and I don't suppose it's been an easy afternoon for you either. I need some time on my own now to think things through. I think you'd better go. Seb and I will stay with Julia for now, and I'll phone you in the week.'

'Can't I even stay and see Seb?'

She shook her head. 'Not today, no. Sorry. I just can't cope. Next weekend maybe, when I've had a chance to think a bit.'

He shrugged, came round the table and kissed her cheek. 'This doesn't change anything between us, Rose. I still love you, and I still want our marriage to work.'

Rose didn't reply. After a moment he walked out and she heard the front door close behind him. She downed the remains of her gin and tonic, then mixed herself another one and sat back down at the table, which was where Julia and Sebastian found her when they came back a couple of hours later.

22

Julia came back to find Rose pale and dazed, staring into the depths of an empty glass which smelt strongly of gin. She took control, gently leading Rose into the sitting room and tucking a blanket round her when she realised she was shaking convulsively. She made beans on toast for Sebastian and a cup of tea for his mum, and helped herself to a few squares of sustaining Dairy Milk. Well, she was pregnant.

Bathing Sebastian was a complete delight. Despite her concern for Rose, a warm glow of contentment spread through her as she watched him giggle and splash in the bath, and then wrapped him snugly in a towel and felt his compact little body nestling against her shoulder. Normally Seb was such a bundle of energy that cuddles from him were few and far between. At bedtime, though, warm and drowsy after his bath, he was more than happy to snuggle up on her rapidly diminishing lap for his beaker of milk and bedtime story. Then he gave her a very wet kiss on the lips and melted her heart further by saying, 'Night night, Auntie Ju. I loves you,' as she tucked him up in the travel cot he almost entirely filled.

However sad and lonely Julia sometimes felt when she thought about Toby, or however trepidatious when she saw Rose's struggles and considered how much harder single parenthood would be, the overwhelming love and tenderness she felt for her godson was enough to convince her that she was doing the right thing having a baby, and even, for a few moments of blissful certainty, that she would be a good mother.

She stood outside Sebastian's door for a minute or two, ostensibly listening to make sure that he had settled okay, but really gathering her emotional resources to go downstairs and hear Rose's story. The baby kicked reassuringly and she stroked her bump, feeling, suddenly, strong enough to support Rose in any way she needed to.

Rose was still sitting curled up on the sofa, cradling the half-empty mug of tea, which had gone cold. Julia took the mug from her hands and then went over to light the ready-laid fire. Neither woman spoke until the fire was blazing and Julia was ensconced in the armchair opposite the sofa, her feet up on an upturned box which was serving as a footstool in her campaign to avoid the varicose veins which had plagued her mother.

'So, you had a lovely time with Graeme then, I take it?'

Rose looked up and smiled in spite of herself. 'You're outrageous, Julia, can't you take anything seriously?'

'Not if I can possibly avoid it. But no, honestly, Rose, of course I take this seriously. What happened?'

Until that moment, Rose hadn't been sure if she would be able to talk to anyone about it, even Julia. Although on some level she knew it was irrational, what she felt most acutely was a sense of overwhelming, sickening shame. How could she have been taken in by such a hoax? How could she have unknowingly lived a lie for five years?

What did it say about her as a wife, as a woman, that her husband would rather have sex with men? But considering Julia's loving and concerned face, and thinking how honest she had been with her in sharing her feelings about Toby and her sense of inadequacy and jealousy regarding Ruby, she knew that she could trust her, at least, with a wholly candid account of the afternoon's conversation.

'Oh, God, Ju. I don't know how to say this. I feel sick just thinking it. Graeme's gay.'

'*What?!*' Whatever Julia had been expecting, it wasn't that. 'You mean he's been having an affair with a bloke?'

Rose shook her head. 'No, not exactly. That might almost be easier. He did have an affair with a bloke in work, just before he met me. It was discovered by his bosses, and he was in the doghouse, and so he basically married me to cover his tracks and prove that he was a fine, upstanding family man. That's why he wanted us to have a baby so quickly, and that's why he's so keen on having a second.'

Julia was temporarily, and unprecedentedly, speechless.

Rose watched, almost in amusement, the changes on Julia's expressive face as she tried to process this information.

'Did he just come out and tell you all this?' Julia winced, realising her choice of words had been unfortunate.

'Not exactly. It's all a bit of a blur. We were arguing, about the second baby thing, it being about him wanting to prove he's still fertile.' She paused, remembering. 'Then I think I said something about that being a bit like getting married to prove you're not gay. And then honestly, Julia, the atmosphere in the room just changed totally. He didn't say anything, but he looked completely panic stricken. It was like something just shifted in my brain at that moment, and I realised that he *was* gay. Suddenly everything added up. Things which had never quite made sense suddenly did.'

'What things?'

Rose ticked them off on her fingers. 'He's never had that high a sex drive, and recently hardly wants sex at all – despite being so keen, allegedly, for a second baby. He's so emotionally withdrawn. He's a workaholic, and seems to use that as a substitute for relationships. Even though he was thirty when I met him he didn't have any ex-girlfriends. I caught him looking at gay porn once. He's never seemed that comfortable with women's bodies – he doesn't like me wandering around naked, and he hated me breastfeeding.'

Julia raised her eyebrows. These points seemed suggestive, but hardly conclusive. 'So, what happened? Did he admit he was gay?'

Rose shook her head. 'Not in so many words, no.' The thought of trying to recount all Graeme's prevarications and denials was exhausting.

'Well, you don't know anything for sure, then, Rosie. Even if he is attracted to men, he could easily be bisexual, and he fell in love with you. I mean, I remember how you made everyone so jealous telling us about all the red roses, and tickets to the opera, and weekend breaks in Paris. He was mad about you.'

Rose shook her head, sadly. 'I really don't think he was, Julia. I think it was all part of this charade. It never really felt real. I always told myself it was just like a dream, and I think I persuaded myself it was genuine because I wanted it to be, and because I couldn't see why he was doing it otherwise, but I think that whether knowingly or not, it was all just designed to get me down the aisle and up the duff as quickly as possible.'

'But you were in love with him?' Julia spoke softly, and it was half question, half statement.

There was silence for a moment or two.

'Yes. Or I thought I was. But if I'm really honest about it, there have been problems right from the beginning, and I've always glossed over them, and told myself that they were normal, or that there was a perfectly good reason or whatever.'

Julia nodded.

'The thing which we've probably argued about the most is his absence – physical and emotional. He works ridiculous hours, weekends as well, but even when he's home he never seems to properly engage with me or Seb. He doesn't want to talk in any depth, and after Seb's in bed he retreats into his study with the computer, or his iPad, or his BlackBerry.' She paused, and laughed satirically. 'I've got a better idea of what he was looking at now, anyway. And then, after being on my own all day and counting the seconds until he's home, actually I sometimes feel lonelier when he's in the house. I've been feeling so guilty about all of this. I've kept blaming myself for not being interesting enough, for being resentful about the move to the country, and all the time I've been trying to maintain a healthy marriage with someone who simply doesn't want to have a relationship with a woman as anything other than a face saver.'

'God, Rosie, I'm so sorry. It sounds horrendous. I feel so guilty that I haven't known about this, haven't been there for you. The awful thing is, I've been feeling jealous of you for having the perfect marriage, and the perfect family. What are you going to do now?'

'I don't know. It's terrible, Julia, but part of me feels relieved, lighter, like a weight I hardly realised was there has gone. I almost feel excited, like my life is full of possibility again, whereas I had felt shut off from everything.'

'That doesn't sound terrible at all, under the circumstances.'

'Yes, but it's not about me, or Graeme really, it's all got to be about Seb. I can't see how I can carry on being married to Graeme after discovering all this, but it's just killing me to think of Seb not having a proper family. And also, sorry to rub this in, but even though Graeme is a long way from perfect, he is another pair of hands around sometimes, and someone to bounce decisions off. The thought of doing it all on my own makes me feel so tired. But I can't carry on either. I feel completely stuck.'

Julia hefted herself out of her chair and went to give Rose a rather awkward hug. 'I don't think you've got anything to feel guilty about, and I think Seb will be absolutely fine because at the end of the day he's got two parents who love him, and that's the most important thing, whether or not you live together. But for the time being you're more than welcome to stay here while you decide what to do. We'll just run a little home for single mothers together.'

Rose returned the hug, blinking back tears, and nodded. Living with Julia was clearly not a viable long-term solution, but for now it allowed her to postpone any of the decision-making for which she felt completely unprepared.

23

It was 3 January, six weeks before Ruby was due to give birth to his first child, and Toby had never felt more in need of a new beginning and a fresh start, or further away from getting one. The festive period had been hell. He had spent it at home with his parents, just the three of them for the first time since he was eighteen. Often Ally and Hugh travelled abroad – Christmas in either the snow or the sun trumping Christmas in the chilly drizzle in their eyes. Those years Toby would always celebrate with Julia, her parents, her brother and sister-in-law, their kids, and a few assorted aunties. If Ally and Hugh were in London, then Julia and he had occasionally spent the time with them.

The previous year Julia had to be on call for work and couldn't go home to Manchester, and so the two of them spent Christmas together at her house. It was one of the most enjoyable times he could remember. Luckily no disasters requiring the intervention of the Deputy Operations Director befell St Benedict's NHS Trust and so they just cocooned themselves indoors from lunch-time on Christmas Eve until Boxing Day evening. Julia cooked up a storm – on Christmas Eve they had sea bass and fennel *en papillote*, smoked salmon for breakfast on

Christmas Day, then turkey with all the trimmings, followed by chocolate and chestnut roulade, as neither of them could stand Christmas pudding. Turkey and ham pie on Boxing Day, and mince pies and Yule log to fill in the gaps. Under his persistent persuasion Julia took a fairly liberal attitude to alcohol consumption despite her on-call duties – after all, he reasoned to her, she didn't drive, and alcohol metabolised at a rate of one unit per hour, so as long as she stuck to one glass of wine an hour, she would be fine. What was really so amazing, though, was just spending so much time with someone he could say anything to. Someone who understood what he was trying to say even before he did himself, and who could finish his sentences. Someone who laughed at all his jokes and made him laugh so much he snorted champagne out of his nose.

He felt so close to her those couple of days that he nearly made his first pass at her since university. They were curled up on the sofa together, her feet in his lap. That was the thing: she clearly felt so comfortable with him, so uninterested in him as anything but a friend, that she wasn't interested in making a good impression. Actually though, close proximity to her long shapely legs in black opaque footless tights, and her still-slightly-tanned-from-autumn-holiday feet with berry-red toenails made him feel all sorts of things which were far more than friendly. He started to gently massage her feet, then her ankles, finding the softness of her skin and her little sighs of pleasure unbelievably erotic. Just as he was making up his mind to try moving his hands a little higher, she broke the silence.

'That's the nice thing about our relationship being like brother and sister, Tobes. Any other bloke doing that and I'd be worrying whether or not I'd shaved my legs, or if I had rough skin on my heels, but it's not like that with you.'

The message was clear. Toby had no idea if it was a deliberate warning shot, or if she was just cheerfully saying the first thing that came into her head in innocent confidence that he would share her feelings. Either way, he abandoned all hopes of anything other than a foot massage, and lay awake on the sofa bed that night in a miserable state of sexual frustration, wondering whether it would be acceptable to masturbate on someone else's spare sheets. Then a couple of weeks later he met Ruby, and was so dazzled and bewitched that Julia passed completely out of his romantic and sexual consciousness.

This Christmas, though, the what-ifs tormented him. As it turned out, Julia did not regard him as a brother (or if she did then she was in serious need of some Freudian psychoanalysis), and if he had pushed his luck back then, things might have been very different. Imagine, he tortured himself, imagine if it was now Julia sharing your house, carrying your child. Maybe because he had spent every Christmas for twelve years with Julia, he was thinking about her more than ever at this time of year. Intense physical longings at the memory of her creamy skin, full round breasts, long legs wrapped round him, soft lips wrapped round him, green eyes glazed with lust. Also just missing *her*. There was no one else he could phone when he heard or read or saw something funny who he *knew* would get the joke, just like that. There was no one else who could make him laugh so much with caustic one-liners and self-deprecating charm. And no one, not even his mum, gave hugs which exuded as much comforting warmth as Julia.

That rainy evening in Covent Garden when he had told Ruby that their relationship was over, he had felt a surge of relief that he didn't have to keep up that pretence any longer, but also a surge of optimism that maybe it wasn't too late to make things work with Julia. That optimism, however, had deserted him. The promise he had made Ruby, that he would remain single until the baby was at least six months old, seemed to completely put an end to his hopes. That would be over a year since his 'Dear John' email to Julia and even if she hadn't met someone else, which seemed unlikely given her innate desirability, she might justifiably be somewhat pissed off with him, and unwilling to resume relations where they had left off in Brighton. Especially – he winced at the thought – especially if Ruby and the baby were still living with him. And that didn't seem unlikely as, even with his generous salary, Toby knew he couldn't realistically pay his mortgage and the rent on a decent flat for Ruby while maintaining both of them and a child. Yet Ruby wouldn't be able to work at first, and even when she did her wages were negligible. Her parents had always financed her lifestyle, but her father had made clear, not unreasonably, that he now saw this as being Toby's responsibility.

That had been another source of Christmas woe. Sir Rupert Anstey had arrived to pick Ruby up and take her home to the country, and requested an interview with

Toby while he was there. Ruby vanished to finish wrapping and packing, leaving Toby to endure one of the most uncomfortable half hours of his life. Sir Rupert had the air of one dying to use the shotgun he no doubt possessed to get his daughter's caddish seducer up the aisle. Modern customs and his wife's strictures ringing in his ears were restraining him, but only just, and Toby had never been spoken to in such terms – indeed, perhaps no one had since 1935. He was a cad, a scoundrel, he had broken his daughter's heart, he had taken his pleasures where he wanted and wasn't prepared to pay the consequences. Not marrying her immediately was bad enough, but now he was saying that he didn't want to be in a relationship with her! Toby had nothing to say which he felt could justify his actions; on bad days he had difficulty justifying it to himself. Saying that he refused to make a relationship with the mother of his child work because she was a little temperamental and they didn't have much in common sounded rather weak; saying that it was because he was madly, irrevocably in love with another woman seemed to justify all the epithets which Sir Rupert was hurling at him.

He retreated to his parents' house to lick his wounds, but they, while doing their best to be supportive, were clearly getting rather impatient with him.

'So are you and Ruby together or not?' Ally asked.

'Not.'

'So then why, in the name of God, have you not got in touch with Julia and told her that?'

'Because Ruby doesn't want me to have a girlfriend. She's worried that if I do I'll abandon her to look after the baby on her own. So to calm her down I promised her that I'd stay single for a while. Well, until the baby is a few months old, anyway. I can hardly phone Julia and say, "Sorry I broke up with you, I still love you and miss you desperately, and can we get back together, but not until I've had a baby with someone else first."'

Ally made a gesture of impatience, and the restraint in her voice was audible as she said, 'Well, no, of course you can't say that to her. But darling, if you and Ruby aren't a couple she really doesn't have any right to try and dictate the terms on which you live your life. You are obviously not going to abandon her or the baby, but equally you can't possibly be expected to stay single for the rest of your life. Any more than *you* would expect Ruby to.'

Toby sighed. 'I know. But Ruby thinks that no one will want her when she's stuck at home with a baby, all fat after the pregnancy, and she doesn't want me to be out on dates instead of at home helping her.'

'Well, it sounds like a terrible idea to me. You've some-how managed the worst of all worlds, Toby. You're not providing a family for the baby because you and Ruby aren't a couple, but you aren't able to pursue the woman you really love because you've got your ex-girlfriend both living with you and refusing to allow you to see anyone else.'

Toby reflected to himself now that Ally was right, as usual. It was a ridiculous situation, it was absolutely the worst of all worlds. Yet he still couldn't for the life of him think how to extricate himself. In some ways things with Ruby were easier now he wasn't expected to perform the boyfriend role. She had moved into his spare room; the third room had been decorated as a nursery for the baby. She was still moody and temperamental, still hated being pregnant, still seemed extremely dispirited, but he now felt far less personally responsible for trying to make her happy, and that took the pressure off.

Toby had never been a great believer in New Year's resolutions: if something needed changing in your life, he thought, you should just get on and do it. No point hanging around for a particular time of year. This year, however, he knew exactly what his resolutions would be, knew what would fulfil him – creating a warm, healthy, loving environment for his baby to be born into, and getting back together with Julia. He just had no idea how these two utterly incompatible aims could be reconciled.

He sighed deeply again as he trudged down the road from his office to the tube station. It was only his first day back at work after the Christmas break, but he was leaving early to meet Ruby and go to their first antenatal class. They had left it rather late as Ruby had been extremely reluctant to commit, and for many months had been very keen on an elective caesarean. Even now he was unsure if she would actually turn up to the class, but as the birth had grown more imminent, and her midwife had explained that a C-section was major surgery and she would not be able to dance or do any other exercise for several weeks afterwards, she had conceded that perhaps some kind of birth preparation might be a good idea. Toby had leapt on this concession and immediately booked a course of six weekly classes which would take them right up to the due date. Tonight was the first, and as promised Toby was doing his duty as a supportive birth partner, but he couldn't imagine that a two-hour session of breathing exercises was going to make him feel any better about his life or the decisions he had to make.

24

Julia lay full length on the sofa, savouring the peace and quiet. It felt like a very long time since she'd had her house to herself. The holiday period had been bizarre, but actually really nice. She had been on call for the second year running, having decided to volunteer so that she could get out of it the following year when the baby would have arrived. Vigorously suppressing the pangs of longing she felt when she thought about her wonderful time with Toby the previous year, she was resigned to spending Christmas completely on her own. In the end, though, Rose's parents had turned out to have a long-standing booking for their first-ever cruise, and so Rose decided that she and Sebastian would stay with Julia, letting Graeme spend time with Seb on Boxing Day. And then Julia's parents had surprised her by booking a room in a local Travelodge for a couple of nights and driving down on Christmas Eve.

The house had been extremely crowded, but that had been fun – everyone chipping in to help with the cooking as Julia was starting to find that too long on her feet made her ankles swell and her back ache. Plus, it was wonderful having a child around for Christmas. Sebastian's non-stop chatter and obvious wonder and delight in his presents, the tree, the fairy lights, were enchanting. Julia also felt that spending time with a delightful toddler was helping her parents to get more excited about their new grandchild, and they therefore gave her a much easier time than she was expecting.

Ironically, now she no longer had to defend her position to her parents quite so vehemently, Julia's own worries about impending single motherhood were growing more acute. Part of that was down to living at such close quarters with a small child. Seb was adorable, but Julia was realising, as she never fully had before, what hard work he was. Sebastian's sleep was disrupted, perhaps by his change of environment, perhaps because he sensed that all was not well with his parents, or perhaps simply because he was a toddler. Either way it meant that Rose was having to get up two or three times a night to soothe, cuddle or cajole him back to sleep. Invariably, too, he was up and about by 7 a.m., meaning that Julia's weekend lie-ins were a thing of the past. She had the uncomfortable realisation that this wasn't just while Seb and Rose were staying: it was going to be a permanent state for her before too long.

So although she had loved playing hostess over Christmas, Julia was rather relieved when her parents went home, and that now Rose's parents were back from their cruise she and Sebastian had gone to pay them an extended visit. Her friend's marital situation was still unresolved. Graeme maintained a stance of absolute incomprehension that he had done anything to endanger his marriage, and Rose felt as if she was banging her head against a brick wall trying to get through to him. This being the case, the last thing Julia was going to do was evict her, and when she hinted that maybe Rose and Sebastian could move back home and Graeme could live at his club for a while, Rose seemed so forlorn and dispirited at the thought of being re-incarcerated somewhere she had never really liked that Julia hadn't the heart to push it.

In some ways having Rose around was great. It was lovely to have someone to have dinner with, and chat about their days, and help her get things ready for the baby. It was lovely to spend time with Sebastian, and to feel that she could be a real, practical help by looking after him for a few hours at the weekend to give Rose some concentrated thinking and planning time. Furthermore, if Rose was still around in March then one of Julia's worst fears – going into labour in the house, by herself, in the middle of the night – would be relieved. On the downside, though, there were evenings when, tired by a long and stressful day at work and a commute home when businessmen would hide behind their broadsheets rather than confront her obvious pregnancy and risk having to offer their seat, Julia just wanted to slump on the sofa with a ready meal and either some moving-wallpaper television or a favourite novel she had already comfort-read many times before. Having to make conversation, even with her best friend, was a strain she could do without. And when she woke up in the early hours with heartburn, as happened with increasing frequency, it was annoying not to be able to get up and walk round without worrying about waking Rose or Sebastian. Most worrying of all, though, Julia was extremely concerned that she would get too dependent on living with someone, having someone to share the little everyday things with, and that when Rose eventually left, she would feel lonelier and more vulnerable than ever.

Julia glanced at the clock. A couple of hours before she had to get ready to go out. She got up, made herself a mug of hot chocolate, put an extra log on the fire, and then curled up again to indulge in a bittersweet pleasure she only allowed herself very rarely – to think about Toby, and to fantasise about what might have been.

In a funny sort of way she had no regrets about their mad weekend in June. Not only had that weekend resulted in her longed-for baby, she felt that there was nothing she would or could or should have done differently then. She had been completely honest, with Toby and with herself, and had enjoyed every second of it. No, her sources of regret, other than the fact that Toby had ever laid eyes on Ruby, concerned her actions over the past twelve years. With the benefit of hindsight, she could now see that she had been in love with Toby for ages, and yet in some unfathomable combination of stubbornness and stupidity she had managed to avoid admitting it even to herself. She had always maintained that she wasn't physically attracted to him, which now seemed utterly incomprehensible. One unexpected effect of her pregnancy hormones was a hugely increased libido, and she would often wake wet and aching with longing after disturbingly realistic dreams of herself in bed with Toby. Or suddenly a vivid mental image of the set of his shoulders, or the line of his jaw, or his long, strong fingers would assail her, and she would literally catch her breath, her knees suddenly weak with desire.

All through the past six months she had been waiting, hoping, every time the phone rang, someone knocked on the door or she logged in to read her emails, that somehow something would have changed, and it would be Toby telling her that he loved her and only her, and she could have her happy ending. Now she was beginning to accept that this wasn't going to happen, that Toby had made his decision. But she was also starting to question her own position. Rose, Simone and her parents had all been unanimous in their conviction that she should get in touch with Toby and tell him about the baby. Pride and fear of rejection had stopped her, but she was now finding herself wondering, uncomfortably, whether that might not be rather similar behaviour to that which had stopped her admitting her feelings for all those years, and had effectively got her into this mess in the first place. After all, while Toby had made his decision, he had made it without knowledge of all the facts. Maybe he hadn't married Ruby. Maybe he would want to be involved with this baby just as much as with Ruby's. Maybe he was missing her as much as she was missing him.

Julia shook herself mentally. This wasn't getting her anywhere. It was time to get ready. She went and ran herself a deep hot bath, and sank into it with her book for a while before lathering and rinsing her hair. She shaved her legs – increasingly difficult with the enormous bump in the way, but ever more necessary with a succession of antenatal appointments which always seemed to involve her being naked from the waist down.

She slathered on rich body cream – she had been lucky with stretch marks so far, but was taking no chances – and then dressed carefully in her best pregnancy outfit, bought for various Christmas outings and celebrations and worn with indecent frequency. It was a bluey-green tunic dress from Zara, not actually from the maternity range, but it was generously cut and skimmed over her bump in a very flattering way. If it was slightly too low cut for casual wear, well, her cleavage was undoubtedly her best feature these days, and this evening was important. She added black opaque tights and her flat, slouchy tan leather boots. Then, in a flash of either sentimentality or defiance, she clasped the turquoise and silver necklace which Toby had bought for her in Brighton around her neck.

It wasn't a long journey. In fact, if it hadn't been dark Julia would probably have walked. In the old days she would have taken a minicab, but now she was conscientiously trying to save every penny for when the baby arrived, so she got the bus instead. The little local bus weaved its way round the side streets, and then through the grounds of the hospital where Julia would be giving birth in less than three months' time. She wrapped her arms round herself to control a shiver of terrified excitement and anticipation.

The house was a large, pretty late-Victorian terrace, with lights blazing welcomingly from all the front windows. Julia felt bizarrely nervous, but gathered her resources and knocked in a determined manner. The woman who answered the door was probably around ten years older than she was, casually dressed in jeans and a chunky sweater. She had a very warm and welcoming smile, and showed Julia through to a room which at first glance seemed full of people, although when she looked more closely it was actually only eight; four couples, she assumed. Well, she had known that they would all be couples, really. For a moment she regretted that she had turned down both Rose's and Simone's offers to come along with her, but then her natural independence reasserted herself – she was going to do this by herself, and she needed to get used to that right from the beginning. They all appeared friendly enough. The two sofas and armchairs were all full, so Julia sank carefully down into a beanbag, knowing that it was unlikely she would be able to get up again without the assistance of a forklift truck, but not quite having the nerve to ask one of the affluent-looking thirty-something males in the group to let her have a more comfortable seat.

The woman who had answered the door looked at her watch. 'Right everyone, we're just expecting one more couple. We'll wait a few minutes to give them a chance to get here, but then we'll get started. In the meantime, if you could just start to get to know one another by—'

The no-doubt hideous icebreaker which had been in store for them was never to be revealed, as at that moment the door swung open again and a woman's voice said questioningly, 'Hi, the little boy who answered the door said to come straight through?'

'Oh, my son!' laughed woolly-jumper woman.

Julia's head jerked up; there was something sickeningly familiar about that voice. She began to shake, and felt herself break out in a cold sweat all over her body. There in the doorway, large as life and twice as beautiful, was Ruby Anstey. Behind her, hand protectively on her shoulder, tall, dark and even more desirable than memory had led her to believe, was Toby.

25

Time slowed almost to stopping point. Julia kept her head down, fixing her eyes on her hands, which were shaking. She clasped them together round her knees in a futile attempt to control the tremors, but her legs were trembling just as violently. A general hubbub of chatter filled the room, but Julia felt insulated from it, as though it were coming from a long way away, or she were underwater. After that first panicked glance, she refused to raise her eyes and so had no idea if Toby or Ruby had recognised her yet. Ruby, probably not. She was so self-absorbed that Julia would have to have a custom-made sandwich board declaring 'I'm having your boyfriend's baby', possibly with accompanying megaphone announcements, before she could grab Ruby's attention. Toby was much more perceptive and observant, but then, Julia reflected wryly to herself, she must be literally the last person he would be expecting to see in his NCT antenatal class.

Julia tried to calm herself and think. She had only seconds to decide on her course of action. If she hadn't been weighted into a beanbag on the opposite side of the room from the door she would have been tempted to make a run for it. But athleticism had never been her strong point, and with her third trimester gait and shape she knew that in the kerfuffle of hauling herself from her recumbent position and then choreographing a route across the crowded room which avoided tripping flat on her face, there would be ample time for Toby to identify her. No, somehow she had to find the wherewithal to brazen it out.

At that moment the fog of voices and panic lifted for her to hear the teacher saying in a cheerful and determined tone, 'Okay everyone, let's get cracking, shall we? As you all probably know, my name's Angie, and I'm your course leader for the next few weeks, helping you all get ready for healthy, happy deliveries, and for life with your new babies. Now, I think I'm right that you're all first-time parents?' A murmur of assent rippled round the room. 'Okay, great. Now, I think the first thing to do is introduce yourselves. A lot of people find that one of the main benefits of a class like this one is that you make friends who will support you through the early days, but will also be around in your life a lot longer than that. I'm still very close to the parents I met in NCT classes when I had my first daughter twelve years ago . . .' She paused. 'And I've had three more kids since, so you see it can't be that difficult, can it?' It was obviously a well-rehearsed remark, but it successfully elicited a wave of slightly nervous laughter.

'So, we need to get to know each other as well as possible to get maximum impact from this class. I'm going to go round the room, and ask you to give your name, your baby's due date, and one fact about your pregnancy or plans for the baby that you haven't shared with anyone else. It can be as major or trivial as you like. So, starting on my left . . .'

Julia almost laughed. A fact about your pregnancy you haven't shared with anyone else? How desperately ironic. She really could help the group get to know at least three of its members a little better if she shared some facts about her baby's conception with them. She wondered how Angie would cope with that. Would the baby love triangle situation have been covered in NCT training? Somehow she doubted it. Peeking up through her lashes reassured her that she was sitting to Angie's right, and so had some time to compose herself before it got to her turn. Toby and Ruby would be ahead of her. Interesting. Agonising, but interesting. She tuned in to the woman currently speaking.

'I'm Anju, this is my husband Vishal. We're having a little boy, due on 28 February.' She smiled mischievously. 'My unshared fact is that we've told our families he isn't due until mid-March, because he is a first grandchild, and both our mothers would fuss so much that we would get no peace. I am hoping that he arrives right on time, and we can tell them he was a little early, and they won't be able to get here beforehand.'

Angie smiled. 'Well, that's one way of handling it. A lot of first babies arrive considerably after the due date, and mums-to-be can find it very frustrating having a constant stream of texts and calls asking what's happening, so being vague about the date is a sensible precaution. It's also important to think carefully about who you want present at the birth, and not feel pressured into decisions you don't feel comfortable with.'

Anju nodded, looking happy to have her decision vindicated, and they moved on to her husband, and then around the room. Then came the moment Julia had been both dreading and waiting for.

'Hi, I'm Ruby, this is Toby. Our baby is due in six weeks' time.' She paused and laughed breathily but self-deprecatingly, and Julia felt a collective intake of male breath as the dads-to-be realised just how sexy this woman was. MILF, indeed. 'I'm not sure there are any interesting facts about my pregnancy, and if there were I'm sure I would already have shared them with someone. I don't really do discretion! Oh, I know. I've been craving chocolate, and practically bingeing on Dairy Milk, a bar a day sometimes – first time it's crossed my lips since I was thirteen.'

Julia was sure it wasn't just the fact that Ruby had stolen Toby that made her want to hit her. Surely all the women in the room were seized by a simultaneous and nigh-overwhelming urge to stuff a Kit Kat Chunky where no sunshine would ever reach?

Then Toby. Familiar, beloved voice, the sound of which made her sick with longing and regret.

'Yes, well, I'm Toby. And my little-known fact? I suppose it's that I find it slightly disconcerting how much men are affected by pregnancy and birth, but how few of the decisions are ours to make. Not that I think they should be,' he added hastily, 'but it's a strange position to be in sometimes.'

Well! Julia stored the words away to analyse later, and tried hard not to think about the implications for what she was about to say.

Angie was speaking. 'That's a good point, Toby, and a brave one to make. A lot of dads feel like that, and it's hopefully something we'll have a chance to explore together over the course.'

A few more people, then her turn. She raised her head, deliberately turning to focus on Angie so as to avoid eye contact with Toby. There was a pulled thread on Angie's sweater, just over her left breast, and she found herself wondering if one of her four children had caught it, maybe in a tantrum, or in giving her a hug. Four children! Once upon a time she had dreamt of a big family like that, but right now it felt as though she would be lucky to survive the emotional stresses and strains of this pregnancy. Right on cue, Angie cleared her throat slightly and made meaningful eye contact with Julia.

Oh God. Here goes. Her mouth was dry, and her voice sounded squeaky and breathless, to her own ears at least.

'Hi, I'm Julia. My baby is due mid-March.' She had contemplated lying, but somehow the correct date was out before she could stop herself. 'I'm a single parent, and my little-known fact is that while my mum, friends and sister-in-law are all arguing about who should be my birth partner, I've got no intention of having any of them.'

At the sound of her voice Toby had jerked his head round and was now quietly hyperventilating. Over the past few months he had indulged in numerous fantasies about seeing Julia again. Maybe they would run into each other in the supermarket, or he would throw caution to the wind and phone her, or open his front door one day to find her standing there. What had never occurred to him, even in his wildest nightmares, was that he would see her here, of all improbable, implausible places. What in the name of fuck was *Julia* doing in an antenatal class?

Angie, oblivious to the earth-shattering impact Julia was having, nodded encouragingly. 'Okay, Julia. So do you want to be by yourself when you give birth, other than the healthcare staff?'

'Umm, no, not really. I was thinking of having a ... doula, is it?'

Angie nodded again, and explained for the group. 'A doula is someone who cares for women in labour and immediately after birth. They're not midwives, or medically trained, but the best ones will have been through extensive training for their role, and be very experienced. They act as a support and advocate for the woman. They can be very helpful, not just for single parents; a lot of couples find their input invaluable.'

Julia, who hadn't been aware that she had made the decision until she heard the words come out of her mouth, felt a little surge of confidence. She hated the idea of being all by herself, but equally couldn't really imagine herself relaxing with any of her friends or her mum; she knew that instead of focusing on the baby she would be worrying about whether they were tired, uncomfortable, hungry or revolted, whereas a doula was paid to be there but was also paid specifically to be on her side, a luxury which she well knew that NHS funding of midwifery services would not necessarily allow any other way.

She was still studiously avoiding Toby's eye, so had no idea what his reaction had been, but she reasoned to herself that there was no need for him to think anything other than that she'd had a one-night stand shortly after they split up. Or had succumbed to her longing for a child and visited the sperm bank. After all, the alternative was just too ridiculous for him to contemplate.

It was too ridiculous to contemplate. Toby just couldn't make his mind work properly. He was suddenly aware of Ruby whispering in his ear, 'You never told me Julia was pregnant!'

'I didn't know!' he whispered back, noting the confusion on her face. Damn. That had been the wrong thing to say. He was going to have to think of a good story as to why he hadn't known now. He shook himself mentally. That was irrelevant. Oh my God.

Toby was a whizz with numbers, and his lightning-fast mental arithmetic was a great asset to him at work. Now, however, the most basic sum in the world, one which had been performed countless times, in hope or despair, ever since Eve first told Adam she thought her period was late, seemed to be beyond him. Mid-March. He had last seen, and slept with, Julia in June. Which was . . . he had to resist the temptation to use his fingers to count and make sure. But it *was* nine months. Surely. Which meant. Oh God. She couldn't have been pregnant already when he slept with her, because he knew it had been a few months since she'd last had sex. And she wouldn't, couldn't, have jumped into bed with someone else immediately after? He felt an immediate sense of angry betrayal at the very possibility. But she had said she was a single parent, so she obviously wasn't with anyone else. A surge of equally potent hope filled him. He *had* to talk to her and find out what was going on.

He gazed with intense dislike at Angie, who was innocently instructing the men and women to split into separate groups.

'. . . So if the women could follow me through to the kitchen?'

Ruby left in the first wave and he saw his chance. Julia looked as though she were struggling to get up, so he leapt to his feet and offered her his arm. She took it, and he could feel the heat of her fingers through his shirt. He gazed down at her, but she was resolutely refusing to make eye contact. A sure sign of guilt, but was it guilt that she had got herself impregnated by someone else within days of declaring undying love to him, or guilt that she had neglected to mention that she was carrying his child? He gripped her wrist and hissed, 'We *have* to talk. What's going on?' Even in the midst of his confusion he noticed how fantastic her tits looked in that low-cut dress.

Julia didn't answer, and then was rescued from having to do so by Angie bustling back in.

'Are you okay, Julia? Go through and join the other women in the kitchen, please. I want to start the men off on their discussion here.'

Her tone was bright and professional, but to Toby's jaundiced ear sounded patronising and fake. Julia pulled away and left the room, and Toby sat, bodily taking part in a discussion about expectations of birth, but mentally just working out how he could outwit that infernal woman (Angie, rather than either Julia or Ruby) and get Julia on his own. He grabbed his chance when Angie returned, announced a coffee break and took drinks orders. He instantly volunteered to come and help her, and set off for the kitchen at a brisk trot. The women were filing back towards the living room, Julia seemingly deep in conversation with Ruby and another woman.

'Hi Ruby, hi Julia. We really need to catch up, Ju! I can't believe you haven't told me about the baby – I know it's been a while since we spoke, but you knew Ruby was expecting, didn't you? Why don't you come and help me with the drinks and fill me in?'

This time it was Ruby who unwittingly rescued Julia. 'Oh, not now, sweetheart.' She gestured at the third woman. 'Lois's husband is a consultant at the local hospital. She's going to introduce us and we can get all the gossip about the best staff to see.'

Toby gritted his teeth. 'I'm sure Julia gets plenty of that sort of stuff at work anyway, don't you, Ju? Come and gossip with me instead.'

Again, Ruby jumped in. 'Oh for heaven's sake, Toby! It's not Julia's fault you're so bad at keeping in touch. You can see her later. I've got to go back to work straight from this, so you two go for a coffee or something then and catch up in peace.'

Julia raised her eyes and met his gaze for the first time, and nodded imperceptibly. He took his cue.

'Okay, do you want to go and grab something to eat afterwards? I've come straight from work and I bet you have too.'

And then Julia said colourlessly, 'Yes, that would be lovely.'

26

Even though it involved such excitements as a life-sized plastic model of a woman's pelvis and a disturbingly realistic and alarmingly large doll to pass through it, neither Toby nor Julia got much out of the rest of the session. As soon as he decently could, Toby managed to shepherd Ruby and Julia through the throng of chatting couples and out into the cold night air.

'Shall we go to the Cuckfield?' Julia suggested. 'There are always plenty of seats, and the food is quite good. I don't feel like a formal restaurant.'

Ruby looked thoughtfully at her watch. 'I'd love to join you both, but as I said, I really should get back to the theatre to catch a couple of people. I'll walk with you, though, and go to Snaresbrook tube.' With that, she linked arms with both of them and they set off, a bizarre little party.

Toby felt even more tense. This was so unlike Ruby. She had never liked Julia much, so where had all this girly bonding suddenly come from? And why the linked arms? She hadn't voluntarily touched him for weeks. She must suspect something. But then Ruby was hardly subtle – if she suspected something then she would be incapable of hiding distrust under a veneer of friendliness.

Julia was equally strung out. She instinctively recoiled from Ruby's touch, then forced herself through gritted teeth to make light and friendly conversation. Luckily Ruby's usual self-centredness meant that she asked no more awkward questions about Julia's pregnancy, but instead prattled on about work in an inconsequential fashion.

Once they were in the pub, having said goodbye to Ruby – Julia astonished to note that she received a triple air kiss for the first time since she had met her – they went to the bar and ordered drinks and a lasagne each. Despite her emotional turmoil Julia was starving, and never, in the whole of her pregnancy-induced teetotalism, had she more regretted the words, 'Lime and soda for me, please.'

Taking their drinks, they settled themselves next to each other in a cosy booth at the back of the pub. Despite the high drama of the situation there was still such a comforting familiarity about being together. There was no pretence at small talk now, though. As soon as they were sitting down, Toby turned and looked Julia straight in the eyes and asked, 'Is it mine?'

She nodded, unable to find the words for the explanation which she knew was so badly needed.

'You fucking bitch.' He responded softly, but with an undertone of venom she had never heard in his voice before. She felt her throat constrict with tears, and still no words would come out.

'I can't believe you didn't tell me. That I would have no idea if it wasn't for this freak of a coincidence.' A sudden thought struck him. 'If it *is* coincidence! Oh my God, did you plan for me to find out this way?'

Still unable to talk, Julia shook her head vehemently.

'Well, thank Christ for that, anyway. But why, Julia? I don't understand how you could keep something like this from me. I just feel so angry, and so let down.'

Up until now Julia had been choked and paralysed by her own guilt. She knew deep down, had always known, that Rose and Simone and her parents were right and that she ought to tell Toby about the baby. It had been getting harder and harder to suppress that knowledge, and when she saw him in the class she could not deny to herself any longer just how big a deal it was. She had been drowning in self-reproach and terrified that Toby would never speak to her again, but now, in the face of his onslaught, she felt the first faint stirrings of anger herself.

'*You* feel angry and let down? Toby, the last time I saw you we had just made the transition from being friends to lovers, you told me that you loved me, that you'd never loved anyone like you loved me, and then you went home to get some clean clothes before, presumably, coming back to continue shagging me senseless. That was over six months ago, and all I've had since is a text message and a fucking *email* telling me that it was all over and that you were having a baby with someone else. How do you think that made *me* feel, Toby? Because believe me, angry and let down doesn't really even begin to cover it!'

'I did what I had to do! It wasn't my choice to go back to Ruby, it was the baby. That changed things.' He glared at her. 'As I would have hoped you had the sensitivity and maturity to appreciate. I can see that you would be upset, but how dare you not tell me about my own child out of some kind of petty revenge?'

Julia could feel tears streaming down her cheeks, but they were tears of sheer fury. 'Revenge? You really think I'd play games with my baby's life and future out of revenge? In your email you asked me not to contact you again and said that you trusted me not to do anything to upset Ruby. So I followed your instructions. If you don't like the result, you've only got yourself to blame.'

'You vindictive cow!'

At this point Julia really saw red and slapped him, missing his face and swiping at his chest instead. He caught her hand to stop her, and she dug in with her fingernails, conscious of nothing but her blinding anger and an overwhelming desire to hurt him in any way she could. Before she really knew what was happening they were kissing, at first too hard for enjoyment, but then softening and turning from anger to passion. His arms were holding her tight, and she buried her fingers in his hair, closing her eyes and trying not to think, trying just to enjoy the experience she had been fantasising about for months.

A nervous cough interrupted them, and they broke apart to see a very young and rather embarrassed-looking waitress standing there.

'Order number twenty-three? Two lasagnes, a side salad and a garlic bread?'

Toby nodded, and there was a slightly uncomfortable pause while the food and cutlery were laid out. When the girl had gone they both turned to each other simultaneously.

'Sorry!' they chorused. And laughed.

Then Toby started speaking again. 'I'm so sorry, Ju. I was way out of order. I've been a complete bastard to you, and I don't blame you for not getting in touch. I haven't exactly been great to Ruby either, spending the last six months fantasising about you. I think I've been trying so hard to do the right thing that I haven't been able to see the wood for the trees, and I've ended up doing the complete opposite. It's all the most hellish mess now.'

Trying to ignore the frisson of pleasure that the idea of Toby fantasising about her caused, combined with the feeling of her swollen and bruised mouth, Julia kept her tone calm and business-like. 'I'm sorry too. I know I should have told you, but it was pride, really. And I suppose panic that you wouldn't want to know, and would choose Ruby over me. It seemed easier for me to pretend to myself that you would have chosen me if you'd known, than to know you hadn't. If that makes sense.'

Now was the moment for Toby's declaration – 'of course I would have chosen you, I've missed you every moment we've been apart, Ruby means nothing to me' – but instead he just groaned, and buried his head in his hands.

Julia sat very still, unsure what to say or do. Up until that evening she had been convinced that she had resigned herself to single parenthood, and that excitement about the coming baby superseded regret about what might have been with Toby. Now, embarrassingly, one kiss seemed to have left her in a state of ecstatic, tortured expectancy. Not since snogging Matthew Edgington in the pub car park aged sixteen, breaking off only when she realised her dad had arrived to pick her up, had one kiss aroused so many conflicting emotions.

'Oh God, I don't know what to do for the best, Julia.' He was looking at her imploringly.

It was hard to believe, but it seemed that Toby was asking her advice about his love life, in much the way he always had, except that this time she was a central protagonist. Part of her wanted to scream at him again, but another part was still consumed by an overwhelming love and tenderness towards him. Also, a new conviction had taken hold of her. Toby *did* love her. She suddenly knew that with overwhelming certainty. And she loved him. Any little obstacles, such as the pregnant girlfriend, could be, would be, *had* to be overcome. The pangs of guilty conscience regarding Ruby, or agonised pride at the thought of putting her own feelings so completely on the line were overtaken by a steely determination to achieve a family for her baby.

'Are you asking me what I think you should do, Toby?' She didn't leave space for him to reply before continuing. 'I think you should sort things out with Ruby, tell her about us, and what happened, tell her that you will always be there for the baby, and will support her in any way you can, but that you don't want to be in a relationship with her. Then I think we should make a go of things, not just for the sake of our baby, but because what we have – had – is really special. It doesn't come along that often. Some people go through their whole lives never loving anyone like I love you, and like I think you love me, and I don't think you can just throw that away.'

She stopped, and started taking deep calming breaths, fighting the tears which were threatening to return. Toby was still sitting in silence. This was agony. It took every ounce of willpower she had not to start retracting, laughing, passing it off as a joke. The blissful certainty she'd had just a few moments before was melting away. Why wasn't Toby responding? She lifted her head up. 'Keep Calm and Carry On', as the vintage slogans which were everywhere at the moment had it. Her baby was going to require more from her than a little humiliation over the next few months and years. She would be strong for them, she had nothing to be ashamed of.

'Have I completely misread things, Toby?'

He shook his head. 'No, you're right. I love you. I've never stopped loving you for a second. But it's complicated, Julia. Ruby needs me; I've made her promises . . . Oh God!' He pushed his uneaten lasagne away from him and stood up. 'I can't deal with this now. I'm sorry, Julia, I do know I'm being a complete bastard, but I just can't cope. I'm going away for work tomorrow. Brussels. I won't be back until a week tomorrow at the earliest. I can't not go, it's a big job and I need the bonus, frankly. I need some time as well, to think all this through. I'll call you when I get back.'

He turned and took a few steps, then came back, stooped, kissed her on the mouth, and was gone before she could think of a response.

Outside he walked fast, and blindly, unaware of where he was going. What the hell had he just done? The woman he adored, whom he had missed every minute of every day for the last seven months, had just told him she loved him, and he had walked out on her. Part of him, a large part, wanted to turn round, go back, take her in his arms and tell her how much he loved her, and then find a way to make things work somehow. But then the other part could only see Ruby's angry face as he told her, could hear her telling him that he would never be able to see his child. Would that eventually make him resent Julia and the child she was carrying? And he still did owe something to Ruby. The stricken look on Julia's face as he left had shaken him, but he knew that she was the strongest and most loving person he had ever met, and he had every confidence that she and her baby, their baby, would ultimately be all right. But ditsy, dizzy, immature Ruby, how would she cope without him around? What would happen to the baby? Toby groaned aloud, much to the distress of an elderly lady walking her dog. He was oblivious to the anxious glances she gave him as she scurried past, trying to weigh up his options once again, to find some magical solution which enabled him to be both happy and ethical and not to end up a stranger to one of his children. But above all, some way of ensuring that he hadn't just kissed Julia for the last time.

Julia felt completely limp, too tired and drained even to be upset. On autopilot, and dimly conscious that even in the midst of emotional crisis her baby needed nourishing, she forked lasagne untastingly into her mouth. When it was all gone she took out her mobile and called a minicab. She might be trying to save money, but the thought of a long, cold, solitary wait at the bus stop now was beyond depressing.

Once back at home, she found she was taking care of herself in the way she would a friend with flu. She changed into the divinely comfortable pregnancy/breast-feeding pyjamas Rose had bought her for Christmas, made a mug of hot milk, dotted 'soothing and relaxing' lavender oil on her bed, and tucked herself up with the complicated arrangement of pillows her bump demanded and *Reading Group* by Elizabeth Noble, which was one of her ultimate comfort reads. She was acutely aware that she could not allow herself to descend into the misery and depression she had experienced when she and Toby first split up. Concentrating on the physical, while resolutely refusing to think, seemed to be the way forward.

27

'He said *he* couldn't cope?'

Six days later Rose was back from her parents, Sebastian was tucked up in bed, and the two women were curled up on the sofa for a debrief. Julia, still wearing the breastfeeding pyjamas which she was now spending all her non-working time in, was recounting what had happened at her memorable NCT class and during the conversation afterwards, and Rose was satisfyingly incredulous.

'So just let me get this straight: you're pregnant with his child, he's asked you not to contact him again because he's having a baby with someone else, you're on the brink of single parenthood with all that implies, but *he's* the one who can't cope? Fucking hell! Men.'

Unsurprisingly, given the state of her marriage, Rose was in a virulently anti-men mood. Julia found herself feeling defensive, wanting to protect Toby from the very accusations which she had flung at him herself.

'To be fair, Rose, he didn't know I was pregnant when he left last time. You said yourself, he was only trying to do the right thing by Ruby and the baby.'

Rose snorted. 'Be that as it may, he knew you were pregnant this time and he's still buggered off, hasn't he?

He needs to think, he can't cope; he's probably taken himself off to a yogic retreat in the Himalayas to "find himself". Meanwhile you and that poor cow Ruby have to sit around gestating his spawn and working out the little practicalities of how you pay the mortgage and put food on the table. You don't really get the luxury of not being able to cope, do you?'

Julia sighed. She knew that this wasn't exactly Toby's finest hour, but, hormonal and filled with all the qualities St Paul told the Corinthians could be ascribed to love, she was willing for the moment to give him the benefit of the doubt.

'The thing is, now I don't know whether to go to my class tomorrow. I mean, I know Toby won't be there because he said he'd be abroad for at least a week, but Ruby probably will be, and I'm not sure I want to see her much. On the other hand, I phoned the NCT and there isn't another local course I can get a place on before March, and I do really want to do the classes.'

This caused a minor explosion from Rose. 'Of course you're bloody going! Don't be such a wimp, Julia. You've done nothing wrong! Why should you be frightened away from preparing for your baby's birth because that dickhead can't get his act together? I'll come with you, and if Ruby even looks at you wrong—'

Julia laughed. 'Okay, okay, I get the picture, you think I should go. I will then, I know you're right. But I don't want you to come with me. It's so kind of you to offer, and I'm really grateful, but I just feel that I need to do this on my own. Anyway, enough about me. How are things with you? Did you have a nice time at your mum's? Have you spoken to Graeme recently?'

Things had gone better for Rose with her parents than she had expected. Their mentality and ethos was very much that marriage was for life, and she had been expecting frosty disapproval that she was walking away from her vows. She had also been dreading having to discuss her husband's sexual predilections with her parents. After all, no one likes talking to their parents about sex of any kind, particularly not anything relating to their own sex lives, and, as it turns out, very particularly not discussing gay affairs which your husband may or may not have had.

However, they had been nothing but supportive and had completely understood why she felt the need to separate from Graeme. Furthermore, they had been full of sensible advice. Her dad had told her, 'Whatever Graeme's done, other than if he was hitting you or Seb, if you loved him then it would be worth trying to make a go of it, for all your sakes. But honestly, pet, if you don't love him any more, and it doesn't look like you ever loved each other properly, then there's nothing left to save, is there?'

'And that's the thing, Ju.' Rose was recounting all this to Julia. 'Dad put his finger on it absolutely – there's nothing left to save. Trying to make my marriage work with Graeme would be just like trying to make it work with a complete stranger I'd picked up on the street. I don't think we ever had a real marriage, I don't think we were ever truly in love with each other, so there's not even a ghost of what we once had to try and revive.'

Julia nodded sadly. 'So what happens next then?'

'Well, Mum and Dad have said that we can move in with them if we want to.' She grimaced. 'It's really good of them, and it's helpful to know I've got a fall-back position, but it's not ideal. I never expected to be back living in my parents' spare room aged thirty.'

'Well, you know you're very welcome here for as long as you need somewhere.'

'Thanks, hun. You've been amazing. If it really is okay with you, then we'll stay a little longer while I sort things out, but it's hardly a long-term prospect, is it? I love this house, but I can't see it working once the baby arrives. You'll need your space.'

'So what would you do in a perfect world?'

'Rent a flat for me and Seb round here somewhere. I love being back in London, I really like this area, and it would be lovely to be near you, for both of us. Plus I've checked, and the local FE college have an accredited aromatherapy course. I've been in touch with a couple of people I used to work with too, and they think I could definitely get some part-time freelance work with them, so that would be a bit of money coming in.'

'Hmm.' Julia paused, thinking how best to tactfully phrase her concerns. 'How much money would it be, though? Because if you've got rent, and childcare, and course fees—'

'No, I know, I can't possibly afford it unless Graeme pays me maintenance for Seb. I wasn't sure if he would have to, because it's me who's left him, and he hasn't had an affair or anything. But I saw a solicitor when I was up in Manchester, and they reckon that he'd definitely have to pay maintenance for Seb, and possibly for me as well.

So that would be okay. But I don't know how quickly it will all happen, and I've got hardly any money in the short term, because Graeme has stopped paying into our joint account. I've got one ISA in my name, for tax reasons, but it won't last very long. Either way, you won't be the only broke single mother around!'

Julia managed the laugh that was clearly expected, trying hard to fight down the feelings of bleak loneliness which the words 'single mother' suddenly awoke in her, when she had thought herself completely resigned to her situation.

'You did *what*?' Alicia was clearly making no attempt to keep the incredulous horror out of her voice.

From the other side of the room, Hugh abandoned all attempts on his crossword. His wife's ten-minute phone call with their son had been punctuated with exclamations and ejaculations of surprise, but he had not been able to make much sense of it. There was something different about Alicia now, though. He had rarely heard her sound so angry with Toby.

'Listen to me, Toby. You *cannot* mess this up. Stop arsing about, take a good look at the situation, and for the first time in the last six months make a sensible decision, or you will regret this for the rest of your life. You just think on that.' She slammed the phone down, and spun round to face Hugh.

Her face was white, and he could see her hands were trembling slightly. The lines around her mouth and eyes were more pronounced, and for once she looked every one of her sixty-three years.

He crossed the room in a couple of long strides and wrapped his arms round her, instantly furious with his son for whatever he had done to bring anguish to his mother. 'Darling Ally, what is it? What's going on?' He gently guided her to the sofa and sat down next to her, taking her hands in his.

'Oh, Hugh, such a mess. The stupid, stupid, *stupid* boy. You know he and Julia had that fling in the summer, and then he broke it off because Ruby told him she was pregnant?'

Hugh nodded, unsure where this was going.

'Well he's just found out that Julia is pregnant too, with his baby, conceived that weekend.'

'Whew!' Whatever possibilities had crossed Hugh's mind, that hadn't been one of them. 'So what's happening now?'

'You may well ask! He only found out because, by some amazing coincidence, Julia ended up in the same antenatal class as Ruby and him. She hadn't told him about the baby because he'd asked her not to contact him again, and she took that very literally. Anyway, from what I can gather, she basically told him that she has always loved him, always will, and asked him if they could make a go of things.'

'And?'

'And the blithering *idiot* told her he was going abroad with work, would have to think about it, and then walked out!'

'Bloody hell. Poor old Julia.'

'Well, exactly. Imagine laying yourself on the line like that and getting that response. After going through the whole pregnancy on her own, as well. It doesn't bear thinking about.'

'But what I don't understand, Ally, is why he's acted like that? He's very much in love with Julia and the only reason he's been trying to stand by Ruby is for the baby. If Julia's having his baby as well, then that sort of evens things out, doesn't it?'

'You would think! Apparently he still feels guilty about Ruby, and responsible.'

'But they're not even a couple any more! He can take responsibility yet still have another relationship.'

'I know.' Alicia banged her hand down on the coffee table in exasperation, harder than she had expected, and winced. 'The thing is, Hugh, while he's messing around indulging his own feelings of guilt or whatever, he might be missing his chance with Julia. He must have hurt her so much, why will she hang around waiting for more? If he doesn't work this out I honestly think it will ruin the rest of his life. But there's nothing we can do about it. Unless, of course . . .' She broke off and glanced somewhat guiltily at her husband.

'Unless what?' Hugh was momentarily confused, but then correctly interpreted the furtive expression in Alicia's eyes. 'Nuh-uh. No way, Ally. Absolutely no way.'

'No way what?' She was all faux-innocence now.

'You are not phoning Julia. Over my dead body.'

'Hugh, just think. They're meant to be together, we've always thought so. If they just need a little push to help them work things out, then surely it's up to us, isn't it?'

'No, it absolutely isn't. Listen to me, Ally. If they're meant to be together then it will work out somehow, but however little he may be acting like it at the moment, Toby is a grown man and he has to work this out for himself. Apart from anything else, you could make it far worse. Imagine what it could do to Julia's pride and self-esteem if she gets the impression that after making such a brave declaration, Toby only goes back to her because his parents told him to. That's no foundation for a relationship.'

Alicia sighed heavily. 'I know you're right. I hate it, but I do know it. Though, Hugh, I just can't bear it if it doesn't sort itself out. Poor Julia, as well. We've always been so fond of her, she's been like a daughter to us in a way, and I've really missed her over the last few months. If Toby doesn't get his act together she's going to suffer so much. Our grandchild as well. We might never even meet them.' Her eyes welled up with tears.

Hugh's arms were instantly around her again, comforting and reassuring. 'I know it's hard, darling. But it's always been hard, hasn't it? Letting him go on the high climbing-frame in the playground when all we could see were broken limbs and concussion. Letting him stay over at a friend's house for the first time, convinced that he'd wake crying for us. Then the day we dropped him off at university – the way he was trying to appear so brave and confident, but underneath there was sheer panic in his eyes. The thing is, though, we had to let him do those things by himself and just be there to pick up the pieces if it went wrong, and that's all we can do now as well. But I tell you one thing, if he and Julia don't end up together,

Julia won't be left unsupported by us, and we *will* meet our grandchild. I'm not saying you can't ever phone her, just that you have to give Toby a chance to do the right thing off his own bat first.'

28

In common with many episodes during her pregnancy, Julia felt sick all day at work. She was planning to work until at least two weeks before her due date in order to maximise time with the baby afterwards, but in actual fact her temporary replacement had already been appointed and she was doing an extended handover with them. This meant that the pressures of her job were greatly reduced, a fact for which she was grateful because at seven and a half months pregnant even doing the daily commute was increasingly taking more energy than she felt she had. Today, though, she couldn't blame pregnancy for how she felt, or only indirectly. It was good old-fashioned butterflies in her tummy, caused by the thought of her second antenatal class that evening.

Despite Rose's robust response to the suggestion that she might not go, Julia still found the question going round and round her mind all day. In the end she came down on the side of going, deciding that Toby definitely wouldn't be there, and that it was entirely possible Ruby wouldn't go without him. Even if she did, well, Ruby had no idea about the situation so it really didn't matter one way or the other. There was even a horrible fascination in seeing and talking to Ruby and trying to gauge the state of her and Toby's relationship.

In the end Ruby did arrive, predictably late and looking rather pale and tired, Julia thought. She seemed subdued throughout, only responding when Angie directly tried to draw her in. Julia found to her amazement that she was really enjoying herself. The other couples all seemed warm and engaging, the kind of people with whom she could easily imagine becoming friends. The level of intimacy which arose so quickly was astounding. She remembered Rose describing something similar when Sebastian was a tiny baby.

'It's really weird, Ju. I'll be chatting to someone I've just met at the baby clinic, and she'll have told me that she needed IVF to get pregnant because she wasn't ovulating regularly and her husband's sperm count was slightly low, and that she had terrible piles while she was pregnant, and that she's avoided sex since the baby was born because she's just too damn tired. And in return I'll have told her the tragic tale of my third-degree tears and infected stitches, and we'll have shared remedies for cracked nipples. Then after all that, she'll ask my name. It's unbelievable. Having a baby means that details you've previously only shared with your doctor and, if he's really unlucky, your husband, you suddenly confide to any chance acquaintance who happens to have a baby the same age.'

Julia was now starting to see that this process began during pregnancy, and rather than finding it off-puttingly cloying as she might have once imagined, she now felt a huge degree of comfort in knowing that there were other women going through the same things that she was. Some of the same things, anyway.

At the end of the class there was a general scrabble for coats, hats and scarves, and Julia became aware of a hand on her arm. She turned round. It was Ruby.

'Julia. I wondered if you'd like to come back for a coffee or something?'

Julia shuddered at the thought of sitting in Toby's kitchen enjoying a private chat with his girlfriend. 'No, sorry, I don't think so. I'm quite tired, and I've got work tomorrow.'

'Please, Julia. Please. *Please.* I really need to talk to you.'

Julia hesitated. Up close she could see that Ruby really wasn't herself at all. There were dark shadows under her eyes, and other than her huge bump she seemed thinner than ever. There was also a note of desperation in her voice, and Julia couldn't help but respond compassionately. 'We-ell.' She hesitated, fatally.

'Oh thank you, Julia! I'm so grateful, you've no idea.'

Somehow, Julia found herself walking along the street making polite conversation with her rival for the second time in the space of a week. Toby's house was fairly near, and before very long she was sitting at the modern glass-topped table in his kitchen, sipping rather distastefully at the mug of herbal tea which Ruby had made for her.

Now she actually had Julia there, Ruby seemed to have lost her nerve for saying whatever it was she had intended. Julia felt a creeping discomfort in the pit of her stomach. Surely, surely Ruby hadn't somehow found out about her and Toby and brought her here for a confrontation?

That didn't fit though. If anything, Ruby was the one looking guilty.

Ruby took a deep breath, a large gulp of tea, and then took the plunge. 'Okay. Look, Julia, I'm really grateful for you agreeing to come back with me, because there is something particular I wanted to talk to you about. Something I want your help with, really.'

Julia nodded, trying to appear as open and responsive as she could, given the weight on her conscience.

'It's really because I know how close you are to Toby. He might listen to you.'

Julia fought the desire to laugh hysterically at the irony.

'I don't know how much Toby's told you about the pregnancy, and how things have been between us?'

Oh God. Julia wanted to run. She was going to have to give *Ruby* relationship advice now. She felt amazingly disloyal; although to whom, she couldn't really work out. However, her curiosity was now proving overwhelming.

'He hasn't said much at all, we haven't been in touch for a few months. I did get the impression that the pregnancy wasn't planned?'

Ruby laughed bitterly. 'You can say that again!' She looked directly at Julia. 'You said you're doing this as a single parent – was *your* pregnancy planned?'

Julia shook her head, again feeling acutely uncomfortable.

'I don't know how you can face it. I mean, it's bad enough doing it with the father around, but completely on your own . . . Why are you doing it?'

Julia thought carefully how best to give the honest answer she felt Ruby deserved, without giving too much away.

'I've always known I wanted a baby. Lots of babies, in fact, it's the thing in my life I've always felt most certain of. So when I got pregnant, albeit accidentally after a brief fling, I was just delighted. Ideally I would have been happily married before I had children, that's how I'd always imagined it, but for me it's just still so amazing that I'm having a baby of my own.'

Ruby regarded her in total wonderment. 'I literally have no idea what you're talking about. I just think that gene must have been missed out of me. I was absolutely horrified when I found out I was pregnant.'

Julia asked boldly, 'So, what made you go ahead with the pregnancy then?'

'I nearly didn't. I got as far as the abortion clinic, and then got all squeamish about going through with it. By the time I got over that it was too late to do it. But I can't tell you how much I regret that.'

Julia was horrified. Although she would completely defend a woman's rights over her own body, her choice whether or not to continue with a pregnancy, there seemed to her to be something obscene about a woman almost at full term, sitting there saying that she regretted her baby's existence. She wondered for the millionth time how warm, loving Toby had ended up with this woman.

Ruby carried on talking. 'I can see that I've shocked you, and I'm sorry. But how would you feel if your pregnancy had come between you and the love of your life?'

It was a rhetorical question, but feeling slightly sick, Julia still felt compelled to answer it. 'Between you and Toby? But surely . . . I mean, I thought that Toby . . . Well, I thought he wanted the baby?'

Ruby laughed again; a laugh which lacked all humour. 'Darling Julia! You are naïve, aren't you? I'm afraid Toby is by no stretch of the imagination the love of my life. As I'm sure you already know, we aren't even a couple any more. I'm only living here so he can help me with the baby. It's separate bedrooms all the way these days.'

Julia's head was reeling. There were so many questions spinning around in her mind that she felt she had lost the intellectual capacity to formulate even one of them.

Ruby's laugh this time was warmer and softer. 'Poor Julia, I've totally confused you, haven't I? Shall I tell you the whole story?'

Julia felt unable to do anything but nod.

'Okay. Well, going back to the beginning of last summer. Toby and I had been together for a couple of months, just having a bit of fun together, I thought. It was never that serious for me, I didn't think I was really ready for a proper relationship. I thought Toby felt the same. Then I met this man at work.' She paused, looking dreamy, remote, and quite remarkably beautiful as she relived this moment. 'Honestly, Julia, it was amazing. I understood what all the fuss was about, all the films and songs. It was just like there was electricity between us. He's incredible. Sexy and funny and so talented and creative. Quite a bit older, which I've always liked. I think it was love at first sight for me, but he didn't seem interested, particularly, and I knew I'd have to play hard to get. It seemed perfect that I was having a casual relationship with Toby because I could exaggerate it a bit – you know how being spoken for always makes you more alluring?'

Julia nodded, terrified of breaking the spell of this fascinating confidence.

'Anyway, that was all fine and I was flirting with this man, Paul, and things were really building up between us, although nothing had really happened. Then suddenly, completely out of left field, Toby only fucking proposed to me! Did you know he was going to?'

Julia nodded again.

'I thought he was completely insane. I had no idea he thought he was really in *love* with me, I wouldn't have been stringing him along if I had known. I'm not a complete bitch. Anyway, even if it hadn't been for Paul, there was no way I wanted to marry Toby, and I told him so. He stormed off in a huff, and that was that, I thought. I spent the next couple of days doing some really heavy-duty flirting with Paul; the tension between us was unbelievable. Then I realised that my period was a couple of days late. I was terrified. I've always been completely regular, and I suddenly remembered that I'd had to take some antibiotics about a fortnight before, and I'd read somewhere that they could counteract the Pill. I went and took a test, and of course it was positive.' She shuddered at the memory, and Julia murmured sympathetically.

'It was a Sunday, and I spent the day in a complete state, knowing I was going to have to have an abortion. I phoned a private clinic and made an appointment for the next day, and I was all set. Then suddenly, I knew I couldn't face it on my own. And I just thought, sod it, why should Toby get away scot-free? So I texted him, and he came round and agreed to come to the clinic with me the next day. Anyway, I had a complete freak-out in the clinic, and decided that I couldn't go through with it. Toby was lovely, so sweet and compassionate, and I panicked and thought that if I had to have a baby, I at least needed some support, and I knew Toby would be a perfect dad, and would look after me, so I told him I did want to marry him after all.'

The words of Ruby's explanation came out quickly, almost without pauses for breath.

Julia exhaled slowly. So that was it. That was the sequence of events which had led to the ruination of her own happiness.

'Toby said that he didn't think we should get married. He'd obviously got a bit offended, poor boy, that I'd turned him down cold. But he said that he'd give our relationship a go; that he'd be there for me and the baby and all the rest of it. He was so kind and caring towards me. And sometimes I thought that it would be all okay, that we could be a family, and I could forget about Paul, and it wouldn't be so bad. But other times I'd be awake at night just yearning for Paul, and I just couldn't stand the thought that I'd never be with him. I was really pissed off with Toby for not wanting to get married, partly cos I knew it would stop my parents freaking out quite so much, and partly because I thought somehow that if I was engaged to Toby and having his baby, then that would stop me thinking about Paul.'

'And did you stop thinking about him?'

'No, not at all! I was a complete bitch to Toby, with horrible hormonal mood swings, and he was still really nice, and patient, and excited about the baby, and I felt so guilty that I wasn't being nicer to him, but somehow the nicer he was the more irritated I was that he wasn't Paul, and the worse I was to him. Then one day, a couple of weeks later, Paul asked me to go for a drink with him after work. I went, even though I knew I shouldn't, but I was so happy he'd asked. We had the most amazing evening, got on so well. And of course towards the end of the night we started kissing, and one thing led to another and we ended up in bed together back at his place. That was it. If I'd thought I was in love with him before, it was nothing to how I felt after that. He felt the same, it was amazing. I hardly saw Toby over the next few weeks. I was meant to move in with him but I just said I needed to be in my own flat so I could get back there easily after a show, and I spent pretty much every night with Paul.'

Julia let out her breath slowly, and some of her sense of guilt went with it. 'So why didn't you just end things with Toby and get together properly with Paul?'

'Because I still hadn't told him about the baby! I didn't really show that much for ages, but then I started to, and it got to the point when I knew I was going to have to tell him, but I was dreading it because I just couldn't see him taking it well. I'd gone through it all over and over again in my head – whether I could face an abortion after all – but whenever it came to it I knew I just couldn't. Anyway, I told him and he was horrified. He felt like I'd been deceiving him. He was furious with me. He said that he'd never wanted children at all, let alone another man's child, and that this was a deal breaker for him. So we split up.

'I was heartbroken. At first I took it out on Toby, and then I thought maybe I should give things another go with him. I even slept with him, for the first and only time since I found out I was pregnant. Then I had a work meeting with Paul, and we ended up back in bed together. And that's how it's been for the last few months. Paul tells me he doesn't want the baby, we decide it won't work, we split up, and then the next time we see each other again it's just like magnets, we end up shagging like rabbits, and then going through the whole thing again.'

'Well, you've certainly had a more eventful pregnancy than I have,' commented Julia wryly.

Ruby ignored the interjection, intent on finishing her story. 'Meanwhile, Toby has clearly got to the end of his tether and breaks up with me. I went off the deep end because I felt like I was going to end up totally on my own. I got him to promise that he'd support me, and that he wouldn't have another girlfriend until the baby was older. I just can't cope at all with the idea of doing the whole baby thing without him.'

Julia drew another deep breath. A lot of things were becoming a lot clearer, if more complicated. Ruby was watching her expectantly.

'Wow, Ruby. Well, I can see that it's all a bit of a mess, but I'm not quite sure what you want me to do about it. Do you want me to tell Toby about Paul?'

Ruby nodded, calmly. 'Yes, sort of. I know this is a huge ask, but I know that Toby will listen to you more than anyone, and I've thought of the perfect solution, if you can just persuade Toby to do it. I want you to ask Toby if he'll bring the baby up for me so that I can go abroad with Paul.'

29

Julia blinked. Whatever she had been expecting, it wasn't that. She gazed round Toby's immaculately designed but rather clinical-feeling kitchen in complete panic. She felt rather like Alice after she had taken the unwise step of following the White Rabbit down the hole. Surrealism bordered normality in a way which made her uncertain whether it was she who was mad, or everyone else. Inwardly cursing the curiosity which had led to her being the recipient of this confidence and this request, she tried to play for time.

'Honestly, Ruby, it's really not any of my business. It's not that I'm not sympathetic to you, but it's got to be something you and Toby sort out for yourselves.'

Ruby shook her head vigorously. 'No, that's just it, we can't. We've just reached a complete impasse, we're barely communicating at all. I've been going out of my mind trying to work out the best way to put this to Toby, but I just couldn't see a way forward. I was even thinking of asking Alicia and Hugh to help me, and God knows they hate me, so I don't expect they would have done. But then when I saw you, I remembered how close you and Toby have always been, and I know you could persuade him, explain to him how things are. I know you could. My idea just makes total sense, Julia.'

'Does it?' Julia asked faintly.

'Yes! Toby has been so enthusiastic about the baby, he really wants to be a dad. He's read all the books, he knows far more about pregnancy and stuff than I do. It was him who booked us on the NCT course; I was planning a caesarean. He'd be a far better parent than I would. After all, why should the automatic assumption be that it's the woman who has to look after the baby if the couple aren't together? That's so sexist and outdated.'

Julia happened to agree with Ruby on this, but she didn't really feel that the time was ripe for a debate on gender politics. She had two options. She could decline to be involved and leave immediately. That was undoubtedly the sensible option, and the one which, lying at home in bed that night, she sensed she would wish she had taken. Alternatively, she could reciprocate Ruby's honesty and tell Ruby her story, and hope that in some bizarre way they could make sense of it between the two of them. After all, if she wanted Toby in her life, or her baby's life, Ruby was undoubtedly going to feature somewhere as well. Also, something inside Julia seemed to have shifted; instead of regarding Ruby's baby as a problem, even an enemy, she suddenly saw it as her child's half-sibling. Normally, of course, confessing to a woman that you were expecting her boyfriend's baby would be unlikely to lead to a positive and constructive discussion, but in this case, first Ruby had said that she and Toby were no longer a couple, and second, she had rather lost her footing on the moral high ground by conducting a six-month-long affair with another man while pregnant. Julia found her mouth in gear before her brain had quite finished its analysis.

'Look, Ruby. It's not that I don't want to help you, but I'm in a very awkward position. I think I'm just going to go for broke and tell you why, and if you want to throw me out afterwards, then you can do.'

Ruby seemed puzzled. 'Why would I want to throw you out?'

'Ahh. Well.' Julia took a deep breath. She felt her baby kicking, and felt reassured and emboldened. 'You know the night that Toby proposed to you?'

Ruby nodded.

'After he left you, he came round to mine, pretty upset, convinced that the two of you had split up.'

Ruby nodded again. 'Yes, that's what I thought myself at the time.'

'Okay, I'm glad you did, because that makes what I'm about to tell you a bit easier. The thing is, without going into details, Toby and I ended up in bed together that night.'

Ruby's eyes grew wide with astonishment. 'Oh my God! No! Not you and Toby? I don't believe it!'

Julia tried to bite back her irritation, but her tone was nonetheless acerbic when she replied, 'It's not *that* astonishing, surely? Or do you just think I'm so hopelessly unattractive that you're amazed anyone would sleep with me?'

'No!' Ruby shook her head vehemently, anxious to reassure. 'No, it's not that, it's just that I never knew you and Toby saw each other like that, I thought you were just friends. I've always thought that when people have been

275

friends for ever like you two have, it would just be too awkward to make the move.'

Relieved that Ruby seemed to be taking the news in a spirit of anthropological interest rather than jealous rage, Julia continued.

'To be honest, if you'd asked me, I would have expected that it *would* be awkward. But without over-sharing, it wasn't. We spent the whole weekend together, and it was amazing. Basically we were planning on staying together, being a proper couple.'

Ruby still appeared slightly bemused, but Julia plunged on.

'Then I guess Toby must have heard from you about the pregnancy, so he went off. Next I heard was an email the following day saying that you and he were having a baby, and that we couldn't see each other any more.'

Ruby appeared genuinely distressed. 'Oh God, Julia, I had no idea. I feel really guilty.'

Refusing, again, to let herself dwell on the bizarreness of the discussion, Julia smiled. 'You've got nothing to feel guilty about. You didn't know about me and Toby. If anything, I should feel guilty for shagging your boyfriend.'

'Oh, that's okay.' Ruby was nonchalant. 'We weren't even together at that point, and anyway, I'd have been shagging Paul given half a chance. Toby and I are hardly Romeo and Juliet, you know.'

'Clearly. Anyway, I was pretty upset, but there didn't seem to be much I could do about it. Then, a few weeks later, I found out I was pregnant too.'

'Oh my God! You mean the baby is Toby's?'

Julia looked at Ruby in exasperation. Over the course of the evening she had warmed to the other woman more than she would have thought possible, but there was no denying that she was not exactly the sharpest knife in the drawer.

'Yes! That's what I'm trying to tell you!'

Ruby grimaced as though in pain, and Julia felt a stab of conscience.

'I'm sorry, I really didn't mean to upset you.'

Ruby didn't reply at once. Her face was contorted, and Julia could see a faint beading of sweat on her upper lip. After a moment she managed to say rather breathlessly, 'Oh no, I'm not upset, not at all. It really doesn't bother me. No, it's just this killer backache I've got. I've been having it on and off all day, but it seems to be getting worse.'

Julia was sympathetic. 'Poor you, all these pregnancy aches and pains are horrible, aren't they? Why don't you get up and have a walk round? I find that often helps.'

'Good idea.' Ruby stood up and then gasped, her hands clutching instinctively at her stomach.

'What's the matter?' Julia stood up too, and walked round the table to Ruby. Her maternity jeans were very obviously sopping. Ruby was white with terror.

'Oh my God. Did you just wet yourself, or is that your waters breaking?'

'I don't know! I don't feel like I peed, but who knows? Oh God, it's still coming!' She looked down at herself in horror.

'Okay.' Julia felt herself switch to her work persona, calm and efficient. 'I think it probably is your waters. We need to phone the hospital to get some advice. Do you know the number?'

'It's in my phone. Toby put all the numbers I might need in there.' Ruby was standing immobile, shivering slightly.

'Right, well you'd better call them, I think. Now, this backache, do you think it could have been contractions?'

Ruby shrugged. 'Wouldn't contractions be in my stomach?'

Julia shook her head. 'I don't think so, necessarily. Angie said they could present like bad period pains in your back, didn't she?'

Ruby gaped at her in horror. 'I missed that bit! That's exactly what they're like.' She winced again.

'Was that another one?'

Ruby nodded.

'Okay, well it looks like you're in labour. That one was at 9.13 by the microwave clock, so we'd better time it till the next one. Meanwhile, you should ring up the hospital.'

Ruby swiped at the touchscreen of her phone with trembling fingers. As she heard the ringtone at the other end she thrust the phone at Julia. 'I can't do it – you talk to them. I hate hospitals and nurses.'

Julia took the phone.

'Hello, Magnolia Ward, Midwife speaking.'

'Hello, my name is Julia, I'm phoning on behalf of my friend Ruby Anstey. Her waters have just broken, and she's been having backache all day which she thinks may have been contractions.'

'Okay. How many weeks pregnant is Ruby?'

Julia gestured to Ruby, who was wincing and grimacing again, but managed to mouth, 'Thirty-five.'

'Umm, she's thirty-five weeks.'

'And how frequent are the contractions?'

Julia glanced at the clock. It now said 9.17. 'I'm not sure, we've only just started timing them, but the last ones were three or four minutes or so apart.'

'Right, well, I think you should bring your friend in straight away. We like to see women anyway once the waters have broken to check that there's no risk of infection, but it also sounds like those contractions are getting pretty frequent, so I think we should see her sooner rather than later. Don't forget to bring her notes and her hospital bag.'

Julia thanked her and hung up. She turned to Ruby. 'Did you hear all that?'

Ruby was still shaking all over. 'Oh my God, Julia, I'm not ready. I'm so scared. I'm so, so scared.'

'Shh, shh.' Julia patted her shoulder in a way which she hoped was soothing, trying to dredge her memory for information gleaned at the two classes she had attended, and all the books she had read. 'Look, you get into the position that feels most comfortable for you, and concentrate on nice slow, deep breathing. I'm going to book a cab, and get your stuff together. Have you got a bag packed?'

Ruby nodded. A ghost of a smile crossed her lips. 'Yes, Toby made me do it the day after the twenty-week scan. It's upstairs, in the room on the left as you go up, and my notes are with it.'

'And do you want me to phone someone else? Who's your birth partner?'

'Toby. And he's in Brussels! No, don't phone anyone yet. I'll see what they say at the hospital, but first babies always take for ever, don't they?'

Julia felt doubtful, but equally didn't want to insist, so just went off to phone a taxi and collect Ruby's things.

The cab arrived almost instantly, which was a minor miracle, but as they set off Julia could see why. The driver was clearly thrilled at his quasi-paramedic role and determined to extract every ounce of drama from it.

'Don't worry, I'll get you there!' he assured them, as he set off at approximately 60mph down the narrow side street, screeching round the corner on two wheels. Unfortunately for Ruby there were several roads of speed bumps between Toby's house and the hospital, and as they took each one at a flying pace Julia would look anxiously across at her, unsure if it was physiologically possible for the baby to be shaken out but not wanting to take the risk. Ruby was sitting on a cushion wrapped in a plastic carrier bag, an emergency resource conjured up by Julia to deal with the worst of the seemingly inexhaustible supply of amniotic fluid.

At one point Julia would have been thrilled to see the woman she had thought of as her rival in such an unglamorous position – white with fear, sweating with pain, and soaking wet from the waist down. Now, though, she just felt compassion and anxiety, combined with a dawning realisation that she could well be in the same position herself very shortly.

At the hospital, Ruby gripped Julia's hand.

'Please come in with me. I really don't want to be on my own, and you're being so calm and sensible.' Julia's heart was racing, and her palms sweating, but she forced herself to keep her tone light and calm, and assured Ruby that she would stay as long as she wanted.

On the ward Ruby was quickly seen by a midwife and examined, Julia remaining discreetly behind the curtain.

'Right.' The midwife pushed the curtain back. 'Well, you're certainly in labour, in fact you're doing very well, between seven and eight centimetres dilated. It's very impressive you've got this far without any pain relief.'

'I have been taking paracetamol all day, I thought I just had a bad back.'

'Well, getting this far on paracetamol is pretty impressive too, my dear. And the good news is that you should have your baby before too long.'

Ruby appeared even more forlorn. 'Should I phone my partner, then? He's abroad, so it might take him a while to get back.'

The midwife frowned in concern. 'I don't know whereabouts abroad he is, but I doubt he'll make it back in time for the birth. I would think you're going to have your baby within the next couple of hours.'

30

Ruby's and Julia's eyes met in horror.

'A couple of hours! But I thought first babies took days. There's no way Toby will get back from Brussels in time.'

The midwife was sympathetic. 'I'm sorry. First babies often do take a long time, but what they really specialise in, I'm afraid, is unpredictability. Is there anyone else you'd like us to contact for you?'

Ruby shook her head forlornly. 'No, it would take my mum or my sister too long as well.' She grabbed Julia's hand. 'Julia. I know this is really weird, but please stay. I really don't want to be on my own.'

Julia felt a mad urge to laugh, which she knew was close to hysteria. Of all the scenarios she had ever envisioned, nothing like this had ever entered her imagination. But what could she do?

'Of course I'll stay, Ruby. But . . .' She hesitated. 'I could do with popping out to get some food. I'm sorry, but I haven't had anything since lunchtime, and I tend to get a bit faint if I don't eat regularly. I'll be as quick as I can.'

Ruby was in the grip of another contraction, and didn't answer, but the midwife examined Julia in concern.

'Yes, you certainly do need something to eat. How many weeks pregnant are you?'

'Nearly thirty-three. Don't worry, I'm not due just yet.'

'No, but you need to take care of yourself. The shop in the main hospital building will still be open and they sell sandwiches and things. You go and get some snacks, I'll be here with Ruby. You'll be much more use to her, and me, if you're not fainting.'

It was a huge relief to be out in the cold night air after the oppressive heat of the labour ward, and as she crossed the car park Julia tried to clear her head. It was no use; images, ideas, fragments of conversation were spinning uncontrollably round her mind, and overriding all of them was the fear and trepidation of having to support a woman she barely knew through labour.

The selection in the shop was limited, but Julia chose a cheese and pickle sandwich which looked as wilted as she felt, some bottles of water and a handful of crisps and chocolate bars which she hoped would get her through the night. A healthy, balanced diet felt both unachievable and undesirable at this juncture. There was a small seating area outside the shop, and Julia sank down gratefully into a scuffed and battered chair to eat her unappetising meal and have a few moments' rest. She did start to feel a little bit stronger and more able to cope as her blood sugar rose, but a wave of dizziness still engulfed her when her mobile rang and the screen revealed it to be Toby.

'Hi Toby, where are you?'

His voice, faint and remote, and surprised, crossed the miles. 'Brussels. I told you that's where I'd be. But listen,

Julia, I've phoned for a reason, and I've just got to go straight ahead and say it. I'm so sorry, I was crap last week. I just got overwhelmed, and I'm so sorry. But I love you. I'm in love with you. You're the one, you're everything. Not because of the baby, just because of you. Oh God. This sounds so cheesy. I'm sorry. But I have to ask. Will you marry me?'

There was a resounding silence. They were words which Julia had longed to hear for months, but they couldn't have come at a more inappropriate time. It wasn't Toby's fault, Julia reminded herself. He had no idea that Ruby was in labour and that Julia was her conscripted birth partner. Yet the timing was still totally wrong for Julia to respond as she wanted, and she had to make a conscious effort to keep her voice calm and unemotional as she replied.

'Toby. I love you too, but I really can't talk about us now. Listen to me. I'm at the hospital with Ruby. She went into labour after the NCT class this evening, and I was with her. Apparently she's quite far on, and the baby will probably arrive in the next couple of hours. She's asked me to stay with her, and of course I will, but how soon can you get back?'

Toby's voice was tight with panic. 'Oh my God! I don't know. I'm sure that the last Eurostar leaves at about nine, so I've missed that, and I don't know about flights. Oh my God. Is Ruby okay? What can I do?'

As seemed to be her role in life, Julia found herself being the calm one, the one who organised and reassured.

'What you need to do is get on the internet and book the first flight or train back that you can. Train might still be better because at least you'll come right into central London and not have to travel in from the airport. You're almost certainly going to miss the actual birth, though, from what the midwife said, but don't worry. I'm here, I won't leave Ruby, and she's fine, doing really well in fact. Text me when you have your travel sorted, and I'll keep you in touch with things here.'

'Okay, you're right. I'll do that. I love you, Julia.'

Overwhelmed by the tenderness in his voice, Julia knew that she had to keep her feelings in check somehow so that she could go back and support Ruby. 'You too, Toby. I'll talk to you soon.'

Hanging up thoughtfully, Julia shoved her phone back in her pocket, picked up her bag of supplies, and headed back to the maternity unit as fast as she could waddle.

Ruby was on all fours on the bed, the midwife talking to her gently and reassuringly. Julia found Ruby's hospital bag and rummaged through it. Her heart contracted at the sight of the almost doll-sized white babygros and scratch mittens, but they weren't what she wanted. She found a water spray and a bottle of relaxing massage oil. Going over to Ruby, who was just coming out of a contraction, she told her that she had spoken to Toby and that he would be arriving as soon as he could, and then she spritzed Ruby's pulse points and offered to massage her back.

'Oh, Julia, that would be fab. Thank you so much. Leonora thinks I'll be ready to push soon.'

The midwife nodded in confirmation and reiterated how well Ruby was doing. By this time Ruby was in the grip of yet another contraction and didn't respond, but

Julia began gently to massage her lower back, ignoring the fact that this put her in the closest proximity to another woman's genitals than she had been since her own birth, and continued to do so, pausing only to re-spritz Ruby and cool her down for the next hour.

At this point Ruby gasped. 'I need a poo. Oh my God, I'm going to poo myself. I need to go to the loo, *now.*'

The midwife laughed gently. 'Don't worry, you're not going to poo, but you are ready to push your baby out.'

Julia moved round to Ruby's head, and began to stroke her hair and make soothing noises as though to an animal in distress.

Leonora was guiding Ruby. 'Okay Ruby, pant now, don't push until I say. Right, now, push down, hard as you can.'

Ruby was scarlet, her face contorted with the effort, and instead of panting was just repeating 'fuckfuckfuck-fuckfuck' between pushes.

It seemed like for ever, but a glance at the clock told Julia it was only ten minutes before the midwife said that the head was delivered. A couple more pushes and she announced, 'Congratulations, Ruby. You have a beautiful baby boy.'

Ruby collapsed onto her side, eyes closed, as Leonora cut the cord.

'Do you want to hold him straight away, or shall I weigh him and clean him up a bit first?'

'Clean him up, please.'

Julia helped Ruby to lie down, and straightened her nightshirt, but all the time her eyes were on the tiny bundle in the midwife's arms. She pulled up a chair next to the bed and sat down, her own legs feeling like jelly after the intensity of what she had just experienced. She felt something on her face, and putting her hand up to wipe it, discovered that tears were streaming down her cheeks.

A few moments later, Leonora brought the baby over, wrapped in a towel.

'He's a lovely, healthy boy, 5lbs 13, which is a good weight for a thirty-five-week baby. Do you have a name for him, Ruby?'

Ruby tentatively put out her arms and took the baby rather awkwardly. 'Yes, I'm going to call him Julian. Partly because I like the name, it was my grandad's, and partly because of Julia – I couldn't have done it without you, and I'm so grateful.'

Fresh tears welled up in Julia's eyes. 'Oh Ruby, that's so sweet. Thank you. But you were brilliant, I didn't do anything.'

The midwife smiled at them. 'You both did very well indeed, and Julian is a lovely name. Now, we'll keep you here while you deliver the placenta, and then we'll move you up to the postnatal ward. We'll probably need to keep you in for a couple of days because Julian was a bit early, but I really don't think there's anything to worry about. Would you like me to help you put him to the breast?'

Ruby stared at the midwife in abject horror. 'I'm not breastfeeding! Absolutely not, no way, no way at all. I've done my bit.'

'Okay.' The midwife nodded her head. 'No one's forcing you, but I do have to ask you if you've been told about the health benefits of breastfeeding, to you and the baby?'

'Yes, I know all that. But I was bottle fed, and I'm fine, and the whole thought of breastfeeding repulses me, frankly. I want my body back now.'

Julia smiled inwardly. However close she had felt to Ruby over the last couple of hours, there had clearly been no fundamental change to her personality.

Three quarters of an hour later, Julia glanced at her watch as she sat in the reception of the maternity unit waiting for her taxi to arrive. Just past midnight. She yawned, and shut her eyes briefly, then the beep beep of a text message roused her again. It was from Toby, in response to her message telling him about Julian.

Thanks for letting me know. Tell Ruby I love the name, and to give Julian a kiss from me. My train gets into St Pancras at 8.57 a.m. tomorrow, so can be at hospital by 10. I love you. T x

Julia reflected on the evening's events as she tried to compose a response. Should she tell Toby that the midwife had let her help dress Julian in his tiny nappy and vest and babygro, or that she'd had the most magical ten-minute cuddle with him before he fell asleep and she had laid him gently in the clear plastic bassinet next to Ruby's bed? Should she tell him that, with his wide, dark eyes and serious expression, Julian looked heart-rendingly like Toby? Or that she was loath to leave Julian with a mother who scarcely seemed to want to look at him, let alone hold him? In the end she decided that these issues were too big and rather bathetic in text message format, and simply replied:

> On my way home now. Julian gorgeous, and he and Ruby both well. I will meet you at station tomorrow. J xxx

31

Running on a combination of adrenaline, sugar, hormones and very little sleep, Julia felt totally wired as she waited in the dramatic but rather cold station the following morning. Behind her stood the famous sculpture of a couple embracing, capturing the romance of meetings and partings at a large railway station. Julia smiled. The female figure was slim and elegant in her high heels and close-fitting skirt and jacket. A very long way away from Julia as she stood in maternity jeans, Ugg boots and her enormous dark red poncho – the warmest thing she could still fit into.

Her heartbeat quickened as the 8.57 a.m. arrival from Brussels was announced and the train slid gracefully alongside the platform. As she had expected, Toby was the first person off the train, his wheelie suitcase bouncing behind him and his manic energy never more apparent as he bounded down the platform towards her. Before she knew what was happening she was in his arms, face pressed almost painfully into his shoulder as he held her tightly and muttered into her hair again and again, 'I love you, Julia. I love you so much. You are the most amazing woman.'

For a few minutes Julia let herself relax into his arms and enjoy a temporary cessation of the feelings of responsibility which had been so overwhelming lately. Then she pulled away. 'Look, Toby, we've got a lot to talk about. And I'm freezing. Let's go and get a coffee in the hotel while we talk.'

Toby was hesitant. 'Oh God, Ju, I really, really want to talk to you. But I told Ruby I'd be at the hospital for ten, and I want to see Julian. I'm sorry, it's not that I'm putting them first, it's just . . .' He trailed off despairingly.

Julia linked her arm through his, and began walking down the platform. 'It's all right, Tobes, I told Ruby you wouldn't be there until eleven. I know you want to see Julian, but an hour probably won't make that much difference – I really think there's a conversation we need to have first.'

Toby paled visibly. 'Does Ruby know that you're meeting me, then?'

Julia nodded, and ignored Toby's look of surprised enquiry.

Toby allowed himself to be dragged along, and they settled themselves in the bar of the luxurious St Pancras Grand Hotel, watching the chaos and drama of rush hour in a busy station unfold around them.

Once they both had their hands cupped round deliciously hot drinks, Julia began. 'Such a lot has happened in the last twenty-four hours, I don't really know where to start. But I'd probably better begin with how I ended up being with Ruby for Julian's birth.'

'Wasn't it just that you were both at the antenatal class when she went into labour?'

'Not exactly. Ruby asked me back to yours after class, because she wanted to talk to me.'

Succinctly, she related the main points of their conversation.

Toby seemed utterly dazed when she had finished. 'So Ruby has been in love with this Paul chap the whole time?'

Julia nodded.

'Little bitch,' he breathed.

Julia surveyed his face anxiously for signs of jealousy, but he just looked furious.

'Why does that make you angry?' she asked softly.

'It makes me fucking angry because all the time I was dancing attendance on Ruby, feeling guilty because I didn't love her, and half out of my mind with missing you, she was shagging someone else! I could have been with you the whole time. Jesus, talk about wanting to have your cake and eat it.'

Julia laughed with relief. 'I know, I do understand. But the thing is, you're not tied to her now, are you?'

Toby shrugged. 'I'm not tied to her, no, but now she wants me to look after Julian full time, and there's just no way I can do that, and have a relationship with you and our baby, *and* work the hours I work. It just can't be done. And honestly, Julia, things aren't going well at work in this financial climate; they're saying no bonuses and a pay freeze this year, maybe even job cuts. Full-time child-care is so expensive, and my mortgage is huge. I just don't see how I can manage. Plus, why should Ruby get away with it?'

Julia chose her words carefully. 'It's not a case of "getting away with it". I know Ruby has behaved badly, but let's face it, we've all made mistakes. I shouldn't have let myself get pregnant, and I should have told you right away when I was. You shouldn't have dumped me by email, and you shouldn't have let Ruby think that you could have a relationship with her when you had feelings for me. And Ruby shouldn't have used you for security when she was in love with Paul. But there doesn't seem to me to be much point on focusing on any of that. What's important now is making everyone as happy as possible from now on, and especially providing love and security for Julian and my bump.'

Toby looked at her in astonishment, and covered her hand with his. 'You really are amazing, do you know that? I suppose you've got it all planned out, then?'

Julia nodded calmly. 'I think so, yes.' She thought back to the night before when she had lain awake for hours, adrenaline coursing through her as she tried to form a sensible plan from the kaleidoscope of events with which life had presented her.

He shook his head in disbelief. 'Go on then, let's see how you sort this one out.'

'Well, first of all I think that Ruby is right. You should bring Julian up, and she should be free to go away with Paul, and just spend holiday time with Julian sometimes. She never wanted a baby, and I don't think it will be good for either her or Julian for Ruby to care for him reluctantly – she'd be giving up her career, and the man she's madly in love with, and I think that would just build massive resentment. Much better that she's a loving visitor in his life than a permanent bitter presence. And you love Julian, don't you?'

Toby nodded. 'Obviously I don't know him yet, but I've loved the baby, the idea of the baby, all the way through Ruby's pregnancy. But I don't know how I can possibly look after him by myself.'

'Who says you're by yourself? You're not getting rid of me that easily.'

'God, Julia. Like I said, you're amazing, but I don't really see what you can do to help. It's all such a bloody nightmare.'

Julia shook her head. 'No, I have a plan. I haven't had a chance to confirm all the details yet, but I think it will work. They're asking for voluntary redundancies at work. Now obviously I wasn't going to take it when I thought I was going to be a single mother, but things are different now. I'd get quite a good payout, I reckon. Then I think you should sell your house and we should live in Walthamstow, not Wanstead.'

'We can't possibly all live in your house! It's lovely, but it's tiny.'

'No, I'm not suggesting that. We should buy a three-bedroom place together, but Walthamstow is much cheaper than Wanstead so it would take the financial pressure off quite a bit. It would mean that we could afford for me not to work, or just to do some freelance, so I can look after Julian and the bump while they're still tiny. And it's too long a story for now, but Rose and Graeme have split up and I think she might like to rent my house for the time being, so that would cover my mortgage. It would be so amazing to have Rose nearby.'

Toby was frowning at her in consternation. 'Julia, you can't be serious. You can't honestly be suggesting that you quit the job you love to stay at home and look after two small babies, one of whom isn't even yours. You can't possibly do that!'

'Why not? I do love my job, but you know how busy and stressful it is, and since I've been pregnant I've been wondering how I can possibly carry on doing it properly, and actually see my child. I've wanted a baby so much, for such a long time, I hate the idea of a stranger getting to spend all their time with them while I worked to pay for them.'

'Yes, I can see that. But Julia, that's your baby – Julian isn't yours. One baby must be hard enough; two at the same time would be impossible.'

'I know it will be hard. But lots of people manage with twins, for example. One of the things I'd use my redundancy money for would be to get help, at first. I know Julian isn't mine biologically, but lots of people have very close relationships with their stepchildren, which is what Julian would be. And Toby, I don't want to be too tactless and go on about it, because you missed it, but I have to say that watching him being born and holding him just afterwards was the most amazing thing I've ever experienced, and I honestly feel like I love him already. I just can't wait to see him and hold him again.'

A huge smile broke out across Toby's face. 'Come on then, let's go to the hospital and see him! There's just one thing that I need to do first.'

'What's that?'

Toby didn't answer in words, but got down on one knee next to Julia. 'When I proposed to Ruby it was all about the dramatic gesture. All I thought about was where I'd do it, what we'd be wearing, eating, drinking, what the ring would look like. Famously, it didn't work at all, thank God.

'And now I'm asking you, and the first time I blurt it out on the phone while you're in the middle of being my ex-girlfriend's birth partner, and now I'm asking you at nine in the morning, when neither of us has had much sleep, in a railway station. I'm sorry that it isn't a big romantic gesture, and that I haven't even had a chance to buy a ring – I promise I'll make it up to you – but this is a proper proposal in a way the other one wasn't, because I love you, and I want us to be together for ever, and I know that we will be, if you'll agree to put up with me.

'Julia Stephanie Upton, will you marry me?'

Julia realised she was crying. 'Yes, Toby. I love you so much too, you make me so happy. And I know that this is all completely topsy-turvy, and not how it's meant to be or how other people do things, but I honestly think it's going to work for us.'

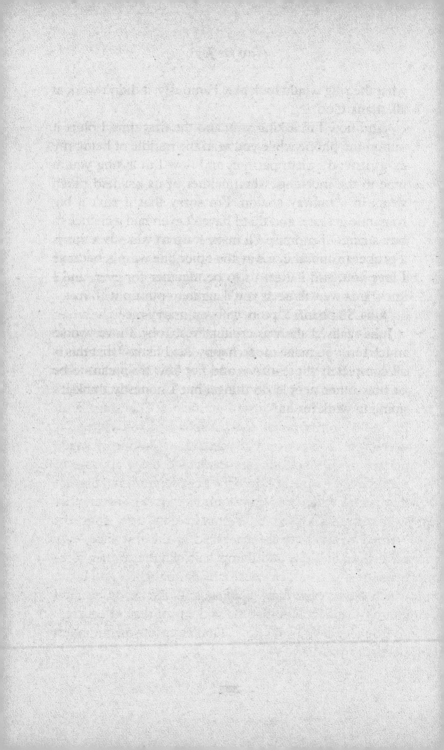

EPILOGUE

Julia smiled up at her parents. She wasn't wearing a scrap of make-up, her face was beyond pale, her hair messy, and a hospital gown flattered no one, but Pat Upton thought that she had never seen her daughter so radiant. Twelve-hour-old Elizabeth Rose Fenton was snuggled in the crook of Julia's arm, fast asleep and totally oblivious to the world around her. Pat looked from her daughter to her grand-daughter, and felt tears springing to her eyes. Julia's eyes met hers, and they shared a moment of perfect under-standing hitherto unknown in their relationship. With Elizabeth's birth, much of what Julia had always seen as over-protectiveness on her mum's part suddenly made perfect sense. And although Pat would never approve of the irregular manner of the baby's conception, and the fact that her daughter was now committed to raising another woman's child caused her a lot of anxiety, these concerns seemed rather petty as she gazed at the tiny face, eyes scrunched in sleep and damp hair clinging to her fore-head. At this point, any decisions her daughter had taken which led to this baby coming into the world seemed entirely justified. Not that she said any of that, of course.

'You look a bit peaky, love. Don't expect you got much sleep, did you?'

Julia shrugged mentally. In a film, her mum would have followed that brief moment of complicity with an emotional outpouring, but real life with northern parents was never going to be quite like that.

'Do you want to hold her?'

Pat nodded. 'If you don't think it'll wake her up.'

Julia shook her head. 'Shouldn't have thought so. Nothing seems to at the moment, just like Julian was at first. I wish that lasted! Anyway. Here you go, Beth, you go to your granny. Mum, you're going to have to take her off me, I can't move while I'm still attached to the drip and the catheter.'

Pat took the little girl tenderly, and Eddie put his arms round both of them. Julia choked up, reaching for her phone to capture a photo of this moment when her parents circled her baby with love.

'So are you calling her Beth, then?'

Julia nodded. 'Yes. It's always been a name I loved, but we decided to go for Elizabeth so that she's got more options. After all, when she's prime minister she might need something more formal on state occasions. And of course Rose is after Rose; I couldn't have got through the last few months without her.' Julia smiled over at where a small slender woman with bright red hair was sitting curled up unobtrusively in the corner.

Pat gasped. 'Oh, goodness, Rose. I'm so sorry, I didn't see you there, love. I was just thinking about the baby!'

Rose stood up and came forward, laughing. 'Don't be silly! I'm sorry for intruding on your first meeting with your grandchild. I popped in to see Julia, and meet Beth, and then Julia insisted that I stay to see you too. She is gorgeous, isn't she? Beth, I mean not Julia.' She grinned at her friend. 'You're normally gorgeous, but you don't look your very best this morning!'

Julia pulled a face at Rose.

Eddie grinned. He had been watching Julia and Rose bicker and tease and support each other since their first day at school a quarter of a century earlier. 'So anyway,' he asked. 'How's the little lad? And where's Toby?'

'He's with the little lad. Hugh and Alicia have been fantastic, but he wanted to give them a break, and also to spend a bit of time with Julian. He was here with me and Beth up until Rose arrived about half an hour ago, and he'll be back in a couple of hours.

'Why don't you two sit down?' Julia gestured at the narrow, high-backed chairs upholstered in a restful shade of bile green. 'There's loads to talk about. Dad, would you mind going to get us some tea, and I quite fancy a Crunchie as well, actually, and then we can have a proper catch-up.'

Rose went to get her coat off the chair. 'I'm going to go, and leave you to it. I've intruded enough.' She leant over and kissed Julia, who clutched at her hand in slight panic. She had an uncomfortable feeling that as soon as Rose left, especially without her dad's laid-back presence, her mum would start on the folly of bringing up someone else's baby, and she wasn't sure she was feeling strong enough to cope.

'No, don't go, Rosie. Stay and have a girly gossip with me and Mum. She doesn't know the latest in the soap opera of your life.'

Pat would have welcomed the chance to have a private word with her daughter, but was far too polite to say so directly. 'No, do stay, Rose. It would be lovely to catch up. Unless you need to get back to Sebastian, of course?' The question was slightly pointed, but Rose succumbed to Julia's imploring look and sat back down, pulling her chair closer to Pat's so that Julia could see both of them easily from the bed.

Julia was giggling infectiously now. 'No, she doesn't need to get back for Sebastian, he's with his father. And his stepfather-to-be!'

Pat was slightly confused. 'Stepfather-to-be? Erm, have you met someone, then, Rose?'

Rose opened her mouth to answer, but Julia had already leapt in.

'No! It's not Rose who's got a new boyfriend, it's Graeme! Isn't that the best gossip ever?'

Seeing that Pat still seemed completely bewildered, and that Julia was on a slightly manic hormonal high, Rose explained more sedately.

'You know Graeme and I split up because I found out that he was secretly gay?'

Pat nodded.

'Basically, he had a brief affair with a man he worked with, called Matthew, just before we got together. In fact, us getting together was a sort of smokescreen for that. I don't think Graeme ever really got over him, and then they met up again at Christmas and got together, properly and openly this time.'

Julia jumped in again, irrepressibly. 'Graeme and Matthew are now madly in love, and Graeme is selling the big house in the country and moving into Matthew's über-cool flat in Shoreditch! So he's going to have loads of money, and he's hardly in a position to be arsey to Rose over the divorce, is he? It's perfect.'

'Heavens above! How do you feel about all this, Rose?' Pat glanced at her sympathetically.

Rose shrugged. 'I am grateful that Graeme isn't going to be in a position to make the divorce difficult. And I haven't been happy recently, so I'm looking forward to a fresh start. Basically I suppose I'm pleased for him, I don't wish him any harm. I just wish he could have come to terms with his sexuality before marriage to me rather than after. But then, I wouldn't have Seb, so everything probably does work out for the best somehow.'

She paused, giving Julia time to interject again.

'It's funny, really. Graeme kept the fact that he was gay a huge secret for thirty-five years, and now, after Rose confronted him, the walls of the closet have just come tumbling down. I haven't seen him, but Rose said that he's at least fifty per cent camper since he hooked up with Matthew again, so I would think that by the time I do next see him, Graeme Harley-Jamieson will be indistinguishable from Graham Norton.'

The three women laughed together, and then Rose got determinedly to her feet.

'Right, I really am going this time, Ju.'

She stroked Beth's sleeping head with one gentle finger, pulled on her coat and moved to the door.

'Lovely to see you again, Pat, say goodbye to Eddie for me. And congratulations on your beautiful granddaughter.'

'Bye bye, love. Good luck with everything. It can't be easy, but you're being very brave. Sebastian's a lucky boy to have you.'

Rose smiled warmly, avoided Julia's eye, and closed the door gently behind her.

Julia sighed inwardly. Where was her dad? How long can it take to buy a chocolate bar? Oh well, better face it. She met her mum's anxious gaze full-on.

Pat took the opportunity with both hands. 'I'm glad to get you on your own for a moment, Julia. It's hard to ask on the phone. Are you really happy? All this about bringing up Ruby's and Toby's son – well, it's hard, love. You'll have seen that over the past few weeks, but now you've got Beth as well . . . plus it can't be easy when they're not your own. Are you sure it's really what you want, that you're not just doing it to please Toby?'

Julia couldn't help but feel irritated at having her expectations fulfilled, but tried to restrain it. Now, as never before, she understood that her mum was motivated by love and concern rather than any malign motivation. Hard though it was to make the leap of imagination, she could vaguely foresee how protective she would feel of Julian and Beth in years to come, and how that possibly might be interpreted by them. So she took a few deep breaths and tried to gather her resources. How best to explain to her mum how utterly and overwhelmingly happy she was?

'Mum, first of all, I love Julian. It isn't exactly the same as what I feel for Beth – that's such a visceral feeling. When they said I needed an emergency C-section I don't think I actually breathed again until I heard her cry as they lifted her out. And then I just felt waves of the most intense, almost hallucinogenic, happiness I've ever experienced, even though I was lying on an operating theatre table, shaking convulsively and about to vomit from the reaction to the anaesthetic!'.

Pat shuddered. 'Thank God you're both all right.'

'I'm fine, Mum. The painkillers they've given me are good stuff, I can't feel anything, even now the epidural is wearing off. But anyway, like I was saying: I'll never feel quite like that for Julian because I didn't grow him in my body, but fathers don't go through pregnancy either, and they don't love their babies any less, do they?'

'Yes, but they are *their* babies, that's my point.'

'Look, I was there when Julian was born. I watched him coming into the world, and other than his mother and the midwife I was the first person to hold him. I've lived with him and his father for the entire eight weeks of his life. I've fed him, and cuddled him, and bathed him, and dressed him, and sung to him. I've got up bleary-eyed seven times a night to soothe him, and he's pooed on me, and thrown up on me, and completely bloody exhausted me. I've done everything for Julian that any parent would do in the first few weeks of a baby's life, and I don't think you can do that without forming an incredibly close bond. I *love* him. It might not be exactly what I feel for Beth, but it's still love, and it's still very strong. And the real proof is that if Ruby came back tomorrow and said that she wanted Julian to live with her after all, I'd be devastated.'

By this time Eddie had come back in, and handed Julia her chocolate, which she unwrapped and began to devour ravenously as her parents started to ask more questions about her plans for the future. With impeccable timing, Beth woke up and began to whimper, so conversation was paused while Julia went through the laborious process of a first-time mum latching on a brand-new baby. When Beth was settled and suckling contentedly, oblivious to the crumbs of chocolate and honeycomb her mother was scattering onto her head, Julia looked up.

'Pass us that water, Dad. I'm so thirsty.'

Her parents were both regarding her expectantly, but, revelling in the feeling of holding and feeding her baby, Julia found she had lost her train of thought completely and had no idea what she had been talking about.

'So what about the house, then? Where are you all going to be living?' her mum prompted.

'Oh God, yes! I haven't told you. We viewed a house the day before yesterday, in Walthamstow Village, which is perfect for us. Three decent-sized bedrooms, a huge kitchen, a nice living room with an open fire, an okay-sized garden, and even a little extra room downstairs we could use as a study, or possibly a guest room if we put a sofa bed in it, although it would be a squeeze. Anyway, we made an offer, and it was accepted the same day, after a bit of negotiation. And then yesterday we had an offer on Toby's house! So, fingers crossed, we just need to wait for all the legal stuff.' She laughed. 'It's funny. It's almost like Beth waited until things were getting sorted before she made an appearance.'

'So what's going to happen to your house?'

'Well, Rose is going to rent it off me for now, which will cover my mortgage, and then we'll just have to wait and see what happens.'

Beth finished suckling, and Julia lifted her gently onto her shoulder and began patting her back to get any wind up. Unbeknownst to her, Toby had returned to the hospital and was standing in the doorway of Julia's private room, Julian strapped to his chest in a BabyBjorn, staring at Julia with adoration written all over his face. Eddie glanced up, catching his eye, and winked.

'So all's well that ends well, pet?'

Julia nodded, emphatically. 'Yep, I think so.' She thought for a moment. 'Ruby and Paul have got together and moved to Germany, which they're both really happy and excited about. Rose and Sebastian like living in my house; Seb is settling well into nursery a few mornings a week while Rose does some work, and she's starting her aromatherapy course in September. Graeme's got Matthew. Julian seems to have settled really well with me and Toby, and Alicia and Hugh are so excited about having two grandchildren.'

'And what about you, love?' Eddie asked softly.

Julia smiled. 'Honestly, Dad,' she affirmed, as Beth let out a resounding burp, 'I've got Toby, and Julian, and Beth, and I've never been happier in my life.'

Pat's and Eddie's eyes met and they smiled, feeling properly reassured about their daughter's happiness and well-being for the first time in months. Then with one accord they slipped out together, leaving Toby free to come over to the bed, unclip Julian, and lay the tiny sister and ever-so-slightly-bigger brother down next to each other, while their parents gazed at them, and then at each other, in rapt adoration.

ACKNOWLEDGEMENTS

There are so many people without whom *Two for Joy* wouldn't exist, and I'm going to indulge myself with a big fat Oscar-winning-speech-style set of acknowledgements.

To Sheila Ableman, my fantastic agent and, coincidentally, mother-in-law, who not only got me a book deal, but spent every Thursday afternoon looking after my daughter so that I could actually write the book.

To Francesca Best, my amazing editor, for loving *Two for Joy* and for making it the best it could possibly be. And to her colleagues Emilie Ferguson, Naomi Berwin, Alix Percy, Lizzi Jones and the rest of the Hodder team for their enthusiasm and support in getting people to read it.

To the lovely people who read, enjoyed and commented on various evolutions of the book, and who believed in me long before I signed a contract – Sue Chandler, Nicola Davenport, Rosalind Taylor-Hook, Margaret Last, Kate Panayi, Jenny Steward, Sallyanne Sweeney and Anna Wetherell.

To Sally Gillespie and Jenny Morgan for giving me the benefit of their professional advice for free!

To the staff at the Deli Café in Walthamstow, who

make amazing hot chocolates, and let me hog a table while I write.

To my daughter Anna, who transformed my life in more ways than one, and is generally fairly tolerant of having to share her mummy with a laptop.

And last but not least, to my wonderful husband, Thomas, who has loved and believed in me for the last fourteen years, and has been passionately enthusiastic in supporting me with *Two for Joy*. Thank you. For everything. I love you.